Cold Gold I

Dennis J. McTaggart

Publishers:
Inspiring Publishers
PO box 159 Calwell ACT 2905, Australia.
Email: inspiringpublishers@gmail.com

National Library of Australia Cataloguing-in-Publication entry

Author: McTaggart, Dennis J.

Title: **Cold Gold I**/*Dennis J. McTaggart.*

ISBN: 9781925346695 (pbk)

Subjects: Abalone industry—Australia—Fiction.
          Detective and mystery stories, Australian
          Short stories, Australian.

Dewey Number: A823.4

Contents

The Vagrant

I had been doing it tough the last couple of years.

I used to drive a van and deliver bread for a well-known bakery, to all the supermarkets.

There was a dispute with our wages and rate of pay.

I dug in and ended up losing my contract and van.

My wife and I weren't doing it that well and the extra pressure of me not working was enough to tip the marriage over and she took the two boys and went to live with her sister.

I stayed in the unit and got behind with the rent and got evicted.

I sold the furniture and other stuff at a garage sale, took the money, and knocked it off on the 'punt'.

I moved into a 'flea pit' boarding house and lived in fear of my life for a couple of years and slowly lost contact with the kids.

They were better off without me.

My friends abandoned me. It was as much my fault as theirs, and so I spiralled down and down until I was homeless and friendless.

I became invisible to ninety-nine percent of the population.

On pension days, I had money and for the rest of the fortnight I was broke and living hand to mouth day to day.

My general appearance got worse and worse.

One pension day, I was refused a haircut by a barber as I was too dirty.

He bluntly told me, 'Fuck off and don't come back. If you sit in my chair, I'll have to get it steam cleaned.'

My beard and hair were long and unkempt. My clothes were dirty and ragged.

It was a surprise when the big bloke with the thickest gold chain I had ever seen walked up to me and said, 'Gidday, mate, do you want to earn one hundred dollars?'

He didn't look like a poofter, so I said, 'What do I have to do? I'm not gay.'

'Neither am I, thank fuck,' He said, 'all you have to do is go in and buy me a mobile phone, that easy.'

'I don't know anything about mobile phones or anything like that,' I answered.

'Don't worry, sport. Just give the people in the phone shop this note and the money and get the phone, in your name, and give me the phone and I'll give you the hundred dollars, that easy. It's not rocket science,' he said with a grin.

He gave me the money and the model number of the phone he wanted me to get for him, so I walked into the phone shop and made my way up to the counter.

The lovely young girl behind the counter walked away from me and looked at a middle-aged salesman who got to his feet and walked over to me and asked in a questioning voice. 'Can I help you?'

'Yes, I want to buy a phone,' I said handing him the note the bloke with the gold chain had given me.

'How are you going to pay, credit card or cash?' he said with a smirk.

'Cash,' I said, deciding that one-word answers would be enough.

I caught sight of myself in the reflection of a display case and realised that I didn't look the best. My hair was sticking out and matted and my beard was dirty. There was a smear of mud or grease on my forehead. I needed a bath.

The sales assistant went to a display case and selected a phone in a box and said. 'That will cost you one hundred and fifty dollars. It's a pay as you go deal. It's got ten dollars credit and you can top it up anywhere, post offices, service stations, seven elevens, anywhere.'

He put his hand out for the money and took it out of my dirty hand and went to go back to his desk. 'Got any ID?' he asked.

I gave him my pension card, and he took note of my name and address.

He held the money as if there was a distinct possibility that he could catch cancer from contact with it and did the paperwork. He soon came back and gave me the phone and the receipt and said in a loud voice. 'Thanks for your business. Where did you hear about us? I hope that you recommend us to all your friends.'

I looked at him and said nothing, turned around, and with everyone looking at me, I walked out onto the street and looked to see where the bloke who I bought the phone for was.

He was leaning against a lamp-post watching me but out of sight of the shop front where the phone people where.

'How did you go, sport?' He asked.

I held it to my chest. He reached for the phone.

'Where's my money?' I asked.

'Let me look at it first, just to make sure that it's the one that I want.' He smiled and said.

He took it and unpacked the phone and said, 'Yep, that's what I want. Well done.'

Handing me a hundred-dollar note, I said, 'Thanks.'

'No problem, sport,' he said and turned and walked away, and I never saw him again.

Start of Cold Gold 1

Dave's untraceable phone rang. It was the one that Teddy got for him.

He didn't know how he did it, but it was a pay as you go that was registered in someone else's name.

It was Teddy, on the line from Melbourne.

He said. 'Dave, I'm coming down with a couple of mates to do a bit. What's happening? What's the weather like? Does it look all right?'

Dave said. 'It looks good for the next couple of days. Very light swell and not a lot of bad weather about,'

Teddy said. 'Yes, the weather maps look good. We should get a couple of days in. I'll meet you at the regular place.'

'All right, mate, what's your ETA?' Dave asked.

'I should be there in about four hours, give or take thirty minutes. If I have a problem, then I'll give you a ring.'

'Oakey, Doakey,' Dave answered and disconnected.

Dave put the phone down and smiled to himself. He hoped that everything went all right, because if they are successful, then there will be a quid in it for him.

Dave used to be an abalone diver. When there wasn't a lot of money in it, just as things started to improve in the industry, he got a severe case of the bends and that put an end to an otherwise brilliant career.

It totally disabled him for about ten years.

He was still not over it, but he would get by because he was good at getting by

Dave waited for a while and then drove into the main street of Bairnsdale and parked in the gardens, across the road from a shop his dad used to run. It was now a bookshop; memories flooded back all good, of the days that he spent working, as a young man selling electrical appliances with his dad many years ago.

Dave's phone rang.

It was Teddy.

'Hey, mate, it's Teddy. I'm in the red Ford Falcon, hire car, and I'm at the water tower. Where are you?'

'Mate, I'm just in front of you. In fact, I can see you.' Dave answered.

'Right, mate, I'll do the old 'loop de loop' and see if I've got a tail.'

'Right, mate,' Dave said, 'I'm all eyes, do your thing.'

Teddy drove past him and then did a right-hand turn around the gardens in the centre of the main street in Bairnsdale, and then another right-hand turn, and headed back towards Melbourne.

Dave watched to see if any other car did the same. None did, and Teddy hung a u-turn and drove back past him.

Dave let him go and started up and followed him out of town. They went through this little precaution most times when Teddy he came down just to make sure that there weren't any fisheries or undercover police on his tail.

When Dave got to the Nicholson Hotel Motel, Teddy was an the bar ordering a couple of pots of beer.

He joined him at the bar and said. 'Good day, Teddy. Mate, it's good to see you.'

Teddy smiled; the overhead light reflected off the gold chain that hung around his neck.

He was a big bloke, ruddy complexion, and always had a smile on his face.

He was a very good abalone poacher, and he always ended up with abalone, plenty of them, never took stupid risks, never dived deep, and always paid everybody quickly.

'Good day, Dave, you have let yourself go a bit, mate. Must be all this "hillbilly" lifestyle you're living,' Teddy said, laughing.

'Yes, mate, it's easier to fit in down here if you look a bit rough,' Dave answered somewhat sheepishly, aware that his appearance differed from Teddy's.

'Yeah, I suppose you're right,' Teddy said.

They moved out of earshot from the barman, an ex-copper.

'Those bastards take everything in and will report you to the coppers if they hear anything; ex-coppers are mostly pricks.' Teddy mumbled.

Dave nodded in agreement.

'What's the plan?' Dave asked.

'Well, we are going to put in at Lakes Entrance and head up the coast towards Gabo Island. Depending on conditions, we'll have a couple of jumps and see what we can find. We'll be away for a couple of days. We'll "coff" up the first day's fish and then shuck out the rest. Bag all the meat, then drop them off to you, and, if the weather holds, we'll drop them off onto the beach and then come back to Lakes Entrance.' Teddy said.

'Have you got a driver?' Dave asked. 'I don't want to be seen with you when the boat arrives.'

'Yes, mate, don't worry. Tony will bring down the boat, launch it, and then take the trailer away and be where we want him to be when we are ready to go home. That's all sorted.'

'Ok, mate, that sounds good,' Dave replied, 'you have got it all covered.'

Teddy said, 'I'll give you a thousand dollars upfront and you will get a cut out of whatever we end up with, OK?'

'Yes, mate, that's perfect. That will do me fine.' Dave replied.

They walked out of the bar and Teddy gave Dave the thousand dollars. Teddy said, 'I'll find somewhere to stay and the boys will come down tomorrow at about noon.'

Dave rang his brother Lee, and told him what was going on. He was happy to know that they were going to earn.

Lee had their four-wheel drive and rubber ducky at his farm a few miles out of town.

The next day, Tony arrived.

Tony was an Italian and had been around boats and the fishing fleet all his life. He was a doer. He always got the job done; no matter what happened, he always was there.

Tony had the boat and three divers.

Dave didn't know any of them, so there wasn't a lot of talk between them.

Teddy and the three divers climbed up into the twenty-three-foot, half-cabin Shark Cat, and Tony backed it into the water.

They swiftly got the boat headed out the entrance at Lakes Entrance and headed towards the oil rigs out in Bass Strait as if they were going deep sea fishing or on a tour around the oil rigs.

Tony drove the trailer away from the boat ramp and went up to Jemmey's point, overlooking the entrance, and watched as the Shark Cat got smaller and smaller as it moved into the distance.

Tony rang Teddy and asked if everything was OK.

'Yes, mate, all's well,' said Teddy.

Tony knew that Teddy would ring him with further instructions when he was ready to come in and wanted to be picked up at the ramp.

Tony made his way to a caravan park where he booked an overnight van for a couple of days. He told the park owners that his boat was in the water and he would be doing a bit of fishing. He paid for two nights in advance.

Teddy headed out to sea.

The boat was moving smoothly over the water; the two, 200 horsepower motors were running smoothly. The boat sliced through the water, sending two rooster tails twenty foot high into the air behind them.

Teddy checked the gauges, everything looked good.

The tachometers hands were sitting on 4500. They still had one thousand RPM's to go. He never pushed the boat to its limit unless he had too. Teddy liked to keep a bit up his sleeve and also it was good to conserve fuel.

Teddy turned to the three other blokes who were sitting and standing beside and behind him and said, 'It looks all right to me.' They all nodded.

Dean, a giant of a man in his early twenties, said, 'Let's hope that we can get some time in the water before the sun goes down.'

Teddy smiled. 'No worries, Deano, we will get a couple of hours in before the sun goes down.' Dean wasn't too happy about diving in the ocean at night. He didn't mind diving in the Port Phillip Bay at night, but the openness of the ocean spooked him a bit.

Dean and Curly

Dean and Curly had been mates forever.

Their earliest memories were of their mothers getting together for cups of teas.

They lived on the same street in Williamstown, a suburb of Melbourne.

There are said to be more millionaires in Williamstown per acre than any other suburb in Melbourne.

Being the same age, they went to school together and started on the same day.

Their mums walked home after delivering the boys on their first day of school and cried together at their little boys' loss of childhood.

Even at that early age, Dean was a big boy, easily the tallest boy in their class, and like most big kids, he had a very gentle nature.

The only way to upset him was to pick on Curly.

Curly was a little bit effeminate-looking and had longish curly hair that he wore almost down to his shoulders. He was a foot shorter than Dean, and they were always together.

They were a formidable duo on the footy field.

Curly was quick, and whenever he got the ball, he would always kick it up to Dean. Dean would run through the packs knocking people left and right and usually mark the ball easily.

While they were eating their lunches at lunchtime, they noticed a little wiry kid eating his lunch on his own. Curly sat beside him and said, 'My name's Alex, but everyone calls me Curly, and this is my mate, Dean. What's your name?'

'My name's Tom and we have just shifted here from Broadmeadows. I've only been here a couple of weeks.'

They all shook hands and they just clicked.

Sometime life-long friendships are formed by the first handshake.

From that time on, they were inseparable; they always had their lunches together and walked to and from school with each other.

They went through school together and hung around together in their teen years. They all got jobs and ended up doing apprenticeships together and ended up as tradesmen.

Tom and Curly worked for the railways and ended up as boilermakers, and Dean ended up as a carpenter.

The money that an apprentice made was very poor, and the three decided to supplement their income by poaching abalone.

They could make more in a weekend than they could all week. All they had to do was rise up early and go for a swim in the bay. It was that easy.

It wasn't hard to dodge the Fisheries as they were more concerned about arresting the Greeks or Vietnamese for taking too many 'Pippies' or undersize fish, the easy stuff.

When they got their driving licenses, they all bought cars; 'shit heaps' mainly, but they were all good with their hands and they always had one going. They started to go further down the coast and soon added to their wares by grabbing crayfish. They could unload these very easily. Anyone would want to take home a crayfish and the big ones always resulted in the best money.

Soon they had people that put in steady orders for the crayfish.

The abalone was harder to sell as only the Asian restaurants wanted them and the Asians were very hard to deal with. They would argue over every cent.

One day, they were approached by a big red-haired bloke. He had an easy nature and a solid gold chain.

He said his name was Teddy and he was always looking to buy cheap abalone. All they had to do was drop it all off at Teddy's and he would pay them cash and they would be away with money in their pockets.

One Sunday night, Teddy suggested that they work in with him. He had a boat and the ready market.

Teddy suggested that they work out of the boat for a while until they all get used to each other and then do it a bit more professionally, that meant more money for all of them.

They all clicked.

There were never any problems. It all worked like a charm and the money flowed in. Soon they were making more money than they ever thought possible.

They were diving at night in Port Phillip Bay, using lights that were strapped onto their masks. Being poachers, they took everything that looked like an abalone.

Teddy's boat was fantastic. It was a twenty-three foot 'Shark Cat' with two, 200 horsepower Mercury outboard motors. It went like 'Stink'. Teddy always drove it, and they split the 'whack' up evenly. Teddy knew where all the abalone were and they always got plenty.

Teddy decided that things were getting a bit hot in the Bay, so they started going up and down the coast, staying away for a couple of days. It was well worth the trouble.

Teddy had everything worked out.

They started calling themselves the 'Dream Team', and in fairness, it was a bit like a dream. They knew all there was to know about each other and valued their friendship, above all else. They ate together and drank together. They spent most of their time together, and when Tom fell for Sandy, they all welcomed his happiness.

Dean was having trouble at home. His gambling was out of control. He would bet all day on the races and lose, and then get on to the 'Dish Lickers' (greyhounds) with much the same result.

He even had a go on the 'Robbers on wheels' (the trots), with the same results.

Dean was a 'dickhead' when it came to the punt and was always broke.

His partner got sick of money problems and took off with an S.P. bookie; much to Dean's disgust, Dean referred to the bookie as the 'Fucking enemy'.

The rest of the boys didn't say anything.

Once when Teddy worked out how much money they were making and how much money Dean had knocked off, he shook his head in disbelief. There was nothing that they could do. It was up to Dean to work his own shit out.

The other two, Tom and Curly, were rocking gently back and forth with the movement of the boat. They didn't mind diving at night or in the daytime, anytime was a good time to dive for abalone.

Tom and Sandy

Tom was tough.

He had to be. It was that simple.

He came to Australia with his parents when he was five years old.

His dad was even tougher.

He was born and bred into a criminal family in London's East End, and he came from the square miles of Government tenement buildings that housed the toughest of the tough.

Murder wasn't unknown, and Tom's father knew that the only way of Tom not ending up living the life that he lived was to move away.

The class system being what it is in England meant that no one had a chance of getting ahead, so immigration was the only option, South Africa, America, or Australia.

Tom's father knew that there were heaps of British in Australia, so he thought, 'Why the fuck not'.

They had nothing at all to lose, and they were taking everyone that put their hand in the air.

So it was settled.

Australia, here we come.

They arrived in Melbourne, and everyone was full of hope. They had left their old lives behind and were starting out fresh. Tom remembered walking off the boat and getting into the bus. The Australian bus driver said, 'Gidday, mate, what's your name?'

Tom was shy and turned into his mum's skirt. His dad said, 'Tell the man, and don't be a baby.' Looking at the grinning man Tom said, 'Tom, sir.'

The driver laughed and said, 'I'm no sir, Sunny. My name's Brian. Pleased to meet you, Tom.' He put out his hand and shook Tom's hand, and Tom never hid behind his mother's skirt again.

Tom loved Australia.

His dad got a job and wasn't put down at by any boss. He joined the union, and suddenly he had a say in the running of his workplace.

Soon he was elected as the union rep.

There were plenty of men from England and it was a new start. He made more friends in a month in Australia than he had in a lifetime in England. Sure things were a bit backward and slow in Melbourne, but nobody seemed to care; if something weren't done today, then it would be done the next day, but everything got done.

Tom went to school and learnt all about the Australian life and the Australian people. The ones who called themselves Aussies were in fact Pommies that had been here longer than the new arrivals, it was that simple.

When he was going to school, he met a heap of kids and became friendly with two.

One was a huge kid called Dean. He was a monster, almost twice Tom's height and very strong; the other was Alex, but everybody called him Curly because he had curly hair and wore it longish.

Tom thought Curly looked like a faggot, but when you had Dean as a mate not a lot of people mentioned their opinions.

They formed a strong friendship. They all played a bit of footy and cricket, but once the three of them stuck their heads under the water that was it. They couldn't spend enough time in the ocean.

They started poaching abalone and crayfish and selling them wherever they could. It was easy to sell the crayfish, but only the Asians wanted the abalone, so they took to hawking them around the Asian restaurants. The Asians were very tough businessmen and would fight over the last cent.

They had been doing it for a couple of years when one day a big bloke with a thick gold chain spoke to them about buying some abalone from them. He said his name was Teddy, and he seemed to have plenty of money and was a good bloke with it.

Later on, he suggested that they do a bit together, out of his boat. It sounded like an excellent plan to them.

When they started poaching abalone with Teddy, everything was easy.

Teddy always had everything worked out, and the abalone was always sold and the money divvied up so that they all got equal shares. They became a team and trusted each other with their lives on a daily basis.

When Tom met Sandy, it was love, at first sight.

Tom was besotted by her beauty.

Sandy was working at a pub that Tom and the boys used to go to once in a while. Tom soon became a regular, and if anybody was rude or back-chatted her, Tom was soon on the scene.

His temper, which bubbled just below the surface, would erupt and would leap to her defence.

Justice was usually swift and the loudmouth was either knocked to the ground or had Tom's stiletto at their throat.

It was common knowledge that Sandy was taken, and if you were stupid enough or drunk enough to flirt with her, then you got what you deserved.

Tom was very jealous and even a sideway glance would have Tom glaring at you.

Tom and Sandy moved in together, and she could do no wrong as far as Tom was concerned. He thought she was wonderful, and Sandy soon learnt what the rules were. She was smart enough to make things work.

Sandy enjoyed playing the 'Pokies', and with the money that Tom made, Sandy really got stuck into them. It was a problem, but Tom overlooked it, nothing took the shine off Sandy.

It was hard to work out who Teddy liked the most out of the three young blokes.

Tom was a small, wiry Pommie, who always had a knife in his sock, a double-edged stiletto, razor sharp, and wasn't scared to stick it into someone if they fucked with him.

He had problems at home with his partner, Sandy. There never seemed to be enough money. Sandy had an issue with the poker machines. She was hooked, and more than once she 'knocked off' the grocery money looking for that 'big win,' but Tom loved her and she had always stuck by him through thick and thin.

Dean was mad on the punt, fair dinkum. He would bet on two flies crawling up the wall, footy, dish lickers, horses, Tattslotto anything that you could bet on he would bet on. He would tell of days when he couldn't put a foot wrong and end up with plenty, and not to mention the days when he didn't have a cracker.

His partner had headed off to greener pastures. She took off with an S.P. bookmaker.

Dean would often mutter, 'Fucken bitch, took off with the enemy.'

Curly kept to himself a fair bit; Teddy reckoned that he just stacked his money away. He probably had a fair bit 'snookered' somewhere.

They were all good blokes, and they had never had a bad word against each other, good mates, it was funny as often three people wouldn't get on.

They seemed to listen to whatever Teddy said and realised that he was the leader.

After twenty minutes of heading straight out to sea, Teddy looked back over his shoulder, and he could just make out the mountain range behind Bairnsdale.

He started to turn to port.

He knew that he was out of sight from the highest vantage point on shore, so he started his run to Cape Conran, some say the end of the famous ninety-mile beach. Ninety miles of unbroken sand, one of the most remote and beautiful beaches in the world.

Teddy turned on his G.P.S., and it gave them a reading of where they were. They headed north, up the coast out far enough that they were under the horizon and couldn't be seen from the shore.

When they went past Cape Conran, they started to move closer to shore, and as they made out the coastline, they headed into shore.

The G.P.S. indicated that they were coming to Pearl Point.

They started to get their diving gear out from undercover in the bow of the boat.

They worked off a compressor and air lines; Dean and Curly worked off a 'T' piece, and Tom worked off a single airline. Teddy would operate the boat and act as a standby dive, if anything happened to one of the other diver, if something went wrong.

This was a formula that had worked before; everybody knew their roles and there were no problems. It was crucial that the person in the boat was a skilled power boat operator and be constantly alert; Teddy had proven himself over many years to be just that.

Their first day's abalone wouldn't be brought to the surface; they would be kept in the net bags on the bottom ready for collection on the final day.

Some of the abalone would die, but most would survive.

If an abalone is wounded when it is taken from the rocks, it will simply bleed to death as there isn't any blood coagulation in them and they bleed out and die. So they would be careful when they 'chipped' them off the rocks.

Some would suffocate, but if the nets weren't too tightly packed, most would be OK. Crayfish, octopus, and other predators would be alerted, but the damage that they do would be minimal.

The three divers got into their wetsuits, and Teddy ran the boat into the shallow water about 500 metres off the rocky coastline.

The two divers, Dean and Curly, were on the 'T' piece and went in first. They were working off the big compressor.

They swam down and started to work.

Tom plugged himself into the air hose connected to the smaller compressor, gave Teddy the thumbs up, and followed them over the side.

The divers knew to keep together so that Teddy could maintain the boat above them.

Teddy slowly started to follow the three lots of bubbles.

When you are poaching, it is crucial to be able to move off quickly, so for that reason you don't anchor your boat. You 'work live'.

You have got to keep the props away from the airlines as if you run over them. You will either cut them or tangle them up around the prop. Either one could end up costing the diver his life.

Below the water, the visibility was good.

They were only in about thirty foot of water and not having to worry about size limits. The divers were taking every abalone that was there off the rocks and putting them into their net bags.

Tom started to 'chip' abalone off the rocks, and when his net bag was a quarter full, he swam across to Dean whose net bag was almost full and swapped them. Tom swam Dean's net bag to a clear sandy spot in the middle of the rocks and left it there. He then swam to where Curly was working and helped him fill his net bag. He gave Curly an empty bag and swam back to Tom's bag and placed Curly's bag next to that.

Because they were 'coffing' the abalone, they put the outer shells against the netting forming a solid wall to protect the tender underside of the abalone from predators.

Tom surfaced and Teddy handed him another ten net bags.

The net bags are bags made of nylon netting with a stiff plastic hose opening at the top end. The bottoms are tied together with a pull line so that by pulling the pull line, the bag opens up and all the abalone fall out very easily.

There are canvas bags that attach to the top ring end and are called parachutes. These are filled with air from the diver's demand valve mouthpieces and take the weight of the abalone so the diver can carry the net bag more efficiently.

The net bags when full take about seventy to eighty kilos of abalone, and when they are shucked out, you end up with about thirty kilos of meat weight.

Tom swam back and swapped an empty net bag for Curly's full one and swam the full bag to where he had deposited the first two. He did the same with Dean's bag.

In between running the bags back and forth, Tom filled his own bag.

Soon there was a pile of bags on the sandy bottom.

When there was a pile of bags on the deposit site, the three divers decided to go up and have a spell. They all surfaced and Teddy helped them into the boat. He took a look at the GPS and marked his position and slowly moved away.

Curly wasn't happy with where the stockpile was placed, and Dean wanted to keep going so they would be able to get out when it started to get dark.

Tom was pretty exhausted.

Teddy expected all this sort of thing and knew it was all part of it. If he could keep them out in the sun for twenty minutes, then they would all warm up a bit and they would give the last remaining couple of hours a real go.

Tom asked Teddy, 'Did you see anyone go past?'

'Yes,' said Teddy, 'I saw a fishing boat from Lakes Entrance go past, heading towards Gabo Island, and another vessel, it looked like a pleasure boat heading the other way. It's been quiet.'

'Ahh, that's how I like it,' said Curly.

'I don't think that they saw us,' said Teddy.

Their boat was coloured to blend in with the shoreline. 'Let's hope anyway.'

'Phew, it's hot in these wetsuits,' said Dean, eager to get back into the water before the sun went down.

'Yeah, let's get going,' said Teddy.

He moved the boat in closer to the shore and the two divers went over the side.

Tom hung back a bit and said to Teddy, 'Do you reckon the passing boats saw us?'

'Well, if they did see us, they would have radioed back to Lakes Entrance and notified the fisheries and they will probably send up a plane. So I'll keep my eyes peeled, just in case.' Teddy laughingly assured his friend.

Tom nodded and fell back over the side. He held up his hand and Teddy threw him a net bag filled with net bags.

Tom swam down and went over to the other two divers who were filling their net bags.

There was plenty of abalone about.

Dean and Curly swam around until they found a good quantity of abalone, and when Tom swam up to them, Curly's bag was almost full. Tom swapped net bags and started another stockpile.

He was swimming back to exchange bags with Dean when a movement caught his eye.

It was a shark.

It looked to be about eight foot long and was a white pointer, nicknamed the white death by divers and surfers all over the world. It circled the bags of abalone that Tom had placed on the sandy bottom. It had its eye on Tom and was watching him intently.

Tom hit the bottom and stayed watching it, and the shark swam off into the gloom.

Bastard, Tom thought, *I hope the other boys don't see it as they will shit themselves. If they do see it, by the time we get back to the pub, it will be twenty foot long and look meaner than that shark in the movie Jaws.*

Tom slowly swam over to Dean and exchanged bags and gave him the thumbs up.

There was no sight of the shark.

Depositing the full bag beside the stockpile Tom headed back towards Curly.

The two divers were working well and their net bags were almost half full.

Tom had a look around. He didn't want to make it look obvious that there was a problem. Because if the divers saw he was worried, then they would have twigged that there was a problem, and maybe there wasn't an issue at all.

Plenty of sharks swim by you for a look and don't bother you; they are just curious, like anyone would be.

Dean was slightly in front of the other two when suddenly, out of nowhere, the shark attacked.

With a flick of its tail, it shot through the water like an arrow.

With devastating speed, it hit Dean's net bag. Dean's net bag smashed into him, knocking his face mask askew and flooding it with water, leaving Dean blinded.

Dean was hit so hard that he spat out his demand valve and he started blindly feeling around for it. The shark started shaking the net bag violently.

The white pointer doesn't have any protective screens over its eyes, so it typically hits its prey hard and spits it out, stunning it or killing it and attacks again.

This time the net bag was stuck in its teeth and it couldn't get rid of it.

It started to violently shake the net bag.

Dean was still holding onto the net bag for some protection. He got the demand valve back into his mouth and started breathing again.

Dean knew that the net bag was his only protection, so he clung to it for dear life.

The shark kept shaking its head trying to get away from the bag. Dean was being forced away from Curly, and as Curly was joined to Dean by the 'T' piece, Curly was dragged backwards through the water away from his net bag.

Curly hit the bottom and clung to a rock for protection.

Tom had glimpsed the shark as it sped through the water towards Dean.

Fuck me, he thought. *This means trouble.*

He saw it hit Dean. He saw Dean lose his mask and demand valve. He saw the shark had his teeth caught in the net bag and was still shaking his head trying to dislodge the net bag.

Tom headed towards the surface.

When he hit the top, he spat out his demand valve and yelled, 'Shark, shark'.

Teddy saw Tom break the surface and knew something was wrong.

When he heard the dreaded word 'Shark', a cold chill ran up his back. No matter how long you spend in or on the water, the mere mention of the word shark is enough to make you stop and think.

Teddy moved the boat over towards Tom.

Tom screamed, 'Shark, shark,, again, 'give me the power head. Quick, the bastard hit Dean's net bag. He's in real trouble.'

Teddy reached down and grabbed the compressed air spear gun with the power head attached.

'Shoot the bastard,' Teddy said.

A power head is simply a barrel about six inches long that screws onto the head of a spear. It contains a spring, bullet, and a firing pin. When the barrel hits something hard, the bullet is pushed onto the firing pin and that sets off the round. The bullet and the charge then go into whatever it hits.

Teddy hurriedly passed the spear gun over to Tom, and Tom swam down towards where the shark and Dean had been wrestling over the net bag.

Tom saw Curly was safe in between some rocks and that Dean had won the battle over the net bag and had the net on top of him and he was backed into a crevice.

Where is the bastard, thought Tom?

The shark was swimming around Dean in a big circle.

It was very agitated.

Its eyes were flicking from diver to diver, and it was ready to attack at any moment. It gave a swish of its tail and it shot across to where Dean was crouched. Dean had got his face mask on and could see what was going on.

He looked up at Tom and gave him the thumbs up, letting Tom know that he was OK, for the present time.

The shark swam under Tom, and Tom lined it up. It didn't matter where he hit the shark, as the power of the discharge would be enough to kill the shark immediately.

Tom took aim and pulled the trigger.

Nothing happened.

Fuck, thought Tom.

He looked at the spear gun and saw that the safety catch was on.

The shark came back for another look at Tom.

This time when Tom aimed, he made sure that the safety catch was off.

The shark moved underneath him, and Tom pointed and pulled the trigger.

With a 'whoosh', the spear sped towards the shark. It hit the beast back behind its head. The shark stiffened, then gave a shudder, and sank to the bottom, rolling belly up.

A surge of relief swept over Tom, and he went down and had a close look at the shark.

It, of course, was dead, its life taken in an instance.

Tom swam over to Dean and gave him the thumbs up.

Curly swam over and signalled that he was going to the top.

They deposited their bags in the stockpile and swam up to the waiting boat.

Teddy saw them break the surface together and gave a sigh of relief.

'Thank Christ for that,' Teddy said under his breath.

'What happened?' He asked as he helped the three divers into the boat.

'Shit a brick, mate, I thought that it was all over,' said Dean, who was a lighter shade of pale.

Curly laughed and said, 'Shit, mate, I've never seen anyone go backwards into a crevice so fast. You would put a crayfish to shame.'

Tom said, 'You weren't too slow getting out of the way yourself.'

They were all talking at the same time.

Teddy asked, 'Will one of you tell me what happened?'

'Well, a shark the size of a "flat head" bumped into Dean's net bag. Dean shit himself and almost fainted, dropped his demand valve and it was up to me to sort things out.' Tom replied.

Dean said. 'Well, I did almost shit myself. The shark was a fucking monster. It hit my bag doing one hundred miles an hour and then got the fucking net stuck between its teeth. So it started shaking its fucking head trying to get rid of it, all the time I'm attempting to hide behind the bloody bag. Fuck me, it was a bit hairy.'

'Did you get it?' Teddy asked Tom.

'Yes, mate, drilled it, dead centre.'

Curly said, 'Tom, you were as cool as a cucumber.'

'Yes, mate an easy shot. Thanks for leaving the safety catch on.' Tom said to Teddy.

'Well, the way you were bellowing and roaring, I didn't want you to shoot yourself or blast the bottom out of the boat,' said Teddy with a laugh.

'Did he make a bit of a racket when he hit the surface?' Curly asked.

Teddy said, 'The only time that I've heard him roar louder was when he was short-changed at the bar by that poofter barman the other week.'

They all laughed.

'Do you want another couple of bags?' Teddy asked.

'Not for me,' said Dean, 'I've had enough for the day. I'm putting the cue in the rack.'

'OK,' said Teddy.

Tom said, 'Come on, Curly, let's go get a couple, and give Dean a bit of time to wash the shit out of his wetsuit.'

'Fuck off,' said Dean.

'Ok,' said Curly, 'I'll see you down there,' and he and Tom swam down and started gathering the abalone.

Teddy helped Dean out of his wetsuit.

Dean said, 'That Tommy is kind of cool under pressure.'

'Yes,' said Teddy, 'he's a good man to have on your side when the pressure is on.'

Tom and Curly worked until it became too dark to see and then came up to the boat and got out of their wetsuits. They dried themselves off, and Teddy wound the hoses up onto spools.

He shifted the boat into a small cove and dropped the anchor.

They settled down for the night and Teddy started to microwave some food for them all. They had a couple of beers and some red wine. None of them drank too much as the next day would be a big day. They worked out who was going to sleep where, seeing that they didn't have any abalone on board there was plenty of room.

Teddy always slept in the open as he was always alert, keeping his eyes open just snatching an hour here and there. He knew if the fisheries came it would be in the middle of the night or the early morning. Seeing that they didn't have any abalone on board, he felt safe, the next day would be a big day.

Through the night, apart from the snorting and farting, all was quiet and calm.

All seemed to be OK.

As the dawn broke, Teddy said, 'Let's have a bit of a go.' They relieved themselves over the side of the boat and had a bit of breakfast, mostly energy bars and short dark coffees. They got into their dry wetsuits.

They always took a second wetsuit as it wasn't any good getting into a wet, wetsuit, as you got cold very quickly, and once you got cold, it was all over for you.

They steamed out of the little cove that they had spent the night in and went to a spot that they had been to before.

As they did yesterday, Dean and Curly worked on the 'T' piece, and Tommy ran the rabbit, back and forth; it all worked well.

When they came up for their third break, Teddy asked Tom how many bags they had got together so far that day.

'Twelve,' was the reply from Tom.

Teddy calculated that they had, with what they had got the previous day, more than a tonne of abalone meat. It was time that they started to shuck out the flesh.

'We had better start pulling them up and bagging the meat,' he suggested.

'Sounds good to me,' Dean said.

They started to bring up the bags of abalone and soon the deck was full of bags of abalone.

Tom began to shuck them out and throw the meat into bins. These bins had holes in them and the blood drained out. As the deck was a self-draining deck, the colourless blood ran straight into the water and the shells flew over the side to the ever-increasing number of fish waiting to pick the guts out of them.

It was all go.

Tom took off his wetsuit top and worked in his wetsuit long johns.

It's a messy job, shucking abalone.

Teddy and the others were aware that this was a dangerous time for them.

If the fisheries came across them and they had abalone on-board, the penalties were very severe, maybe ten dollars per abalone and a heavy fine as well as confiscating the boat and all their gear.

The radar was on with a ten-mile radius, but if the fisheries came, then they were in real trouble.

Dean and Curly stayed in their wetsuits. Teddy took the boat back to where they had stockpiled the abalone that they had gathered the day before and they went down and started to bring them to the surface.

Teddy and Tom dragged them into the boat and the other two swam down for more. Some abalone had escaped from the nets, but most were still trapped inside the net bags.

Soon they had all the abalone up in the boat, and they headed out into the ocean where they had plenty of vision.

Teddy said, 'Let's get into it.'

They all started shucking out the abalone meat and soon they were getting through the bags of abalone. When the bins were full, they would put the abalone meat into clear plastic bags, squeeze out all the air, and tie the top closed with wire ties. That stopped any blood escaping. It took hours of hard work, but it had to be done.

The Shark Cat was low in the water, and Teddy was worried about its speed being cut down.

The fisheries had a couple of very fast boats, but what can you do? Just keep on doing what you do best.

When all the abalone was shucked out into plastic bags and the decks and cabin were full, there wasn't a lot of room left on deck and in the cabin.

Teddy started the motors and jacked them down, and as he pushed the throttles down slowly, the big motors roared into life. The boat began to move quickly through the water; slowly, it climbed onto the plane and it increased its speed.

They had been working all day and the sun was starting to sink in the west. Everyone felt as though they had done a couple of hard days' work. They all felt tired and happy as there was money in the bank. All they had to do was unload the fish.

They headed back towards Lakes Entrance.

Dave's untraceable mobile phone rang. It was Teddy.

'What's doing, mate?' he asked.

'Not too much,' Dave replied, 'how did you go?'

'A full house,' Teddy replied.

'Sounds good to me,' Dave said, 'what's the deal?'

'We are on our way,' Teddy said, 'is there any action?'

Dave said. 'I had rung my mate in Paynesville and there was a bit of action from the fisheries. Their boats are still tied up, but they are all there getting ready to mobolize, so we might have a visit from them. What's your ETA?'

'I reckon that we will be at the spot at about nine thirty tonight.' Teddy replied.

Dave knew exactly where he meant. 'OK, mate, I'll be there,' Dave said and shut his phone.

Dave rang his brother Lee and told him to bring in the four-wheel drive and the rubber ducky into town and he'll meet him.

Dave told him everything was set. He said that he would meet him at nine o'clock.

He drove up to Jemmey's Point and saw the police Shark Cat coming down the channel from Paynesville.

Dave's mobile rang, and it was his mate in Paynesville. He told him that the fisheries and police boat were on the move and that they were heading down towards Lakes Entrance.

It looked like there was going to be a party and Teddy and the boys were going to be the surprise guests.

Dave rang Teddy and said that things were going to hot up a bit and there was an ambush coming his way.

Dave said, 'We had better revert to plan "B".'

'Right,' Teddy said.

They had worked out a few plans as things might change.

Plan 'B' was he would meet him on the beach before he came into Lakes Entrance and ferry the abalone from his boat to their truck via the rubber ducky.

It was a good plan, and as the sea was calm, there would be no problem.

Dave rang his brother and said that we are going with plan 'B'.

'That's easy,' Lee said, and they decided to get started.

Dave rang a mate of his, Pete, and said. 'We need a hand. I'll pick you up in half an hour.' Peter was a diver, a gold dredger, and they had done a bit together for a while. He was to be trusted and was always eager to do a bit of work for cash.

Dave's brother, Lee, picked him up and they swung by and picked up Peter. He had a mate with him, Paul.

Dave knew him, and he was all right.

They all headed off towards Nowa Nowa They got to the turn off to Petterman's Beach, a deserted ocean beach.

Lee got out and let a bit of pressure out of the tires to give them better traction on the sand and drove the four-wheel drive up onto the sand dunes and over to the ocean.

The sea was smooth, and there was hardly a shore break.

When they hit the hard sand, Lee accelerated and they drove away from where they crossed the sand dunes. When they reached the spot, where they had arranged to meet Teddy, they stopped and got into 'steamers,' very thin wetsuits that surfers wear to keep them warm, or 'Board Shorts'.

The weather was warm, and it was very pleasant in the moonlight.

Dave's phone rang and Teddy said, 'Give us a light and let us know where you are.' Dave turned on a spotlight and shone it out to sea.

Teddy said, 'Yes, mate, I've got you. I'm a bit to the left of you. I'll bring the boat up to you.'

They backed the 'rubber ducky' into the water and Dave jumped in with Peter. He started the small outboard motor and moved out to sea.

Dave saw Teddy's boat sitting off the shore. He didn't have any lights on. It was hard to see the Shark Cat.

Dave moved the rubber ducky towards them and was soon beside the boat.

As the noise travels very well over water, they kept our voices down. The boat crew started handing down plastic bags full of freshly shucked abalone. When the rubber ducky was full, Dave moved slowly back towards the beach and ran it up onto the sand. They all started to unload the bags.

Lee asked, 'how many trips to go?'

Dave said, 'Three or four I reckon.'

Lee nodded, and they turned the dinghy around again. Dave jumped in, and Peter and he headed out again.

They did the exercise four more times and until the boat was empty and all the abalone were on shore.

The whole operation only took about half an hour.

They loaded the 'ducky' up with abalone and then put what was over in the back of the four-wheel drive and headed off to Lee's place.

Teddy took off towards Lakes Entrance. He was still running without navigational lights. Visibility was good with a full moon and stars shining brightly.

As there was no problem in being seen, Teddy was running close to shore. They had been going for about half an hour when suddenly the Fisheries Shark Cat appeared. It was heading straight for them with lights flashing and sirens screaming.

Teddy laughed and said to Tom, 'See anything, mate?'

'No, mate, not a thing,' said Tom.

Teddy pushed both throttles down almost all the way and the Shark Cat leapt forward.

'I reckon that there will be a reception committee waiting for us when we get in,' said Teddy.

'Yes, mate, I reckon that you're right,' Tom answered.

The navigation lights of the entrance were in front of them and Teddy headed straight for them. The fisheries boat had dropped behind them, and there was minimal swell. Teddy surged through the entrance.

The police 'Eden Craft' was beside them in an instant. The police craft was a twenty-five-foot 'mono' hulled speed machine powered by two, 300 horsepower Mercury outboards, a very fast craft.

Teddy knew that there was no way in hell he could outrun a unit like that, so he throttled down and slowly his Shark Cat came to a slow speed. The police officers gestured to Teddy to pull into a wharf, and Teddy obeyed.

The Fisheries Shark Cat came up towards them and fisheries inspector, Wallace P Trotter, bellowed into his bullhorn. 'You are ordered to stop your craft immediately. Turn off your motors, and prepare yourself to be boarded.'

Wallace (Piggy) Trotter

Wallace P Trotter had always been a fatty.

He was a little round kid with a round face and a squat round nose stuck in the middle of his face.

When he was at state school, a teacher had asked what does the initial 'P' stand for, and the local wit had jumped in and said, 'Piggy. As the saying goes, 'the heaviest load that the devil can bestow on you is a cruel nickname.'

Piggy struggled through school and was at best described as an underachiever. He tried a few jobs, but nothing really seemed to work for him.

He, like most 'bush' kids, decided to join the Police Force but didn't get through the exam. He thought about the army but decided that that was a bit dangerous. He wandered from job to job. He either got sick of them, or they got tired of him.

One day, he saw an advert for fisheries officers and decided to give that a go, and guess what? He easily passed the entrance exam, did the training, and started out as a fisheries officer.

He loved it.

He was very good at detecting offenders.

If he saw a Vietnamese driving a van down a country road. He knew that the bastard had a net and he was going to set an illegal net across a river and catch a heap of undersize bream.

If he saw a bloke sitting an the end of a jetty with a plastic bucket, he knew that the bastard had undersized fish in the bucket.

He wouldn't approach him when he was out on the jetty, because all he had to do was tip the bucket over and the fish would go back into the water. He waited until the fisherman was getting into his car and then he would suddenly appear from nowhere and arrest the hapless victim.

If he saw a bus load of Asians, he just knew that they would all have an amount of abalone on their bodies or bags.

He never stopped watching and listening. He loved his job, and in fairness, the job loved him.

He was soon promoted, and as he made his way to the top, he took great delight in taking young blokes under his wing and giving them advice. The poor recruit would have to sit, trapped in a fisheries four-wheel drive, or office, and listen to the same stories over and over again, about some arrest that Wallace had made. Wallace seemed to think that the telling of these stories was in some way mandatory for the young officer.

No one called Wallace 'Piggy' to his face, and he was the butt of a lot of jokes. But when the department had a problem, it was always Wallace that they called in to fix it up.

Wallace knew that Teddy and his gang were poachers, abalone poachers, and he knew that it was his 'God-given right' to track the bastard down and arrest him. He almost nailed him a couple of months ago, but that slippery bastard had slipped through his fingers.

'I'll get the bastard,' Wallace muttered to himself, and anyone else that was listening.

When he got the phone call from a 'concerned citizen,' that Teddy's boat was up the coast, he immediately leapt into action

'He'll come into Lakes Entrance. I'm sure of it. He'll have his trailer somewhere and a bloke sitting waiting for him to come in, and they will be away before anyone has a clue that he's in port. Things will be different this time.' He assured the assembled fisheries officers.

'We'll get the bastards as they come in through the entrance. I'll get support from the water police, and we will surround them. We will confiscate their boat and their four-wheel drive and all their diving gear that will slow the bastards up a bit.

Wallace was beside himself, this looked like it was in the bag.

He jumped into his fisheries 4WD and headed to McDonalds' drive-through and ordered up big as there was a lot to organise and you can't think on an empty stomach.

He was half-way through his second 'Big Mac' when he had a thought, *maybe I can confiscate his gold chain, on the claim that it was brought by the proceeds of crime. Yes, that would slow the bastard up.*

Teddy pulled up to the wharf. Dean and Curly tied up.

The police boat pulled in behind them and the fisheries boat pulled up alongside them.

'What's the problem, officers?' Teddy asked, with a smile. 'You're all out getting a bit of overtime, good for you, keeps the money rolling in.'

Wallace P Trotter heaved his considerable bulk over from the fisheries boat and said to Teddy. 'We have been waiting for you. We know you were up the coast. What have you been doing? I hope that it's nothing illegal. With the power vested in me, we want to search your boat.'

'Mate, help yourselves. What are you looking for?' Teddy asked.

Wallace drew himself up to his full height and said. 'We are searching for any illegal fish, abalone fishing gear, or other illegal items. Let's start with names and addresses.'

A number of four-wheel drives, with the fisheries logo on them, were drawn up to the wharf and fisheries officers were getting out.

A police divvy van was also on hand to take away the evil-doers, should there be any.

Tommy, Dean, Curly, and Teddy all gave their names and addresses while Wallace huffed and puffed his way around the Shark Cat, opening and closing hatches and cupboards. He dragged out all the wetsuits and diving gear.

'Been diving have you?' suggested Wallace; with a gleam in his eyes.

'Obviously,' said Teddy, 'it is a diving boat, after all.'

'Well, what have you been diving for?' Wallace asked.

Teddy looked at him as if he was a slightly retarded child and said, 'We've been diving on, and looking for shipwrecks, off the Victorian coast. It's our hobby. We all get together when we get some time off and just go and look for wrecks.'

Wallace asked. 'Where is the proof that that's what you have been doing?'

'Where is the evidence that we haven't been doing just that?' Teddy asked.

'It was reported that you were diving close to shore up past Pearl Point.' Wallace stated.

'Yes, mate,' Teddy answered, 'that's where most shipwrecks happen when the ship runs into the land when they are not expecting it.'

Tom, Curly, and Dean sniggered and Wallace went a deep shade of red.

One of the officers said, 'There doesn't seem to be anything illegal aboard, sir.'

A light seemed to light up in Wallace's eyes. 'Yes,' he said, 'they have dumped the load somewhere, unloaded it at sea. Yes, that's what they have done.'

'Or maybe we really are social divers who just enjoy looking for and diving on wrecks,' Teddy suggested.

Suddenly Wallace jumped to life. 'Radio base and tell them to set up road blocks either side of Lakes Entrance, and we'll get the bastards on the road,' he yelled to an underling.

'Yes, sir,' was the brisk reply.

'Can we go now, or do you want to hold us up further? Like we have got homes to go to, you know, and unlike you blokes, we aren't getting paid for this.' Teddy asked politely.

'No way,' roared Wallace, 'I want to see the boat out of the water to make sure that there aren't any secret compartments.'

'For fuck sake,' said Teddy, 'I'll give my mate a ring and tell him to bring the boat trailer down to the ramp so I can load the boat onto it.'

'Bullshit, you will,' roared Wallace, 'I bet he's got the illegal abalone, where is the bastard?'

Teddy said. 'I don't know exactly where he is, but I do need him down here so I can put the boat on the trailer. I don't like to leave the trailer in the car park as if we don't come in of a night. People may think that we are in trouble and contact the water police who would spend time and money looking for us.'

Wallace thought for a moment and said, 'All right, get him down here, at once.'

Teddy rang Tony. 'Where are you, mate? We are ready to put the big girl up on the trailer.'

Tony laughed and said, 'Mate, I'm up on the point overlooking you. What a fucking circus! There are more "Swinging Dicks" gathered around you down there than there is at a Collingwood, Footscray footy match.'

'Right, mate,' said Teddy, 'I'll see you at the boat ramp.'

Teddy, Wallace, and a couple of Officers took the Shark Cat around to the boat ramp, and Tony had the trailer backed into the water.

One of the fisheries four-wheel drives was parked in the front of Tony's F100, so he couldn't make a run for it.

Teddy ran the Cat up onto the trailer; Tony hooked up the boat to the trailer and jumped into the four-wheel drive. He looked at the driver of the fisheries vehicle that was parked is the front of him and shrugged.

The fisheries officer waited for Wallace to give him the OK. Wallace nodded and the fisheries vehicle backed away, and Tony towed it out into the car park, where they were immediately surrounded by fisheries and police officers.

Wallace eased his bulk out through the diver's door and lowered himself to the ground.

'Torch, torch, I need a torch,' he demanded.

One of his underlings rushed a torch to him and Wallace started to go over the twin hulls of the boat looking for a secret compartment, finding nothing.

'Come on,' said Teddy, 'there's nothing here. We haven't been doing anything wrong. Can we go home now, or will we sit out here all fucking night?'

Wallace looked around for something to materialise out of thin air, but when nothing did, he said, 'Let them get going.'

Tony went around the Shark Cat and secured it down onto the trailer.

Dean, Tom, and Curly climbed up into the four-wheel drive, and Teddy said, 'I'll catch up with you at the "Billabong" road house'.

The 'Billabong' was an iconic roadhouse petrol station that was open twenty-four hours. They could get a steak and a cup of coffee and relax a bit. They were all hungry as they hadn't had a lot to eat in the last twenty-four hours.

Teddy walked back to his motel and picked up his car. He wondered how Dave and his brother were going and where they were.

After they had got the abalone off the Shark Cat, Dave drove the rubber ducky up onto the beach, and the boys unloaded it and Lee backed the trailer down.

They hooked the winch up to the duck and winched it up onto the trailer. They started loading the abalone into the duck, and what was left over, they chucked in the back of the four-wheel drive.

The men made it back to Lee's farm and drove into his large shed.

Lee has a ten-tonne furniture van with a hydraulic back; he does a bit of furniture removal and anything else he can do to get a quid. They loaded twenty tea chests into the furniture van. These were plastic lined and the abalone was put into them and put up the front of the truck.

The thick mats that Lee uses to cushion between the furniture were placed over them, and then they all started to load up furniture that Lee had stored in the shed. Soon the tea chests were out of sight under a house full of furniture.

Dave paid Peter and Paul and told them to take his car into town and that he would pick it up on his way back.

Dave said to Lee, 'Let's hit the road, mate.'

They drove out of the shed and into the night.

Teddy pulled into the 'Billabong' roadhouse. It was almost midnight. He pulled up behind the Shark Cat. It looked huge on the trailer with the two big black motors across the stern.

I love that boat, he thought.

He walked in, and all the boys were there tucking into a steak, eggs, and chips, a real truckies' meal.

He ordered what they were having and the tired waitress wandered off to organise it.

'How is the boat towing?' asked Teddy.

'Sweet as a bun,' said Tony. 'It should be a good run, barring accidents,' he added.

It was an unwritten law that no one mentioned anything about abalone, so they ate mainly in silence.

Dave, Lee, and the furniture van made it out of Bairnsdale.

There was a truck weighing station out of Bairnsdale and that was where the police and fisheries were set up.

They were doing checks on every car, looking in the boots and backs of utilities.

They pulled in, and the police and fishery officers came up to the window.

Lee looked at them and smiled and said, 'What are you blokes after?'

The fisheries officer said, 'There was a team of poachers operating out of Lakes Entrance, and we are checking out all the vehicles to see if we can come across the illegal abalone.'

'Where did you come from?' The young officer asked.

Lee said, 'Bateman's Bay, mate. I've got the paperwork here if you want to have a look at it. It's all clear, Bateman's Bay to Richmond, just another day at the office for us.'

'We'll have a look in the back if you don't mind,' said the police officer.

'No wukkers,' said Lee and jumped out and opened the rear door.

The door opened and the officers were confronted with a house full of furniture all covered with thick rugs. The police officer laughed and said, 'You wouldn't get a match in there, would you?'

'No mate.' Lee smiled, 'there's never enough room. It's surprising what people cart around with them.'

'Yeah, no worries mate,' the police officer said, 'off you go, have a good trip.'

Lee smiled and climbed up into the cab and they drove off.

It was smooth sailing all the way to Melbourne.

Lee and Dave got onto the freeway and they got to Richmond in good time.

Dave rang Derek, the processor. He was ready to go.

The processor. Derek.

I've always been a percentage man. I've always thought that a bit of a million is better than all of a hundred.

I've tried fishing, diving, buying, and selling. I've done everything that there is to be done in the fishing industry.

I've seen heaps of fishermen, some, a minority, have made a lot of money, but the largest percentage have ended up broke or at least working for wages or less.

I brought a small seafood processing plant with a 'Fish and Chip' shop out the front.

There is real money in fish and chips, especially the chips. You buy a few potatoes for a few cents and peel them and cut them up and then you sell them as a 'minimum chips' for three dollars and fifty cents. It's all cash and you pay your workers in cash; everyone's happy

I looked at the processing area and realised that it could be upgraded to export quality, very simply. A lot of my mates were abalone divers and when I explained to them what I was going to do, they all said, 'Go for it', so I did.

I went from processor to processor and told them that I could provide them with abalone meat. All legal, and I explained that by buying the abalone from me, it would save them all their labour costs. They were all eager to be part of my team, so away I went, into my own seafood processing business.

I had a lot of loyal divers who supported me, and my business grew. I soon found a way to get around all the paperwork, and it was easy to buy off divers who were diving for the original license holders. It was a closely kept secret and all went well.

One day, one of my friends came in and he had a big bloke with him. He was a big, happy bloke who was always smiling. He introduced him as Teddy. He had a good, firm handshake and a big, thick gold chain. I liked him from the moment I set my eyes on him.

'Hello, Derek,' Teddy said, 'maybe we can do some business together.'

I smiled and said, 'I hope so.'

The diver that had brought Teddy in said. 'Teddy does a bit of poaching, abalone. Of course, he's got a crew together and they are pretty successful. He needs to be able to unload a big quantity now and then.'

I felt my pulse quicken. This is what I've been waiting for, big loads.

'That sounds all right to me,' I said. 'How much would you have and how often?' I asked.

Teddy smiled and said, 'let's hope there's more than a tonne, any less than that, and it's not worth the risk.'

That was my thoughts exactly.

'How much do you want a kilo?' I asked.

Teddy looked at me directly, and I saw a glimpse of a hard business man. 'I know how much you get, and I want forty dollars a kilo.'

I said, 'Has it got to be forty?'

'Yes, mate, we can't do it any cheaper. We'll end up broke.'

That was that we started to do business together.

Teddy would ring and say, 'We are going away for a couple of days and I'll give you a ring when we are on our way back. There are a couple of blokes that I work with; you'll get to meet them. They are good blokes.'

Everything went smoothly and I started doing Teddy's abalone and I got bigger and bigger and made more and more money. I was happy with the way things were going.

Being a small operator he bought off the legal divers and also bought off the poachers.

A lot of his abalone was purchased off legal divers who were diving for units that belonged to the original license owners and they had gotten too old to dive.

An abalone licence could be divided up into units and the units sold off to legally registered divers. These divers were paid as little as the original owner could get. Say, maybe the abalone was worth forty dollars a kilo, in the shell. Then the original diver would be prepared to pay fifteen dollars a kilo and they would keep the rest, a pretty sweet deal. This is where Derek would come in, and if he could get the abalone through without paperwork, then he would buy the abalone straight off the sub-contractor and pay him in cash.

Derek would still get top dollar from his buyers and the sub-contractor diver would still have the paperwork so he still get the same amount of fish and no one was out of pocket, everyone was happy.

Lee and Dave drove the furniture van into the yard of a factory and the roller doors opened and saw Derek standing there. He motioned them into the factory and they pulled up beside his van.

He had a bloke with him, a solid-built Italian, one of Tony's cousins.

Tony had about one hundred cousins. They all were always available to help out, no matter what the time or the place.

They started to unload some of the furniture. Although it looked packed to the roof, there was a way to get to the tea chests very easily and soon they had some of them out and they were loaded into Derek's van.

Tony's cousin and Derek drove them to the factory where they unloaded them and returned to the furniture van.

In their absence, Lee and Dave had unloaded the other tea chests. Derek drove in, and they all threw the rest into his van. Derek and Dave headed off to his factory. Lee and Tony's cousin stacked the furniture back into the furniture van.

Lee laughed and said, 'The people who have this in storage would be surprised to find out how many times it had been to Melbourne.'

They both laughed at the thought.

Derek and Dave headed back to his factory. Dave started to weigh up the abalone. The plastic bags were ripped open and tipped onto a draining table. All the blood dripped through the drainage holes and the meat was weighed.

Teddy had told Dave to keep one hundred kilos for another client, the Vietnamese bloke, called Henry.

Dave weighed up a hundred kilos and said to Derek, 'The rest is yours.'

Derek said, 'Right, let's get this done.'

They weighed it all up, and when they agreed on the total.

Dave rang Teddy and said, 'there are fifteen hundred kilos, not counting the one hundred kilos that we kept aside for Henry.'

Dave double-checked the opened plastic bags and rechecked the amounts from each bag.

Tom, Curly, and Dean would be able to guess almost to the kilo how much they had so if Dave made a mistake, then there would be trouble.

Derek drove Dave back to the truck and Lee was asleep on the front seats and was instantly awake when we got there. They unloaded all the tea chests and put them into the back of the furniture van, shut up the van, and Dave shook Derek's hand and they started the long drive back.

Teddy fingered the gold chain that was around his neck. He always did that when he was thinking.

We ended up with sixteen hundred kilos, not too bad for a couple of days work, he thought.

He had driven back to Melbourne and was at his home. A tidy little terrace that he rented off a company that was owned by a corporation that was owned by a trust account that was owned by an offshore company that was owned indirectly by him. It was a confusing arrangement that was set up by his younger brother Shane, who was an accountant. He assured him that there was no way that it was able to be traced back to him. He knew that if he were caught and arrested for poaching abalone, then the fisheries would try and take all his assets.

He had a shower and headed off to bed. He was exhausted.

His partner Rita was awake and asked, 'How did you go?'

'No problem,' he answered. 'Everything is sweet.'

He almost instantly went to sleep.

It only seemed like minutes that Teddy had been asleep when his mobile rang.

It was Tom, and Tom wasn't happy.

'That fucking Sandy hit the casino, just as soon as I left to go with Tony and the boys. She wiped out all the money she had and cleaned out the credit cards. Then she borrowed money off the loan sharks. She's into them for two thousand dollars and they are charging ten percent a fucking day.'

'Calm down,' Teddy said, 'what do you need?'

Tom took a breath and said. 'I need a couple of grand quick as you can get it to me. I'll go and fix those pricks up. Otherwise, I won't be able to get on top of it.'

'I'll pick you up, mate, you can come with me and we'll drop off the hundred kilos to Henry.' Teddy suggested.

The restaurant owner.

My name is Hung Lee, and people call me Henry, or Hung Low, depending on how long they have known me.

My parents fled from Vietnam, by boat, with their two-year-old son, me, and made it to Australia. They braved terrible abuse and death at the hands of fishermen and pirates. My mother supported me in a sling and never put me down until we were safe. My father had sold everything he owned and turned the money into American Dollars and then into gold bullion and hid it in and on their bodies. They also filled my nappy with gold.

That wouldn't have stopped the pirates as they would have stripped everyone of all their clothes and murdered the men, thrown the naked babies overboard, and raped and killed the women.

We ended up in the high-rise commission units in Richmond, near Melbourne with a heap of other 'New Australians', all new to the country and all willing to make something of ourselves. My parents had another two babies; both girls and they worked very hard to keep the family well fed and happy.

My parents didn't find it easy to speak English, and we spoke Vietnamese at home.

When I went to the state school, I picked up English very quickly from the other kids, so when the family had to do something in English, it was left to me.

I soon became a translator for my family and other families that weren't confident enough in English.

Of course at school, I was called, plate face, power point, ching chong Chinaman, gook, and a heap of other names. But I soon learnt that I was being called all these names by wogs, dago's, wops, slimy Greek bastards, Jew boys, spud heads, Pommies and skippies. They all looked the same to me.

There were a few of us Viet kids and we all stuck together so all in all we were all right and we got through school pretty well.

Mum and Dad loved Australia and they did everything they could do to make a success of their new life; they worked long hours and prospered. They both wanted me to get an education and go to university, but I wasn't that great a student and my heart wasn't in it.

Mum and Dad borrowed some money from the Vietnam community and leased a small restaurant. They worked very hard at it and it became quite successful. When I left school, I went into the restaurant and worked eighty hour weeks.

The restaurant was a great success, and as it grew in popularity, we could put on more staff.

Because my English was excellent, I went 'Front of house' that meant that I was out there meeting and greeting people.

I really enjoyed that aspect of the restaurant trade.

Abalone was a great treat, very expensive; and whenever we had a big function on, we were always asked for it. At times, people would come in and offer us the abalone, but it wasn't the best quality and the supply wasn't constant. It was taken by illegal divers and there was a bit of a risk involved in buying it.

One night, in the restaurant, a client came in. He was a big bloke, had a great smile, and had the thickest gold chain that I had ever seen. His name was Teddy. When he introduced himself, he said, 'Gidday mate, my name's Teddy. What's yours?'

I took his outstretched hand and his grip was firm and said, 'Hung Lee, Henry, or Hung low, whatever you want to call me.'

He laughed and said, 'Henry, it is, Henry, I need a table for six people, with a dash of speed and a bit of humility.'

I didn't get quite what he meant, but it was impossible to take offence. 'No worries mate,' I said, 'walk this way.'

'Good thing that you don't have a limp.' He laughed.

I still didn't get it, but he seemed to have a great confidence about him.

He and his guests really enjoyed themselves, and when they left, Teddy paid with a credit card and then gave me fifty dollars in cash.

'I never put the tips on the credit card, Henry, I always tip in cash.' He said.

Teddy became a regular, and I found myself looking forward to seeing him and his friends come into the restaurant. At the end of one meal, he asked me if he brought some abalone in could the chef 'knock' up a meal for him.

I said, 'Yes Teddy, no worries, mate.'

A few days later, Teddy rang and said. 'Henry, mate its Teddy, can I book a table for six and can I bring in some abalone for your kitchen to knock up for us for tomorrow night?'

'No worries mate,' I said.

Whenever I spoke to Teddy, I always resorted to an Aussie accent.

Teddy came into the restaurant the following night and gave me a polystyrene cooler with about five kilograms of freshly shucked abalone wrapped up in a plastic bag.

'Mate,' he said, 'just knock us up a couple of serves done different ways and whatever is over, keep yourself. Split it up amongst the kitchen staff, have a meal when you knock off, enjoy.'

He made his way to his table and said to the waiting others, 'Wait until you taste this, you will realise why the Japanese pay top dollar for it.'

My father and I looked at the abalone. It was of excellent quality, and when we had done it in four different ways and served it to Teddy's table, there was still about half left.

My father looked at me and I said, 'Teddy said we could keep what's left.' My Father was jubilant and nodded; he had a big smile on his face.

'What do you know about this man?' My Father asked.

'He is a very good custome, and a very good tipper. He seems to have plenty of money. You should see his gold chain.' I replied.

My Father nodded slowly and asked, 'Can he get more abalone?'

When I spoke to Teddy about buying more abalone, he looked at me and asked, 'How much do you want?'

'That would rely on the price and the condition,' I said.

'Teddy said that the price is forty dollars a kilo and that was fresh abalone, same price for frozen, I.Q.F. (Individual Quick Frozen).'

I laughed and said that people come into the restaurant and offer it to us for as little as ten dollars a kilo.

Teddy laughed and said, 'Next time they come in, buy some for me as I can sell all I can get for forty dollars a kilo.'

We left it at that.

The price for abalone was about thirty dollars a kilo in the shell to the legal divers, and when you 'shuck' it out of the shell, you get about one-third recovery. So for every ten kilos of shell weight, you end up with three kilos of meat weight. Before you pay to pick it up, process it, store, freeze or chill it, that three kilos owe you over three hundred and fifty dollars, then you have to sell it.

After careful consideration, I decided that next time Teddy called me I would buy twenty kilos of abalone meat. Keep some for our restaurant, and sell the rest to our friends in other restaurants at sixty dollars a kilo.

In the restaurant, you can sell a small platter of abalone for about one hundred dollars, that platter may only use two to three abalone, and there is about eight or nine abalone to the kilo. That makes it a very profitable dish.

When Teddy called, I said for him to get me twenty kilos of fresh abalone meat.

'That wasn't a problem,' he said, and he delivered and I paid him his eight hundred dollars. I spoke to other restaurants and sold what I didn't want. This was a very profitable operation, and soon I was buying from Teddy every time he had some. I bought as much as I could as I had no problem getting rid of all I could get.

If I bought one hundred kilos off Teddy for four thousand dollars and sold it all to my friends, I ended up with a two thousand dollar profit, tax-free, easy money. That's how it started!

Teddy said to Tom, 'He'll have the cash ready, I'll give him a ring, and I'll pick you up in twenty minutes.' Teddy hung up and got out of bed. His partner Rita had gone to work, and she was a librarian and worked for the local council.

Teddy jumped into his van and drove to Tom's place. Tom was waiting for him, and he climbed in and they headed around to Derek's factory.

He pulled up in the delivery area and Derek came out.

'Are you here for the hundred kilos, mate?' He asked.

'Yes, mate, I've got to drop them off,' Teddy said.

'No worries,' said Derek, 'I'll get them for you.'

He went into the factory and came out with four fish bins of abalone. They loaded them up into Teddy's van and then headed off to Henry's family restaurant.

They pulled up at the rear of the restaurant and after having a quick look around, they started to carry the bins in. It was reasonably early and the streets were deserted.

Apart from a 'hotted' up Commodore, there was no one about at all.

Henry's father opened the door and smiled when he saw Teddy.

'Hullo, Tiddy,' he said.

Henry laughed to himself; his father hadn't really mastered English. He always called Teddy, Tiddy, and he also called eggs, eggar's.

Henry's mum blushed when Teddy walked in as Teddy always called her beautiful.

'Hello, Beautiful,' Teddy said, 'when are you and I going to run off together?'

It was the same old joke that Teddy always said.

'Where do you want these little beauties?' Teddy asked.

Tom and Teddy went out and brought in the rest of the abalone.

'There is one hundred kilos there for you, Henry. They have been in the cool room all night so they are nice and cold.'

'No worries mate,' Henry said, reverting to an Aussie accent, 'I'll grab the money for you.'

Henry went to the safe and opened it.

He grabbed four thousand dollars in cash and was just about to hand it to Teddy when the door burst open and three Vietnamese rushed into the kitchen. They wore balaclavas and were armed with machetes. Everyone stopped.

The leader said something in Vietnamese.

Teddy said. 'Speak fucking English. I don't talk Asian.'

The leader said, 'We want the money and the abalone, give it to me now.' He was shouting at the top of his voice.

Tom said, 'Don't hurt us, we are not armed,' and he sat on the floor.

The Vietnamese, who was doing all the talking, shouted, 'Give me the money, now, or you die.' He was hyped up and probably running on drugs and adrenalin.

Tommie's stiletto flashed across the room and lodged into the Vietnamese's shoulder. He dropped the machete, and Teddy lunged at him and belted him across the face.

The Vietnamese fell to the floor. The other two were confused.

'Take him to a hospital,' Teddy ordered, 'before he bleeds to death.'

Henry and his father picked up evil-looking stainless steel cleavers. The two remaining Vietnamese looked at each other confused.

'We don't know who you are,' Teddy said, 'go; now, in peace, and we will forget all about this.'

The remaining Vietnamese grabbed their wounded mate and were about to carry him out to the hotted up Commodore when Tommy said, 'What about my fucking knife?'

Teddy pulled out the knife; it made a sucking sound and blood started to run down the chest of his 'T-shirt'. He handed it back to Tommy.

'Good shot mate.'

Tommy just nodded.

The Vietnamese ran out of the rear of the restaurant, taking their wounded mate with them.

Teddy said to Henry, 'Well, that's all the excitement over for today. Let's hope that tomorrow is a bit quieter.'

Henry handed the four thousand dollars over to Teddy.

'Thanks, mate,' said Teddy. 'Will you blokes be all right?' Teddy asked Henry.

'Yes, mate, we won't have any more trouble out of those blokes. They'll be gone and licking their wounds somewhere. Boy, oh boy, you really whacked the front man!' Henry said.

'Yes, mate, when I hit someone, they stay hit.' Teddy laughed.

Teddy and Tom went out into the street and got into Teddy's van.

Tom rang the number that his partner had given him to contact the loan sharks that had lent her the two thousand.

At ten percent a day, they were earning two hundred dollars a day interest.

Big money, thought Tom.

His phone was answered by an Italian, who asked, 'What do you want?'

'*Rude bastard,*' thought Tom.

The loan sharks.

Mario and Nick were brothers.

Both were big men in their late thirties.

Their late father Bruno had come to Australia just after the Second World War, like thousands of others, to escape the poverty of Europe. He and his young wife Maria had walked off the ship and walked up to the desk that was set up as an employment office for the 'Ford' motor car factory at Broadmeadows.

They both signed up, on the spot, to work on the assembly line, and did that for the rest of their lives.

Bruno worked double shifts, and Maria only had time off to have the two brothers, one year apart

They bought their first home and moved in.

Over the years, they bought two more homes and rented them out to other 'New Australians'. They lived well and paid their bills on time and sent their two boys to school, and let them get an education.

Bruno died when he was fifty, and Maria only lasted a few years. Her heart was broken by her loss.

The boys were left with a house each to live in and another house, their parent's home, to sell; this left them with in excess of two hundred thousand dollars in cash to invest. They were very close and their parent's death left them even closer.

Given their size and lack of intelligence, security work was their specialty.

They excelled in security work; with massive bodies and shaved heads, there weren't many who disputed what they said. When they said it was time to leave premises, people left.

They started to work at the 'Crown Casino' and saw first-hand how some people would gamble everything that they had away. It seemed like they would go into a trance and only awake when everything was lost, even when they won, the people would keep betting, eventually ending up with nothing.

They saw the Vietnamese and Chinese enchanted by the tables and the spinning wheels and the non-stop dealing at the green felt tables. They also saw the people who fed off these poor souls, lending them money at exorbitant rates and how grateful the people were to be offered money, and they started to think.

Their first victim was a Chinese restaurant owner, who after a run of bad luck was broke.

Mario, who was working as a security person, said to the man. 'I couldn't help but notice that you had a terrible run of bad luck, I'm sure that your luck will turn, if you stick at it.'

The desperate man looked up at the massive security man and said. 'Yes, I just needed some more money. I'm sure my system will work eventually, but I've run out of money.'

Mario said.'You look like a smart business man. What if I lent you some money and you continued.'

The smaller man looked at Mario and said, 'How much you charge?'

Mario, who was well aware of the going rate, said, 'ten per cent, then ten per cent a day.'

The small man thought for a moment and said, 'Yes, yes, how much can you lend me?'

Mario said, 'One thousand dollars.'

The small man nodded and said, 'Yes, I will do it.'

Bruno went to the toilet and gave the man his one thousand dollars; he took his driver's license for identification. They parted and the man went back to the tables.

Mario said to Nick, 'we are away, mate, we just hooked our first fish.'

'Good work, Mario, this could be the start of something big.' Nick answered

As word got about, Mario and Nick became very popular with the punters. In fact, they became so popular that their company decided that it wasn't a good look to have these two gorillas running a loan shark operation wearing their uniforms. So the two brothers were given the option, either abandon the loan sharking or give up their security positions.

The answer was easy; give up the uniforms and still operate the loan sharking. So the brothers went to the casino of an evening and looked for prey. It was easy; soon people approached them when they needed a cash injection. They stationed themselves at a table near the bar, so they were easily accessible.

When Tom's partner, Sandy, approached Mario and said, 'Hullo, Mario, I need some money. I've had a bad run of luck.'

Mario, who had seen her around and was on a nodding acquaintance with her said, 'Yes, love, how much do you need?'

'A pair of gorillas, (two thousand) will see me through,' Sandy said.

'You know the rules,' Mario said, 'ten per cent on getting the money and ten per cent a day after that. Give us your license and I'll give you the money.'

Sandy handed her license over and Mario gave her the money.

Mario thought that Sandy was a good-looking woman. He asked as a way of engaging in conversation with her, 'What's your old man do?'

Sandy said, 'He's an abalone diver, but he's away at the present moment. He'll be back in a couple of days.'

Sandy walked away, eager to get back to the machines.

Mario said to Nick, 'Mate, that's a license to print money. I wonder if he's a poacher or a legal diver.'

'Who gives a fuck?' Nick said, 'as long as he pays us our money, he could be the prime minister.'

'Yes, yes, good point,' said Mario.

A couple of days later, Mario's mobile rang and a voice said, 'You lent my wife two thousand dollars the other night at the casino. I want to pay it back. Where can I meet you?'

Mario explained that that he was at the 'Tower Pizza' restaurant and asked, 'Why don't you join us?'

Tom gave his name and said. 'You loaned my wife two grand and I want to repay it. Where can I meet you?'

'Splendid, my name is Mario, and I'm having lunch at the 'Tower Pizza' restaurant in Lygon Street, Carlton. You can join us if you like.'

'All right, I'll be there in twenty minutes,' said Tom.

'Lygon Street,' Tom said to Teddy.

They drove there in silence through the traffic.

'These pricks are bottom feeders,' said Tom. 'They see someone with a weakness and they pounce. They hope that the person can't pay them back and then they really put the pressure on, drive them mad, they end up taking everything that they have. Bastards, someone should shorten them up, fucking wogs.'

Teddy could see that Tom was getting worked up more and more and as they neared their destination, Teddy knew that there could be trouble.

Tom had been in trouble before and Teddy knew that Tom wouldn't take a back step from any problem.

'Don't start something that we can't get out off. We are in their territory, and they will have some back-up.' Teddy said stating the obvious.

Teddy and Tom parked the van outside the restaurant and walked in.

It was lunchtime and business was a bit slow.

These restaurants really came to life in the evenings when everyone came to Lygon Street to get a bit of the Italian culture. There were a few full tables, and well-dressed Italians were sitting at them drinking coffee and eating pizzas.

Tom pressed the redial on his mobile and Mario's phone rang.

Teddy and Tom made their way across to the table.

'Gentlemen,' Tom said, 'I've got something for you.'

'Please sit down,' Mario gestured to the two empty seats at the table. 'You are the abalone diver, Sandy's husband.'

Teddy and Tom sat down with their backs to the door.

This wasn't good, Sandy had broken the unwritten law about mentioning abalone diving.

Tom didn't answer the question, instead he said, 'How much do I owe you?'

Mario said, 'I make it two thousand and six hundred dollars.'

There was a stony silence, broken when Tom asked, 'How the fuck do you come to that?'

Mario smiled. 'Let me explain. You pay ten percent when you get the money. In this case, it was two thousand dollars, so that equates to two hundred dollars. Then there is a ten percent, per day interest charge, for two days, that is four hundred dollars. That makes six hundred dollars, plus the original amount, that comes to two thousand and six hundred dollars.'

Mario smiled and expanded his chest. 'Did Sandy end up winning on the night?'

Tom looked at Mario and his brother and said, 'No, she fucken didn't, that's why I am here to pay you.'

'Oh, she had more bad luck, did she?' Mario looked concerned, 'perhaps she will have better luck next time.'

Tom looked at Teddy.

Don't do anything stupid, Teddy thought.

Tom put two thousand dollars on the table and then counted out six hundred dollars. He held the six hundred dollars and looked at Mario. Mario gazed back; he knew that they had the money and that it would be paid.

It took Tom a little while to pass the money over, but he did and Mario accepted it without comment.

'Would you join us for some lunch?' Mario asked.

'No, mate, we will head off. We have a bit to do.' Tom said.

'Well, give Sandy my best,' Mario said.

Tom and Teddy walked out of the restaurant and got into the van and drove off into the traffic.

'An evil pair of bastards,' Teddy commented.

'Yes,' said Tom, 'you wouldn't want to meet them in a dark alley late at night.'

Teddy nodded. They drove on in silence.

Teddy dropped Tom off at his place and then drove over to Derek's factory; he walked into Derek's office and said, 'Hello, mate, what's happening?'

Derek looked at Teddy and smiled, 'Mate, all's well. The abalone should be boxed up and frozen. We are happy little Vegemite's", everything is under control. The money has been transferred to my account and I'll get it out at three o'clock. I've notified the bank. They are used to this sort of thing, and they are expecting me.'

'Well done, Derek, do you want to meet me at the bank or back here?' Teddy asked.

'Mate, if you don't mind, back here, I feel safer in my own factory.'

'No worries,' Teddy said, 'I'll be here.'

Teddy decided to go and get some lunch.

Dean and Curly were sitting in a pub in South Melbourne, deciding on what to have for lunch.

'Let's give Teddy a ring and see what he's up to,' Curly suggested.

'Yes, good idea,' Dean said.

They gave Teddy's number a ring, and Teddy agreed to meet them in fifteen minutes. 'Can you order me a stake and a pot?' Teddy asked.

Teddy arrived and filled the two in about what had happened earlier on with Henry at the restaurant.

'Fuck,' Dean said, 'you were lucky to get out of that without a split head. Those fucking Vietnamese are tough bastards, little but tough. That Tom is fast with the blade. He's a bit scary.'

'That's not the end of it.' Teddy said, 'Sandy got on the punt and knocked off all the money that Tom had left in their house. She "snipped" two of the biggest loan sharks in fucking Melbourne. We had to go over to Lygon Street and "square up".'

Dean and Curly looked at Teddy and shook their heads. 'That fucking Sandy is mad when it comes to the punt,' Curly said. Dean, who was as bad on the punt, said nothing.

Their meals arrived, and they got stuck into them and ate in silence.

Mario turned Sandy's license over and over in his hand and said to his brother, 'Nick, I fancy that Sandy. I reckon that she would be a decent root.'

Nick looked at his brother and shook his head. 'Mario, your dick will get you hung. There're plenty of blondes that you can fuck. They throw themselves at you at the casino.

Everyone wants to be with us. We are big time. We spend more on our shoes than most of them do on food for a month.'

Mario looked at his brother and said, 'It's not the same. I enjoy the chase. Those sluts that will do anything for a dollar just aren't the same, and I reckon that Sandy will be easy once I get close to her.'

'How are you going to do that?' Nick asked.

Mario held out Sandy's license and said, 'Her dickhead of a partner forgot to take her license. This will tell me where she lives. I can be there in twenty minutes. I wonder if she will be happy to see me. I think that maybe she will be happy. Why don't you come and see how a smooth operator works? You can stand guard as we won't want to be interrupted.'

Nick smiled and said, 'Maybe she will be happy to see the both of us.'

'Let's go,' said Mario.

The brothers walked out and got into Mario's Mercedes Benz. They sped off.

They arrived at the address. There was no car in the drive, so Mario took the punt that Tom wasn't home, and they walked up the drive and knocked on the door.

Sandy opened the door with the chain on and looked through the gap.

'What do you want?' She asked.

Mario smiled his killer smile and said. 'Is Tom home? I need to talk to him about something urgent.'

Sandy hesitated and shook her head. 'Tom should be home after four.'

Mario hit the door with his shoulder and the door flew open. Sandy, was violently pushed backwards.

'Good,' Mario said, 'it's just the three of us then.'

Sandy was in trouble and she knew it.

The two brothers grabbed her and dragged her by the arms back into the house.

Mario ripped her top in half and Sandy's breasts were revealed. She was braless. She tried to cover herself up, but it was to no avail.

Nick pulled down her tracksuit pants and knickers.

She was naked and at their mercy.

'Hold the bitch down,' Mario ordered to Nick. Nick pushed down on her breasts and held her to the floor.

Mario dropped his pants and got on top of her.

Sandy started twisting her hips and kicking with her legs.

Mario said, 'Fucking bitch', and smashed his fist into her face.

Sandy saw stars and stopped kicking and moving. She felt blood run down from her nose.

'That's better, you fucking whore,' Mario said.

Mario violently entered her.

Sandy cried out in pain.

Mario thrust into her for what seemed like a long time.

He gasped when he finished.

'That's what it feels like to be fucked by a real man.' He sneered.

The brothers changed positions, and Nick thrust his penis brutally into Sandy.

He slapped her across the face and said. 'Move you, fucking bitch. You're lying there like you're fucking dead. Show a bit of fucking life.'

He gave her another slap and felt good.

'Fucking blonde bitch, you'll remember us. You'll remember that you've been fucked by real men.' He twisted her breasts cruelly and climaxed.

He stood up and said, 'Tell anyone about this, and we'll be back and next time we will fuck you up properly.'

Mario looked down at her and said, 'By the way, here's your license, you dumb slut.'

They walked out of the house and drove off.

They were pleased with the outcome of the afternoon.

'That showed the bitch,' Mario said to Nick.

'Yep, it sure did. Next time, we see her at the Casino, I reckon that we should just grab her and give her a fuck, whether she likes it or not.' Nick suggested.

'That sounds like a good plan.' Mario laughed.

They drove off happy with their afternoon.

Teddy walked into Derek's Factory and knocked on the office door.

'How did you go, mate?' Teddy asked.

'All's well,' Derek said. 'The money is all here, mate, safe and sound. Do you want to count it?'

Teddy laughed and said, 'I'll give you a ring if it's short.'

They both trusted each other as they had been doing business together for a long time.

Teddy shook Derek's hand, and they smiled at each other, and Teddy walked out.

He carried the money in a plastic 'Target' bag. He always thought that briefcases attracted attention to them; nobody noticed a plastic shopping bag.

Teddy had worked out what the 'Whack up' was and knew how much everyone got. He remembered that Tom had already got a couple of grand to pay those low life loan sharks and that would be deducted from his earnings.

Teddy felt good as he drove to the arranged meeting place. They were all there waiting and the money was divided up and everyone went their ways, all happy.

Tom arrived home, and when he opened his front door, he noticed that the security chain had been ripped out of the wall.

Fuck, he thought, *some bastard has broken in. Shit, Sandy, where is she?*

He called out to her and heard a reply from the bathroom.

He hurried into the bathroom and saw Sandy was in the bath.

Her face was bruised. One eye was swollen and she had a fat lip. There were red marks on her body and the bath water was red from her blood.

She was crying.

Tom rushed to her side.

He held her gently and said, 'Sandy, it's all right. It's all right. I'm here now, and it will all be okay.'

He gently held her and said, 'Can you tell me what happened?'

Sandy swallowed. 'They hurt me. They hurt me bad. There were two of them, and they were strong and I didn't expect anything. They took me by surprise.'

'That's OK. It wasn't your fault. It wasn't your fault. Please don't cry. Everything will be all right. I'll fix you up. Come on, get out of the bath and I'll tuck up into bed.'

'Tommy, I'm scared. They said that if I told anyone that they will come back and really fuck me up.' Sandy cried.

'Hey, hey, come on, Sandy; let me dry you and we'll get you into bed. I'll get you something to drink, some Irish cream. It will help you sleep. I'll ring Teddy and get him to come over and bring his girlfriend for some company. Did you recognise the men that did this?' Tom asked gently.

Sandy stopped crying and said. 'It was Mario and his brother Nick, the ones that I borrowed money off the other night. They had my license, and they got my address of my license.'

Tom nodded. 'It will be all right. Don't worry. Here, drink this, and I'll ring Teddy.'

After giving Sandy a couple of painkillers, she gulped them down with the alcohol. Tom made her as comfortable as he could and went into another room and rang Teddy.

Teddy picked up his mobile and saw that it was Tom. 'Yes, mate,' he answered.

Tom was calm and said, 'We've got a problem. Sandy has been raped and bashed by them two loan sharks that we paid the money to today.'

'What the fuck!' Teddy asked.

Tom explained. 'She is pretty upset. Can you bring Rita over to sit with her?'

'We are on the way. I'll ring the boys and tell them to meet us over at your place,' Teddy said and disconnected.

Teddy yelled out to his partner and said, 'Rita there's a problem over at Tommie's place. Sandy is hurt and he wants you to sit with her for a while.'

Teddy's partner nodded and said, 'What happened?'

'I'll fill you in on the way,' Teddy said and hit the fast dial for Dean's number.

Dean picked up immediately. 'Yes, mate, what's up?'

Teddy explained what had happened and told him to pick up Curly and bring some sort of weapon as he thought that things were going to get rough.

Dean said that they would be there in fifteen minutes.

Teddy and his girlfriend arrived at Tom's place and walked up the drive. He tapped on the door, and it was opened by Tom. Tom put his fingers to his lips to say to keep quiet.

'Is Sandy all right?' Teddy asked.

Tom nodded and said, 'She's asleep. I don't want for her to wake up alone.'

Rita said, 'I'll go in and sit beside the bed so if she wakes up, she will know that someone is here with her.'

There was a tap on the door, and Tom went and let Dean and Curly into the kitchen.

Dean came in. He looked huge, but somehow he looked even bigger with the baseball bat that he had by his side. Curly had a leather cosh in his hand. He had it made at the local shoe repair place. Curly had filled it with lead shot and it was a lethal weapon, one 'whack' from that over the head, and it was a good night, nurse.

Tom got down to business. He explained what had happened and who had done it, and then he explained what he was going to do to the loan sharks. He added that if anyone wanted to come along, they were welcome, and if they didn't, then it didn't matter. They all knew that there was no way in the world that they were going to let Tommy go and walk in on his own.

They looked at each other, and Teddy said. 'Fuck it all, let's teach these pricks a lesson. Try not to kill anyone.'

They walked out as one.

They decided that they would start at the 'Tower Pizza' restaurant as that's where they went to meet the loan sharks the first time. It was a bit early for them to be at the casino.

Sure enough, when they pulled up, they could see the brothers sitting at the same table that they were sitting at the first time they saw them.

Teddy said to Dean and Curly. 'You can be our "ace" up the sleeve. They don't know what you look like if you can get behind them when we attack. If anybody jumps in, you can start to bash them.'

Tommy said. 'I want the bastards hurt, really hurt. I want them to think of Sandy every time they sneeze or cough, every time they roll over in bed, every time they reach for something. I want them to hurt. I want their legs broken and their arms broken. I want them to be in pain for the rest of their lives.'

Teddy nodded and said. 'Yes, mate, we get the picture. Try not to kill them or we'll end up in the shit.'

Dean and Curly walked into the pizza shop and looked around. They made a point of, not looking at the two brothers. They chose a table at the rear of the restaurant, behind the two brothers and waited.

Dean wore a three-quarter leather jacket that concealed the baseball bat held to his body by the pressure of his arm, and Curly had his cosh in his pants pocket.

They sat at the table and studied the menu.

The two loan sharks were talking to a couple of other tough-looking Italian blokes and it was obvious that they were well known in the restaurant. Everything was quiet. Some other tables were occupied by elderly men who were drinking coffee and talking quietly.

Teddy and Tom walked in the door side by side; they made a 'B' line for the two brothers.

'Remember me, you dump fucks?' Tommy enquired and smashed Mario square in the face. Mario's nose exploded and blood started to pour down his face.

Teddy hit Nick on the jaw, and Nick went over backwards off his chair and onto the floor. He quickly scrambled to his feet.

There was plenty of fight left in him.

Two of the tough guys that had been talking to the brothers ran in. One hit Tommy on the back of the head and Tommy went down. The other went for Teddy. He hauled back his fist just as Dean's baseball bat hit him across the back, winding him, he hit the turf gasping for breath.

Curly missed the tough guy's head that had floored Tommy, with his cosh, but managed a sound hit on his shoulder.

The tough guy couldn't lift his right hand.

Tommy sprang up from the floor and started to beat Mario.

Mario was blinded by pain, blood and snot.

His face was a mess.

He covered up as best he could.

Tommy gave him a roundhouse swing that rocked every tooth in his head.

Mario was in trouble, but he was smart enough to hunch up and most of Tommy's blows landed on his shoulders and back. He let one go at Tommy, and Dean swung the bat at him and caught him halfway between the elbow and the wrist. Mario felt a bone break. Now he was in real trouble.

Tommy started to do some real damage, and Mario's face was almost unrecognizable. Blood was running down his shirt front. Tom showed no sign of slowing down. Nick had got to his feet only to be confronted by Teddy, who landed a couple of blows to his body. Nick started to fight back, but his heart wasn't in it. He was hurt and had had enough.

Dean levelled one of the tough guys with his baseball bat; he was out of the picture. Curly and Dean then swung onto the last tough guy, his race was soon run, and he was left a bloodied heap on the floor.

Teddy was well in control of Nick, and when Curly hit Nick across the side of his head, with the cosh, he hit the deck.

Mario was unconscious, and Tommy said to Dean, 'Give me the bat.' Dean handed the bat to Tom, and Tom said, 'This is for Sandy, you pricks.' Tom swung the bat at Mario's kneecaps with a sickening thud. He hit his knees and legs four times, and Teddy said, 'Tom, Tom, be careful, you'll kill him.'

Tom came back from wherever place in his mind that he had gone to and said, 'Fucking dog, he deserves to die.'

Tom then went to the unconscious Nick and whacked his knees with the bat. 'I'm done,' Tom said.

Teddy had a look around the room.

Nobody moved; all the older men just sat and watched. They knew that they would be next if they stuck their heads in.

'Come on, boys, our work here is done,' said Teddy, imitating an actor from the seventies crime show. The four of them walked out of the restaurant and got into Teddy's van and they drove away. They passed an ambulance heading towards the Tower restaurant.

Tommy said. 'Thanks for the help, boys. I would have been fucked if it wasn't for you all.'

Teddy laughed and spoke for all of them. 'Mate, that's what we do, if one of us is in the shit, and then we are all there to pull him out.'

Curly laughed and said, 'The way you got into that big bloke, it looked like you didn't need a hand.' They all laughed.

'Let's get an alibi,' Teddy suggested.

They headed to a small hotel in Ascot Vale, Teddy said to the barman. 'Stanley, we have been in here for an hour, if you remember we came in just as the news started.'

Stanley, the gay barman, looked at Teddy and said. 'Right you are, Teddy, I'm sweet.'

Teddy laughed and said, 'I just bet you are Stanley.'

They stayed for a while and calmed down.

When they had been there for an hour or so, they all headed back to Tommy's place.

Dean and Curly went their way, and Teddy and Tom quietly went inside.

Teddy's girlfriend Rita was asleep in a chair beside Sandy's bed. Teddy gently woke her, and she awoke with a start.

Teddy motioned her to come into the kitchen, and Tommy asked, 'Did Sandy wake up?' She shook her head and said, 'No, she's been through a lot. She must be exhausted.'

Tom nodded and said. 'Thanks for your help. I'll talk tomorrow.'

Teddy and his girlfriend headed back to Teddy's house.

There wasn't enough room in the ambulance for all the injured men, so the ambulance officers called for back-up. The police arrived, and as there weren't any witnesses, they couldn't do a lot. The detectives knew that news of what happened would trickle down to them by and by, they didn't expect there to be any arrests. The four men were rushed to the hospital. Two brothers were seriously injured and were transferred to intensive care; the other two had mainly their pride hurt, but even so they spent more than one night in the hospital.

Teddy relaxed and thought, 'Well, that's that, another day over and done.

I wonder what the boys are up to.

Tommy will be looking after Sandy.

Dean will be at the races or at some card game, and Curly will . . .' Well, Teddy didn't know exactly what Curly did with his money, probably he stacked it away somewhere.

Teddy would give them a few days or weeks off, and when the weather was good, well, they would be off again. They would all be broke and keen as mustard, to fire up again.

The Black Devil
Prelude AD 1678

A timeworn old man was sitting in the sun, reminiscing the past.

He was a storyteller, the local historian, and when prompted he would tell the tale of the Black Devil.

'He was known as the Black Devil. He was a pirate captain that everyone feared. He and his crew were merciless to whom or whatever ship they boarded on the open seas, they killed and robbed and were a menace to all.

It was said that he was the son of an African chief and was taken by blackbirder or slavers, on a slave raid.

Pirates intercepted the ship he was held captive on, and, as was the Pirates' custom, after taking everything of value, they offered the slaves their freedom. If they joined forces with the pirates, of course, the biggest and strongest were accepted first. He readily joined the pirates. He had the courage and soon was seen as a leader of men. His strength and his eagerness to kill were soon noted by the captain and crew and he was promoted up from a lowly position to one of importance.

Soon he was by the captain's side whenever they encountered and robbed a ship. On one fierce battle, the captain was killed by a musket ball to the heart. After a bitter fight amongst the remaining crew, The Black Devil was elected to be the captain.

And so the legend was born.

In the late sixteen hundreds, there were plenty of ships laden with gold and treasure. Some were poorly armed and had unreliable crews. Men that were dragged drunk on board with the promise of a better life only to find out that they were signed on forever to work and live worse than dogs. They were easy targets for The Black Devils pirate boat, which was renamed, Kumali, and soon their tally was becoming a real threat to the big companies.

The companies soon approached the government, and the government of the day decided to send out a trio of naval vessels to catch and hang the Black Devil and his crew.

It didn't take long for the Navy to intercept the Kumali, and after a short battle, the Kumali was damaged and the pirate crew decided to make a run for it.

They threw their dead over the side and fled for their lives.

The pirate crew knew that if they were caught, then they would all swing, so there was nothing else to do, but make a run for it. So they sailed off with the trio of naval vessels behind them.

The Kumali was a fast boat, faster than the navy vessels, so there was little to do, but get the wind in your sales and go for the horizon.

This is what they did.

Unfortunately, the naval crew was more experienced than the crew of the Kumali, and they couldn't lose them.

The naval crew knew that if they didn't put an end to the crew of pirates, then they would pay for it themselves on their return. They were promised riches and promotion if they were successful and disgrace if they returned and were unsuccessful, so they followed the pirate vessel.

Sometimes it would look like they were getting closer and then the next morning they would awaken and just be able to make out the Kumali on the horizon. They doggedly hung on.

Days turned into weeks and weeks turned into months.
They were never seen again.

My name is Lumumba.

I was next in line to the throne.

My father is a feared and respected leader, and when he dies, as he one day must, I would have sat on the throne and ruled the empire known as Utoomba.

When I became a man, my father had the head witch doctor and foreseer of the future to tell me what the future held for me.

He stared into the smoke of the fire and threw the bones onto the ground; he called on all the distant members of our tribe that had passed into the heavens before us to tell him my future.

He went into a trance and told us that I would be a much-respected and feared leader, but I would die on a faraway shore; and my bones would one day be bleached in the sun.

My father thought about this and accepted it, for who can comment of the ways of the unknown.

I had a loyal band of followers that would have been by my side on the day that I was elevated to the throne. But for the evilness of my younger brother, who was jealous of my position. He plotted with the Slavers and arranged for us all to be captured as slaves when my father was away on important business.

When my father returned, he was told that the village was attacked by Slavers and luckily my younger brother escaped, but, unfortunately my men and I were all taken.

He told my father that he and the rest of the village did all they could, but it was to no avail as the Slavers had formidable weapons and the villagers were outnumbered.

My father would have saddened by my loss as he thought that I would have been a fair and just king. But life must go on and he would have accepted the story and then made my younger brother next in line to be king.

My men and I were chained and marched to the port.

For days, we were beaten, flogged, fed and watered very little until we had no strength left in us.

Finally, we were loaded onto a slave ship and then it set sail for a far off country.

I told my men to be brave and, if we were as one, we would survive.

We endured many hardships, sea sickness, starvation, and cramped, filthy conditions below decks; we hardly saw the sun, but we stayed united.

One day, we heard the sailors yelling and running around on deck as if they were in danger and heard the term Pirates.

A fierce battle followed, and our ship was boarded by the pirates. Anyone that resisted them was killed and thrown over the side to feed the ever hungry sharks.

In the end, the captain surrendered his ship to the pirate captain.

The pirate captain and his crew ransacked the vessel looking for bounty and liquor and if possible any women that might have been on board. When they had loaded everything of value aboard the pirate ship, they bought us slaves up on deck. Through an interpreter told us that if we wanted to join them and be free we could, but we must swear loyalty, on blood, to the pirate captain.

Of course, we agreed, and we became pirates.

We soon learnt what we had to do when we were in battle; we even enjoyed the thrill of taking over vessels and killing anyone that stood in our path.

My men and I became a force to be reckoned with.

We talked together and decided that it would be better for us if we overthrew the captain and his most loyal followers and take over the ship ourselves.

As we didn't have any idea of navigation, we decided we needed some experienced navigational crew. So we spoke to the existing crew members and soon found some men that were more than happy to come over with us, for a bigger percentage of the take.

When we encountered the next ship, we attacked and in the confusion we were able to kill some the captain's loyal crew. As luck would have it, the captain was felled by a musket ball and died almost immediately.

We took over the hapless ship and killed everyone that we didn't want and threw their bodies over the side. We then had a vote and I was elected to be the new pirate captain.

We were by all means free men, but we all yearned to be back on solid land in the arms of our loved ones. But alas we had seen a side of life that we wouldn't have seen if we hadn't have been taken by the slavers.

The gold and trinkets meant little to us but to the others on board they meant everything.

When we called into a friendly port to trade whatever spices or materials, or other valuables we had, we saw that gold was power. We could buy whatever we wanted with gold.

The fair-skinned ladies were generous with their favours and the Tavern owners were friendly and helpful to us. They didn't care about the colour of our skin, or the fact that we could hardly communicate with them. Just as long as we had gold and anything else of value to trade with them, everything was good.

We came up with a plan that we would take as many ships and get as much gold as we could in the period of a year and then return to our homeland and claim what was rightfully ours. We would have plenty of gold, and we could buy mercenaries and overthrow the present ruling party and then I would be king and be returned to my rightful role as king.

I would slaughter my brother and all his followers and let the people realise what injustices had been done. I would make our kingdom great and all will live in peace and harmony.

My ship's crew consisted of my closest followers that kept me constantly guarded and other crew members, that we had taken on board.

I felt that the gold kept them loyal, but I was always aware that treachery was always there so I was constantly alert.

We became very successful at what we did and soon we were feared; for our ruthlessness was beyond compare.

We would sail up in the direction of a merchant ship, and when we were challenged, we would lower the black flag and turn towards them and unleash a barrage of cannonballs that would cripple their rigging. Leaving them slow in the water. Then we would lash our ship to theirs and board them, cutlasses at the ready.

We would swarm across their decks slaughtering all before us and soon the decks were awash with blood. Nothing could stop us and we felt that we were invincible.

One morning, I discovered a hidden compartment in the captain's cabin that I had taken over. I only found it by chance. When I opened it, I found a heavily fortified Sea Man's chest. My crew and I smashed it open and the contents were revealed. It was a jewel-encrusted golden chalice.

Some of the crew had knowledge of such treasures and confirmed to me that this chalice was very valuable.

My former tribal crew mates and I laughed at such talk. How can something that weighs as much as ten coconuts be worth such a fortune?

The others explained that, in fact, this was a gift from one king to another king and that this sort of thing was normal and correct in these times. It was something of great importance. We wondered about such things as it was customary of great kings, in our country, to do the same.

Maybe we were all the same? Even if our skin was a different colour!

When we entered a friendly port, we discovered that the British government had, due to our constant pirating of their bullion ships, decided to unleash three 'men of wars'. To capture and hang me and all my crew. They were prepared to follow us to the end of the earth and our destruction was their sworn duty.

Early one morning, out of nowhere, we were suddenly surrounded by the British trio. They raked our ship with cannon balls and soon we were severely damaged. Luckily, a storm came at us and we were lashed by rain and hail. We decided it was time to run for our lives and so we did. We sailed with the wind behind us off into the distance.

We were slightly faster than the three 'men of wars', but due to their navigational skills, they kept us in sight. We weren't getting away. We were just keeping in front of them. We sailed with them in pursuit for many days and then many weeks, and then many months.

We called at some ports and stocked up on supplies and fled before we were trapped by the 'men of wars'. We kept running as our lives depended on our agility to remain in front of our pursuers.

Some of the crew were superstitious and thought that there was a possibility that we would fall off the edge of the earth. I assured them that that was a better proposal than being hung by the neck until we had kicked our lives away.

We came across the great southern land, a land so isolated that people from our world had never explored it, and we hadn't seen the sails of the 'men of wars' for some time. So when we saw the smoke of fires, we went ashore and witnessed a primitive race of people, dark of skin, like us, but very backward. We slaughtered the strange two-legged beasts that 'hopped' around and cooked and ate them. The meat was very good, but being what we are, we killed the primitive men and took the women aboard.

We soon were tired of the women, as they were very different to our women back in the land we were taken from. They didn't speak our language, so we slit their wrists and threw them overboard; they were soon eaten by the sharks.

We had a meeting. Confidence was high now that we had eaten and with full bellies we decided that we would press on. We hadn't spotted a sail for some time, we were sure that our freedom was assured. We decided to go ashore and bury some of our looted treasure on the theory that whenever we needed it, we could come and get it. We looked for a natural harbour and when we found one, we went ashore and buried some of our vast wealth. I couldn't bear to part with the golden chalice, so I left that on board with the rest of our cache of treasure. We decided to head back.

We still had plenty of provisions, but on the return trip, we were hit by a savage storm and the ship foundered.

We were crashed into rocks; there was nothing that we could do.

We could only ride the storm out.

The waves pounded our craft and it was torn to shreds. We were doomed, on the other side of the earth, far from our homes, in a country so desolate that only strange animals and primitive people could survive.

Most of the crew were drowned or were killed by falling masts and spars; the rest were eaten by the ever present sharks.

A few of us made it to shore, but we were doomed to die a lingering death from injury and starvation.

Our bones were slowly bleached by the sun.

The Monumental City AD 1853.

Captain William James squared his shoulders as he looked over his craft from the wheelhouse, the Monumental City.

What an excellent ship, he thought to himself.

One hundred and seventy foot and ten inches long, from stem to stern, an exceptional craft, in fact, the first steamship to cross the Pacific Ocean.

The Monumental City was built in 1850 by Murray and Hazelhurst in their Baltimore shipyard.

She was a 737-ton wooden-hulled screw steamship with a single deck and auxiliary ship-rigged sails. The vessel had two oscillating engines, also built by Murray and Hazelhurst, powering a single Smith's propeller with a diameter of twelve feet. An account of the New York Herald shortly after she was launched described the Monumental City as having a first and second cabin, affording accommodation for about two hundred and fifty passengers. Her passenger accommodations are of the most superior character, the staterooms being fitted up with much elegance and abounding with conveniences.

It was a leisurely trip taking only sixty-five days; they had stopped it Hawaii and Tahiti, an exceptional voyage enjoyed by all.

After an unsuccessful career taking miners from Panama to the gold fields in California, she had been sent out to Australia to take gold miners from Sydney to Melbourne and back.

This was her first voyage, and she was on the return leg back to Sydney.

Captain James asked his Chief Officer Edward Van Syce, 'Is everything fully prepared for our journey?'

'Yes, captain, everyone is aboard, and we are fuelled and ready to leave an your command.'

Syce replied.

'Then give the order to cast off and we will be on our way,' Captain James ordered.

With that, the ship cast off.

The Monumental City steamed out through the heads and turned to run towards Sydney Town.

She was soon on her way up the coast.

Dinner was served and the captain shared his table with some of the wealthy miners. There was much laughter and plenty of wine was consumed; all in all a most pleasant time was had, the sea was smooth, and they were making good time.

Captain James made his way to the wheelhouse and checked with his chief officer to see that everything was 'Shipshape' before he retired to the saloon and once again taking up the company of the wealthy miners.

This became a habit with Captain James and the next night he welcomed miners to his table and enjoyed their company and the tales of the adventures that they had encountered on the Australian gold fields.

As was Captain James habit, after he had eaten his dinner, he entered the wheelhouse and made sure that everyone was alert and standing at their posts. He checked that the officer-in-charge was alert and not drunk. A problem that he had never had with Chief Officer Syce and proceeded to head to his cabin and go to bed, where he slept soundly until he felt the ship thud into something solid.

He realised, without being briefed, that the ship had run aground on the sand.

As he hurriedly dressed and made his way to the wheelhouse, he was confronted by panicking passengers. He assured those that he came across, not to worry as it seemed to him from his limited knowledge that the ship had only 'ran aground'. A change in the tide would see them all clear, nothing to worry about, it often happened, please remain calm, and that he would get to the bottom of the problem.

When he got to the wheelhouse, there was panic.

So he calmed them down by saying, 'Just be calm. The weather is smooth, and there are about four hours till daybreak. We will stay as we are and then unload the passengers onto the island at first light.'

Over the next couple of hours, the breeze strengthened and swung from south-west to south, south-west, causing the vessel to thump heavily on the sea bottom.

Captain James ordered that the fore-mast be cut away and the boats be lowered to evacuate the passengers. But many refused as the seas were starting to become very rough and they feared for their lives in the pitching ocean.

Captain James ordered that a rope, a 'lifeline,' be strung between the vessel and the shore. This was done and soon some of the passengers and crew made their way to the shore.

The weather deteriorated and soon the waves were washing over the ship's decks, causing many people to be washed into the sea and drown.

Some of the miners were wearing money belts that were filled with gold, coins and bars, and these poor souls went rapidly to the bottom. The only way off the ship was the lifeline as the seas got rougher and rougher and the ship broke up more and more.

There was little that the captain and crew could do but try and get everyone to go over the side and use the lifeline to get to shore and safety.

The vessel eventually broke up and a total of thirty-seven people died; the survivors made their way to safety at Two Fold Bay.

Later on at an inquiry into the loss of vessel. The court found that Chief Officer Edward Van Syce was guilty of unofficer-like and unjustifiable conduct. The court severely reprimanded Captain William James for incautiousness and indiscretion: when approaching a coast to which he was a stranger and con-fessedly out of reckoning as to the position of the ship.

Alas, they were broken men!

They blamed themselves for the death and injury of the passengers.

Present day
The Golden Chalice

Teddy fingered the solid gold chain that he had around his neck and said to his partner, Rita. 'It's funny, but you get used to the weight around your neck, you don't really notice that it's there at all.'

'Some day, someone will thieve that off you,' Rita said looking up from her morning paper.

Teddy laughed and said, 'I've already thought of that, they will have to cut my head off as I've 'Super glued' the clasp up.'

Rita looked up from her paper, laughed and said, 'Some of the dickheads that you hang around with would do more that cut your head off to get their hands of that much gold.'

'Yes, you're probably right,' said Teddy, 'I'll just have to be careful of who I hang around with.'

Teddy's phone rang, and it was Dave, from up the country.

'Hello, Dave, what's up?' Teddy asked.

Dave, who spent a fair bit of time hanging around the fishermen and the abalone poachers said. 'Mate, there was a couple of blokes in the pub last night and they were talking about one of their mates getting a handful of gold coins off a shipwreck just off Mallacoota.'

'That's all we need, some bastard telling sunken treasure stories to get everyone excited,' Teddy said.

'There might be something in it,' Dave replied.

'What sort of ship was it?' Teddy asked.

'Well, it wasn't a treasure ship,' Dave replied. 'It was a passenger vessel, the Monumental City. It was taking miners from Melbourne to Sydney and it went the wrong side of Gabo Island.'

Teddy asked, 'Didn't they see the lighthouse on Gabo Island?'

'No, mate, that's the reason that they erected a lighthouse on Gabo Island. Because so many people lost their lives, at first it was a wooden one, and then they built the one that's there now out of granite,' Dave explained.

He continued. 'There has been a period of shit-house weather up here and the heavy seas must have uncovered some of the wreckage. That's all I can put it down to. If you were to come up for a look, then maybe you can do a bit on the border between Victoria and New South Wales. There's plenty of reefs there, and it's not too deep.'

Dave knew that Teddy didn't do too much in deep water.

'All right, I'll check with the boys and see if they are interested. At any rate, I'll get back to you and tell you what's going on.'

Teddy pressed 'end' and sat down and thought about how he would set things up.

Maybe get Tony to tow the boat up to Eden and then come down from there. He wondered if the entrance to the ocean was open at Wonboyn.

He would give the bloke that ran the caravan park a ring and see if they could unload in there. Yes, that would work. There also was a bay that offered all-weather anchorage, Bittangabee Bay; it would be hard to unload the abalone there, but it would be all right to stay there overnight, yes, that would work.

Teddy thought about it and rang the divers.

He told them that they could go up and have a look for some gold coins and then on the way back knock off some abalone. Same story as always, they would be away for a couple of days.

Tony would tow the boat up to Eden and they could fly up and meet him at the Merimbula Airport. He would put the boat in and disappear and meet them when they had done their thing.

All the boys agreed, and Teddy gave the 'OK' for Tony to tow the boat up to Eden.

Teddy rang his mate at the Wonboyn caravan park and asked him if the bar was open and could he get out to do a bit of fishing.

The caravan park owner said that due to the recent bad weather that the bar was, in fact open and there was plenty of clearance and Teddy could get his Shark Cat out easily. Teddy thanked his friend and put a plan together.

Teddy rang Dave back and gave him the all clear as to what they were planning to do.

Dave was happy to be doing a bit. He rang his brother Lee and told him that there was something on the go and to be prepared for a trip to Melbourne. All they could do was wait to hear from Teddy.

Tony did the checks around the trailer and pumped grease into the waterproof wheel bearings, (bearing buddies) on the boat trailer. Filled up all the fuel tanks in the four-wheel drive and the Shark Cat, and headed off towards Eden, probably an eight-hour or a nine-hour tow.

Tony didn't mind the solitude of driving and towing the boat.

He didn't fancy being a diver as he had a great fear of sharks, and he would be well paid for whatever he did. It was lucky for him that he and Teddy were mates as he didn't need to work a normal job. He was on a disability pension, so he was on call twenty-four hours, seven days a week. He was doing it easy.

✧ ✧ ✧ ✧

Wallace, Piggy, Trotter was leaning his large body back in his chair, feet up on his desk. When the news came through, from a fellow fisheries officer, that the Shark Cat that Teddy used was heading towards Bairnsdale.

'That bastard is at it again,' Piggy roared. 'He's on his way down here to rub our noses in it again. This time I'll fix the prick. I'll get him red-handed. I'll get the bastard with a boat load of abalone. He won't know what hit him. I'm ready for him now.'

Piggy marshalled his troops. It was obvious that he was a 'driven' man.

'No excuses, men, we'll stay on his trail, don't let him out of your sight.'

The other fisheries officers looked at each other and thought it was going to be a long night. They knew that Piggy was adamant that he would one day get Teddy and his gang. Maybe this would be the day, and they wearily got themselves ready and hoped that it wouldn't end up like the other times that they had tried to intercept the poachers. Long days of surveillance with nothing at the end.

Teddy, Tom, Dean, and Curly got out of the taxi at Essendon airport and walked up to the ticketing area and picked up their tickets from the R.E.X. Country Airlines counter and sat down to wait to be called to get into the plane.

Tom was a bit worried about leaving Sandy on her own as she was still getting over being attacked and raped by the loan sharks. Rita, Teddy's partner, had suggested that Sandy come over and stay at their place while the boys were away. This suited Sandy, as well as Tom, as Sandy wouldn't sneak away to the pokies if Rita were there.

Dean was quiet as he had knocked off most of what he had made the last trip in a card game that had lasted for days, and Curly didn't say much at the best of times.

Teddy did most of the talking and kept their spirits up; they didn't bother about having a drink as they had started work, so to speak.

Piggy Trotter, dressed as a tourist, with a baseball cap pulled down and 'reflector' sun shades on, kept Tony and the Shark Cat in sight.

This was easy. He reckoned that Tony didn't have a clue that he was tailing him.

In fact, Tony realised that he was being tailed almost as soon as Piggy got behind him. Through a series of speeding up and slowing down procedures, Tony soon established that the white falcon sedan was 'on his tail.'

He made a mental note to mention to Teddy that he should change the colour of the Shark Cat so that it wasn't so readily recognisable.

When he passed through Nowa Nowa, he wondered how much fuel that the white falcon had and how far it would tail him.

He rang Teddy and told him he had a tail.

Teddy didn't seem too worried, just told Tony to keep going and see what happened.

Tony pulled into the service station at Newmerella and topped up the four-wheel drives tanks. He noticed the white falcon had pulled up on the side of the road, just within sight of the service station. He knew that as soon as he pulled out, the falcon would pull in and get a fill-up and then be on their way after him.

He smiled and thought, *Well, soon they would know just where he was going.*

The plane landed at Merimbula Airport, and the four men walked into the terminal and asked for a taxi to take them to

Eden. The girl behind the counter directed them to where the taxis were waiting. They all jumped into one and headed towards Eden. They didn't speak too much as taxi drivers were all ears and they talked to everyone.

The driver, a youngish Australian, asked them what they were doing up here, and Teddy said. 'We are going to do a bit of fishing, try and hook a big one, just go out and spend a bit of time on the water.'

The taxi driver then went on to tell them all about how the marlin were being caught down off Eden and how strange it was for them to be down this far. Must be global warning, he commented.

Teddy agreed and the others remained silent.

Soon the driver had them in Eden, and Teddy asked to be dropped off at the Eden fisherman's wharf.

When Tony crossed the New South Wales, Victorian border, and the Falcon kept following him, Tony thought that now they will know that we are going interstate. He wondered if they had power over the border, but he thought that the Victorian Fisheries would team up with the New South Fisheries and work together to get rid of the evildoers. He only had an hour or so before he could put his feet up.

Teddy paid the taxi driver, and he drove off, wishing them the very best of luck.

The boys saw Tony in the four-wheel drive and walked over.

Tony was ready to launch the boat, so they all got on board and Tony backed the boat down into the water.

Teddy started the engines and they ticked over smoothly. Tony unclipped the bow, and Teddy reversed the boat off the trailer and out away from the boat ramp.

Teddy and Tony gave each other the thumbs up and Teddy slowly cruised out into Two Fold Bay, the second deepest natural harbour in the world. They picked up speed and were soon going past Boyd Town Tower down south towards the Victorian, New South Wales border.

The lighthouse on Green cape came into view and Teddy said to the boys. 'We will probably unload our fish (abalone) off into Wonboyn. There's plenty of depth on the bar. I spoke to the manager of the caravan park last night and he reckons that it's all good.'

The boys were comfortable as the sea was calm and the sun was shining.

They crossed Disaster Bay, named after a couple of wrecks that had gone on the inside of Green Cape in the middle of the night and continued down towards the border.

Teddy checked the GPS and saw that they were in Victorian waters. He slowed the boat and then brought it to a halt, and the divers started to get their gear ready.

Teddy said, 'Well, here we are Dean and Curly, jump over and see what's down there.'

'Isn't this where that white pointer bit that abalone diver?' Dean asked.

'Yes, mate, sure is,' Tommy replied, 'but he didn't like the taste of him and spat him out.'

Curly laughed and said, 'He ended up on American television, a real-life shark attack victim.' They all laughed.

'That's one way of hitting the big time.' Teddy laughed.

They were well over the Victorian side of the border, and as usual the boys went about their business without any fuss. Tom swam down and started to pile up the net bags of abalone in a pile as Dean and Curly chipped them off the rocks.

As always, they took everything, size wise, big and small, and soon had ten bags stockpiled up. Tom had to swim further and further between the divers and the stockpile so he gave them the thumbs up and they headed for the surface.

Teddy brought the boat over and they all climbed on board.

'We'll move over a bit and see what there is to be had over there,' Teddy suggested, marking the spot on his GPS.

They were all soon back in the water again, Dean and Curly chipping off the abalone and Tom running the rabbit across to another stockpile.

It started getting dark, so Teddy called it a day and the boys got into the boat and Teddy rolled the hoses up onto the spools that were fitted to the boat.

'Get changed and we can go back to Bittangabee Bay or we will shelter in the anchorage of Gabo Island.'

'Which is the closest?' Tom asked.

'I reckon Gabo Island,' Teddy answered.

'Well, let's spend the night there,' Curly said.

So it was agreed.

They got out of their wetsuits and headed off towards Gabo Island.

They were all sitting around talking when Teddy asked them when they wanted to have a look at the wreck site. They all agreed that it should be before they started to shuck out the abalone.

After some consideration, they decided that they should have a dive in the morning and then spend a couple of hours in the shallow water looking for some gold coins; they probably wouldn't find any. Then maybe Tom and Curly would continue to get abalone while Teddy and Tom started shucking out the abalone from the first stockpile.

They all agreed that this was the best way to go; so they all settled down and had a bit of tea and a drink. Soon they were all ready for bed, and after sorting who slept where, they put their heads down.

Teddy was awakened by the noise of a boat coming into the anchorage and thought that it might be the fisheries or water police. As they had nothing on board and all their abalone was coffed up in their net bags, there wasn't anything to concern them. But he was surprised at how they got so close without him hearing them or seeing them.

It wasn't anything to worry about as it was an older couple who were probably sailing around Australia to keep away from their kids and constant demands for their hard-earned money.

When the sun came up, the boys got ready for the day ahead. They had breakfast, short black coffees, and energy bars. They didn't get into their wetsuits, and they would wait until they got over to where they were going to dive.

Teddy hoisted the anchor and they got under way.

They headed back towards the New South Wales, Victorian border, and moved close into shore.

Wallace, Piggy Trotter, drove down the hill towards the Eden Fisherman's Wharf and saw Tony pull up and light a smoke.

Tony walked around the Shark Cat and checked to see if everything was sound. He unhooked a couple of straps that held the boat to the trailer and looked to be happy with the way that the boat had travelled. He didn't appear to notice Piggy looking at him.

Wallace had spoken to the New South Wales Fisheries department and told them what was going on and they had offered to give him all the assistance that they could possibly give. Any arrests on New South Wales soil, or water were going to go to New South Wales Fisheries and not Victorian fisheries.

Piggy wanted a boat to go up and see where exactly Teddy and his band of desperadoes were; unfortunately, this wasn't possible immediately, so Piggy seethed inwardly.

Bastards, he thought, *what will I do next? Should I stay in Eden and wait for them to come back or should I watch Tony and the trailer? Well, Teddy needed the trailer to put the boat on, so I'll watch the trailer. Yes, that ought to do it, keep my eyes on the trailer.*

Piggy waited and watched the trailer, and when Tony drove off, Piggy couldn't have been happier; he followed Tony at a discreet distance.

Tony headed off towards Merimbula, and when he saw that the white falcon was behind him, he smiled a bit. *That's one problem fixed*, he thought to himself, *that's one Fisheries officer gone on a wild goose chase.*

Tony booked himself and his trailer into a caravan park and decided to head down to a club for a bit of dinner.

He rang Teddy and told him he and his tail were in Merimbula getting ready to eat.

Dean and Curly hit the water together and swam to the bottom. Curly looked around and decided that they would start to work on a section of reef that had plenty of abalone. They began to fill their net bags and when Tom arrived on the scene, they were almost ready to exchange their net bags for empty ones. Tom started to make a pile ahead of where the two divers were working so as they would be working towards the stockpile.

A large wobbegong shark slinked by, these were also known as a 'carpet shark' as their skin was of a mottled kind of colour. It had a big broad head and was relatively harmless. They normally lay concealed in the weed and the rocks.

The only way of getting into trouble with it was to startle it, and it would then, with incredible speed, snap out at you. Some divers had been bitten by a wobbegong, and as it had fine razor-sharp teeth, some damage was done, but mainly to the diver's pride.

Soon they had enough abalone stockpiled to stop for a spell, so Tom gave the boys the thumbs up and they took whatever abalone they had and put them onto the stockpile. The three of them headed to the surface, and Teddy brought the boat over to pick them up.

'How many bags have we got?' Teddy inquired.

'There's about twelve down there that we got so far,' said Tom, 'and about twenty from yesterday, so that makes about thirty-two, all things being equal.'

'That should give us about eight or nine hundred kilos of meat,' Teddy reckoned. 'We should get another ten bags just to make sure of making the whole deal pay.'

They all knew what they needed, but Tom said, 'Let's go and have a quick swim on the wreck site and see if we can spot anything. If not, then we can have a quick jump in somewhere and finish up while we are shelling out the abalone.'

'Sounds good to me,' Teddy said. 'In fact, I wouldn't mind having a bit of a look around for myself, just to make sure that you blokes don't miss anything.'

Tom laughed and said. 'Fucking treasure hunters, you are all the same. You stop earning and waste your time looking for treasure that's not there, "Dickheads", I don't know what goes on between your ears, fair dinkum.'

They all laughed and got prepared for the short trip around Cape Howe and in between Gabo Island and the shore, heading towards Tullaberger Island.

Teddy pulled the boat around to the eastern side of the island and said to the divers. 'You will see a shaft lying on the bottom among some rocks. It's covered in weed and barnacles, but you can still make out the straight lines, that's where she ran aground, the rest of the wreck is scattered all over the place.

Just remember that Mother Nature doesn't do things in straight lines. If you see anything straight, then it's man-made.'

He started the compressors and the divers went over the side.

They swam down together, and as it was only about twenty foot deep, the visibility was good.

Tom indicated that they swim together in a straight line about ten feet apart, and he gave them a sweeping motion. They all concentrated.

The bottom was sandy and there were a lot of ripples in the sand about twelve inches high. It looked like the bottom had been ploughed a long time ago.

They covered a lot of ground quickly and it soon became apparent that there weren't piles of gold coins lying out in the open, but they stuck to it.

Every now and then one of them would stop and pull a bit of rotten timber up or move a small rock away to look at it, but all in all it was pretty uneventful, almost boring. They started to become bored with the whole operation. Secretly, they all hoped that the bottom would be littered with gold coins and all they had to do was pick them up by the hand full, but alas it wasn't to be.

Curly, who was on the outside of the three divers, noticed something sticking up in the sand away to his left. He slowly made his way across to it, and it looked like the side handle of an urn or something like that.

He grabbed hold of it and gently tried to lift it out of the sand. It offered some resistance, so he worked at it.

The other divers noticed that Curly was attempting to get something out of the sand, so they swam over and Tom started to fan the water with his hand. Then Dean also began to fan the sand out of the way.

Soon the water was cloudy with sand and mud. Small fish started to come around, then bigger fish and then bigger fish. Soon they were surrounded by literally hundreds of fish all looking for something to eat out of the sand and mud the boys had fanned into the water.

Curly kept hold of the handle as it was his find. More and more sand and mud went into the water making visibility almost impossible to see beyond an arm's length.

Suddenly and from out of nowhere, a massive form streaked through the water leaving a wake of bubbles behind it. It sped through the water and grabbed a large trevally in its mouth and was gone.

Dean looked at Tom and moved his hand in a biting motion; Tom shook his head and gave Dean the all-clear signal, thumbs up.

Dean wasn't convinced that everything was all clear and started to look around, but the visibility was so bad that he couldn't see anything.

Meanwhile, Curly was working on getting the object up from the sand and the mud. It finally came clear.

He started to swim up with it and saw a large seal swallowing a fish, head first.

Ugly big bastard, Curly thought.

He swam up towards the surface and the visibility got better and better. He saw Teddy moving over towards him and held up his free hand.

'Did you see that big seal?' Teddy asked.

'Not really,' said Curly, 'but I did manage to find this.'

Teddy reached down and grabbed the other handle and lifted it onto the boat. It gleamed dully in the sunlight. The light reflected off the jewels that were inlaid in it.

'What the fuck is that?' Teddy asked.

Curly asked, 'Do you reckon that it's real?'

'I fucking well hope so,' Teddy said.

The other two divers came up and asked. 'What is it? Is it worth anything?'

They all clambered into the boat and sat there staring at what was the most valuable item that any of them had ever handled in their lives.

Before them was the golden chalice that the Black Devil had found, in a hidden compartment in the cabin of the ship. That he and his crew had overtaken. They had been forced to run for their lives, only to wreck their boat on exactly the same treacherous coastline that 200 years later the Monumental City had also come to grief on. And now that our current-day divers were diving on, 400 years after the first wreck.

They all looked at the golden chalice and wondered how much it was worth.

'I wonder where it came from.' Teddy asked, almost to himself.

Tom said, 'Fuck knows, I wish it could talk.'

They all nodded, a silence surrounded them.

'What are we going to do with it?' Dean asked.

They were all silent for the moment trying to figure out what would be best.

Finally, Teddy spoke, 'Here's what we should do. We should take it back to Melbourne and get it valued. We will have to take it somewhere that is a bit dodgy, somewhere that knows how to keep their mouth shut as, as we all are aware this is a 'No Take' site. We can look, but we aren't supposed to remove anything.'

'That would be fucking right.' Said Tom. 'We just leave it there for some other bastard to pick up and sell and we are left with our dicks in our hands and fuck all else.'

Teddy said, 'We will take it back to Melbourne and get it valued, and then we will work out what we will do about it.'

Curly spoke for the first time, 'How do we whack up whatever it's worth?'

Teddy said, 'Like always we split it up evenly between ourselves.'

'What about the others, Tony, Dave, and Lee?' Curly asked.

'Well, we will work all that out when we sort out how much it's worth, but we can give them a little extra. It all depends on what we end up getting ourselves.'

'Yes, let's see what we end up with,' Tom suggested.

Teddy stowed the golden chalice up the front of the boat and they all started to get about their business.

Teddy took the boat back to where they had stockpiled up the abalone and they loaded up the accumulated bags. They then went around and Dean and Curly grabbed what they could as Teddy and Tom started to shuck out the first load of abalone.

When they were shucked and the abalone meat was in the bins, they started on bringing up the rest and soon the boat was full of abalone. They all got into it and finished shucking out the rest of the abalone.

Teddy phoned Dave and told him they were going to unload at Wonboyn and should be there in about five hours.

Teddy described a jetty that was privately owned on a property that he knew wasn't habituated and where they could unload unobserved.

Dave immediately got in touch with his brother Lee and said, 'Mate, we are away, I'll be out there in half an hour. We will be picking up the gear at Wonboyn tonight.'

'Good as Gold!' Lee replied.

Wallace 'piggy' Trotter waited until Tony had ordered his meal at the club. When Tony waited for his meal to be prepared, Piggy went up and ordered a wet dish, which is a meal that is already prepared and just needs to be put onto a plate.

Beef curry and rice was the one that Piggy chose, and he hoped that the beef curry wouldn't make him fart too much. You had to be careful when you were on a stake-out.

When Teddy and the boys had finished shucking out all the abalone, they washed everything down and got ready to get into Wonboyn and unload the meat. They cruised into Disaster Bay and headed towards the bar at the entrance to Wonboyn Lake, all looked smooth and easy.

They cruised up the lake and saw the jetty.

Dave was standing on the end of it and he had a trolley.

Teddy pulled the Shark Cat up to the jetty and the boys started to unload onto the jetty.

Dave began to wheel the abalone meat up to the rear of the truck, and Lee started putting the plastic bags into polystyrene-lined tea chests and stacking them in the back of the furniture van.

Soon it was all loaded and Dave and Lee headed off towards the highway.

They had a long drive in front of them.

Teddy took off in the boat and they prepared themselves for the trip back to the Eden boat ramp.

He rang Tony to give him their ETA.

As it was getting dark, Teddy had the navigational lights on. The boys were quiet and a bit tired, but the excitement of finding the golden chalice kept them on a high.

Curly asked, 'What do you think that it's worth?'

Nobody answered as they didn't have a clue.

Teddy said, 'Maybe it's worth one hundred thousand. It's hard to tell. Where we sell it, will be the big question. Because if we put it to a public auction, we will have to tell everyone where we got it and that site being a "look-only" site, then we will be fined and have it taken off us. They might also confiscate the boat and all our gear. I've got a friend in Melbourne who does a bit with gold and jewels. In fact, I brought my gold chain from her. I'll give her a ring and she can tell us what we can do. Meanwhile, let's just keep it low key until we know what we are going to do.'

The boys all agreed and they headed around the corner of the coast and into Two Fold Bay.

As soon as Tony saw them come across the bay, he backed the boat trailer into the water and Teddy slowly drove the Shark Cat up onto it. Tony clipped the bow of the boat onto the trailer and he went into the four-wheel drive and pulled the boat up into the car park.

The New South Wales Fisheries and Piggy surrounded the boat, and with a confident tone, Piggy said. 'Right, you blokes, you are all under arrest. Let's see what you have got in the boat.'

Teddy smiled and said. 'Fisheries Officer Trotter, I presume, what are you doing here? Did you come up all the way here to give us a "howdy doody"?'

'No,' said Wallace, 'I've come up here to arrest you for poaching abalone, as I know that's what you have been doing.'

'Once again, please come aboard and have a look around. See what you can find.

There's nothing here that would interest you lot.'

The boys all climbed down and stretched their legs; they walked around and looked at the assembled fisheries officers. The fisheries climbed over the sides of the boat and had a quick look. It was obvious that there wasn't any abalone on board.

They hardly looked in the front cabin. Teddy knew that even on a close inspection that they wouldn't find the compartment where he had hidden the chalice.

Wallace Trotter realised that once again he had been outwitted.

He made his way back to the offices of the fisheries department and sat down. He explained to the assembled officers that in fact he couldn't prove that Teddy was a poacher, but he knew that the bastard was.

He apologised to his counterparts and climbed into the white falcon and drove away.

He was halfway the Bairnsdale when he came up behind a lumbering furniture van and didn't have the opportunity to pass it for about ten kilometres.

'Ignorant prick,' Piggy snarled and wondered what kind of dickhead would work at carting other people's furniture around. Piggy accelerated away from the lumbering truck.

Dave and Lee saw the white falcon coming up behind them and Lee thought that it might be a problem, but when it eventually passed them, he began to smile to himself.

No problems, he thought, *we'll be in Melbourne in about five or six hours.*

Dave rang the processor and gave him an ETA.

Derek was happy and said that all will be ready, when they arrived.

Teddy and the boys decided that they may as well hire a car at Eden and drive themselves and the chalice to Melbourne. They arranged this and decided to have a quiet night in a hotel in Eden and head off in the morning.

They booked into the Australasia Hotel in the main street, one of the two hotels in town, and they all had showers and headed down to the bar for a few beers.

There were a few locals in the main bar and the barmaid asked what they wanted.

Teddy said, 'Four pots of beer, thanks, love.'

She smiled and asked, 'Mexicans?' Meaning they were from 'south of the border'.

'We call them "middies" here, love.'

Just as long, as they are wet and cold.' Teddy laughed.

The barmaid smiled as she was used to serving Victorians.

'Are you up here fishing, for fun or for profit?' she asked.

'We are just having a couple of days off, hoping to hook a marlin,' Teddy answered.

She nodded and went about her business serving other customers.

The boys relaxed and started to drink their beers.

They were into their third round when the door opened and a group of younger blokes came in and noisily started to drink up the front end of the bar.

One of them had on a 'Biker T-shirt'. They were looking for trouble and were trying to intimidate the other customers in the bar.

The loudmouth with the 'Biker T-shirt' looked at Dean and said, 'What the fuck are you looking at? You long streak of pelican shit.'

Dean looked at Teddy and said. 'Fuck me, it can talk as well, didn't you say all Bikie shitheads were so dumb that they couldn't fucking feed themselves, and they all copped it up the arse.'

Tommy said.

'No, mate, Teddy said that they weren't all dumb shits and that some of them could actually feed themselves and walk the streets like normal people. Granted they are not the sharpest tools in the garden shed, poor things.'

Teddy laughed and said. 'Now, now, you fellows, don't you know that it's bad manners to hang shit on the disabled. Just let the halfwits dribble and drink their beers and they will soon go out and chase parked cars or something like that.'

Curly spoke for the first time and said, 'From the looks of it, most of them have chased parked cars and caught those cars' head first.'

All the boys laughed and ignored the assembled 'Bikie' group.

'Muddy,' the leader of the Bikie crew, was a little taken back by the response from the four strangers.

He was a man to be feared. He was, as he told his image in the mirror, daily, someone not to be 'fucked with'. Anyone that did fuck with him was either drunk or a fool, and these shit-heads were a bit of both.

Muddy looked at Curly, the smallest, and said, 'Hey, pretty boy, want to suck my dick?'

Looking at his crew he said, 'I reckon that he's thinking about it.'

They all laughed. There were six of them and only four of the strangers.

Teddy and the three boys looked calmly at the group, and one thought went through their heads, if you pick on one of us, then you are signing up to fight all of us.

Teddy looked at the smug want-to-be gangsters and said, almost to himself, 'Let's rock and roll.'

With that, Teddy and the boys moved, as one, towards the group of bikers. Teddy led the display by smashing his fist into one of the unfortunate bikers' face. He fell back into the arms of the rest of them, and Teddy kept smashing blows into whoever came in front of him. Tom didn't have his stiletto, as he had flown up to Merimbula, but that didn't slow him down; he started hitting anybody that was within reach. Dean grabbed one hapless victim and head-butted him in the face. Blood poured from the victim's nose, or what was left of his nose, and Curly just started like a thrashing machine.

Muddy was astounded by what was taking place.

He and his gang were in desperate trouble, and they were on unaccustomed ground. At least two of them were down and all the fight knocked out of them. One had cleverly rolled under the pool table and had his eyes closed, that left him with three and they were in trouble, it had all happened too quickly for them.

He decided that they should bolt and come back later on and sort these bastards out. That thought had barely crossed his mind when Teddy smashed his fist into the side of his head, making him see stars.

Fuck me, Muddy thought, *we are in real trouble. How did this happen?*

Muddy didn't see the roundhouse swing that sent him to the hospital.

Dean saw Teddy hit him, and when Muddy wasn't expecting anything, Dean let a wild right-handed roundhouse go. It connected with Muddy's temple and that was it, 'Good night nurse'.

After Muddy had hit the deck, there wasn't too much fight in the bikies.

The barmaid said to Teddy and the boys. 'You have created a bit of a problem for yourselves. These boys have a lot of mates around here. I reckon that as soon as they can get themselves organised, then they will be back, and they won't be coming to say howdy, they will want to revenge themselves. I've called the ambulance and I can tell the coppers what happened, so you should be in the clear there. As soon as they hear that you were picked on by a larger group, you should be all right. I would fuck off if I was you, and don't come back for a while.'

This sounded like good advice, so the boys grabbed what little gear they had, and the chalice, and went down into the car park and took off for Melbourne.

Dave and Lee made it to Melbourne and drove into the factory yard where Derek, the processor, was waiting. He had his van ready, and they unloaded all the tea chests, containing the abalone meat, into his van. Dave and Derek drove around to Derek's factory and they started to weigh up the abalone.

Dave ripped open the plastic bags and put them in a heap so he could count them, and Derek weighed up the meat and put it into bins ready to be repacked into frozen export boxes. It only took them a short time, and Dave rang Teddy to see if he wanted some separated to sell to Henry, the restaurateur.

Teddy said, 'Yes, keep one hundred kilos for Henry.'

Dave did this and when they had finished and agreed on an amount, Derek drove Dave back to the van that Lee had got organised for the return trip.

Dave rang Teddy and told him how much was there and they got going.

Teddy and the boys pulled into the 'Billabong' service station and went inside for a meal.

It was late and the same tired-faced waitress was on duty as she was the last time that they had stopped.

She smiled and said, 'Would you like four steaks, eggs and chips, lads?'

'Yes please, love,' Teddy replied, and as it was quite late, Teddy asked, 'What hours do you work? Like every time we come here, you are on shift.'

She replied. 'Me and my old man run the place. We are on duty twenty-four seven.'

'That's hard work,' Teddy replied.

'Yes, we reckon that if we stick to it a couple of years, then we can sell it and maybe buy something with not as long in the hours.' She replied, as she went into the kitchen and started to prepare their meals.

Curly said. 'I wonder how much the chalice is worth. Do you reckon that it's worth one hundred thousand dollars?'

Teddy looked at him and said, 'We will see what it's worth as scrap and then double it and see how we go at that.'

They all nodded and waited for their meals.

Wallace 'Piggy' Trotter was back in his office and completed a report of what happened on his trip to New South Wales.

His colleagues looked on and listened to Piggy's description of how the events unfolded.

With restraint, they swallowed their sniggers and put on concerned faces. Piggy went into great detail about how he was almost invisible as he trailed the boat and four-wheel drive up the coast and how Tony, the driver of the four-wheel drive, was completely unaware of his presence. In fact, Piggy gave the less experienced a lesson on how to become almost invisible when on 'Stake-out.'

They all listened as Piggy explained that if he could have commandeered a boat, then he would have caught them out. Yes, he would have caught them in the act.

Bastards, they will get what's coming to them next time they show their heads in his area.

Teddy and the boys drove into Melbourne. As the sun was appearing above the horizon, they were all pretty well bushed.

Teddy dropped Dean and Curly off and headed for home with Tom. As Sandy had spent the time Tom was away at Teddy's and Rita's place, they walked in and both had showers and hit the sack.

When Teddy awoke, Sandy and Tom were talking quietly in Teddy's kitchen. They had the gold chalice on the kitchen table and were looking at it. Teddy came out of the bedroom, and said. 'Good morning, I could kill for a cup of coffee. Has Rita gone to work?'

Sandy smiled and said, 'We didn't think that you would ever wake up. We were just about to run off with the treasure.'

Teddy poured himself a coffee and said. 'Well, I suppose we will have to shop it around a bit and see what the offers are. It's going to be interesting.'

'That's for sure,' said Tom.

'But first let's go and deliver the hundred kilos of meat to Henry at his father's restaurant.' Teddy said.

Teddy drunk his coffee down, and he and Tom decided to make tracks.

They went out and got into Teddy's van and drove around to Derek's factory. When they got there, they walked in. They saw that Derek was talking to a factory hand. When he saw the two men, he asked them, 'Are you here for the hundred kilos, boys?'

'Yes, mate,' replied Teddy, 'when can we come around and pick up the money for the rest?'

Derek smiled and said, 'I've been on to the bank and they said that they will have the money ready for me to pick up at about three o'clock this arvo. Is that all right for you?'

'Yes, mate, I'll drop around and see you at about three thirty.'

'No worries,' Derek said.

Tom and Teddy loaded the hundred kilos into Teddy's van and they headed off to Henry's restaurant. It was a pleasant drive and the boys were relaxed. They pulled up outside the rear of the restaurant and Teddy knocked at the rear door. They checked the street to see that there weren't any suspicious-looking cars about and when the door opened, Henry's father looked out and said, 'Hullo, Tiddy, how you are?'

Teddy answered. 'Right as rain, old mate, how are you and your beautiful wife going? I hope that you are both well.'

Teddy and Tom hurried the abalone into the kitchen where several kitchen hands were getting ready for the lunchtime trade.

Henry was organising the front of the restaurant. When he saw Teddy, he said to his mum, 'Look out, Mum, Teddy is here to carry you off to a life of luxury.'

'Hello, beautiful,' Teddy said with a smile. 'Are you ready to elope with me yet?'

Henry's mother blushed and said, 'No, Teddy, but maybe someday, who knows?'

It was the same old joke that Teddy said every time that he came into the kitchen.

Everyone laughed, more out of habit than anything else, it was a good feeling.

Henry got the money out of the safe and gave it to Teddy.

Teddy didn't count it as he knew that if it were short, then it would be an innocent mistake, and He thought that Henry would lose face if it looked like Teddy didn't trust him. So he put the money straight into his pocket.

They picked up some bins that they had left last time and made their way out to their van.

Tom said to Teddy, 'That was a bit quieter than the last delivery when those three Vietnamese tried to rob us.'

'Yes, mate, it sure was,' Teddy said, 'thank Christ for that.'

The golden chalice was in the back of the van, and Teddy gave one of his friends a ring. Her name was Martha, and she did a bit of buying and selling of gold and diamonds. She was a smart, good-looking blonde who knew her way around.

She knew what was going on in the shadowy underworld. She was always in the know and somehow she always made money. She was what's known as a 'Good Earner', and Teddy trusted her completely.

Martha answered the phone with, 'Good morning, sweetheart, how have you been? Long time, no speak. How can I help you?'

'Well, Martha, I've got something that you might want to have a look at. I reckon that there will be a bit of an 'earn' in it for everyone.'

Martha laughed a throaty laugh and asked, 'Can you bring it around?'

'We are on our way,' Teddy replied, 'see you in thirty minutes.'

Martha laughed and said, 'I can hardly wait, see you soon.'

The two men drove to an affluent suburb and down a leafy street.

Teddy parked behind a late model 'Mercedes Benz', and he and Tom got out with the chalice and walked up to the front door.

Teddy pressed the button and looked into the surveillance camera and smiled. A small dog started barking furiously on the inside of the door and was dealt with a swift boot to the rear. The door opened and Martha stood in front of them with a radiant smile.

'Come in, boys,' she invited, 'can I get you a beer or coffee or tea?'

Tom and Teddy smiled, and Teddy said, 'I reckon that champagne will be in order when you lock eyes on what we have brought you.'

With that, Teddy walked across to a kitchen bench and pulled the chalice out of the bag. He placed it on the bench, and there was silence in the room.

Martha said, 'Fuck me dead,' completely dropping any poshness in her voice, 'where the fuck did you get this?'

Teddy said, 'Mate, it's off a shipwreck. We were down the coast, and Curly just pulled it up out of the sand and the mud.'

'Jesus Christ all mighty, I reckon that it's worth a fortune. I'm speechless,' Martha said.

'Well, we hope that it's worth something.' Teddy said. 'Our problem is that if anyone finds out that we got it from a wreck site, then the government will take it from us and we will get fined for disturbing a wreck site. They are a bit dark on that sort of thing.'

Martha had got over her initial shock of seeing such a splendid item and her mind was racing.

She picked it up and said, 'Scrap value alone I reckon that it's worth a couple of hundred thousand, in the right hands I reckon that it could be worth more than that.'

The boys started to think. They were really in the money, one hundred thousand dollars each, that's a lot of money.

'How will you go about seeing what it's worth?' Teddy asked.

'I'll give it some thought,' Martha said, 'it will take a fair bit of planning. Can you leave it with me and I'll have a bit of a think?'

Teddy said, 'Why don't you take a couple of photos of it and go and show them around to people who you think will be able to price it before we actually show it to someone.

It's just that there are a couple of other people in the whack up and they don't want to let it out of our sight, no offence, Martha.'

'I can understand that,' Martha replied. She got out her phone and took some photos.

'This is really something,' Martha said, 'really something; I can't believe that you just picked it up on the ocean bottom.'

Teddy assured her that there was a bit more to it than that, but Martha wasn't really listening. She was a little overcome by the beauty of the chalice.

They made arrangements to talk later on in a couple of days' time when Martha had 'shopped' the chalice around.

Teddy and Tom walked out into the street and Teddy laughed at Tom and said, 'Did you see Martha's face light up when she got a look at the chalice?'

'Yes, mate, she is one happy little Vegemite.' Tom laughed.

Martha didn't muck around.

She knew and liked Teddy but knew he wasn't the hardest bloke around. She desperately wanted the chalice as she recognised as being something of high value, maybe something worth killing for. Martha connected her phone up to the computer printer and printed off a couple of copies of each of the photos she had taken of the chalice. She jumped into the Merc and headed off towards the city. She felt the excitement growing in her stomach. This was something she could really earn on; a once in a lifetime opportunity, something that she could actually gain out of.

She put the phone onto 'hands-free' and drove towards the city.

Her first call was to an old friend, a Jew, who dealt in gold and jewels.

He answered his phone with a simple 'Yes?'

'Eddie, it's Martha, I've got something that you might be interested in, something that you haven't ever seen before.'

Eddie was suddenly interested, very interested.

He and Martha had done a lot of deals together and he knew that if Martha were excited, then he should also be.

Eddie was an old man and didn't need the money that he got from dealing in gold and jewels; he just loved the excitement of 'wheeling and dealing.'

Eddie also had a soft spot for Martha. She was half his age and was, he considered, a very smart operator.

Over the years, he had seen them come and go in the gold and jewel business. Some struggled and hardly made any money and others burnt brightly for a short time and then vanished, but Martha kept going through good and bad times.

Some of the gear that she brought him was stolen.

He knew that; in fact, he recognised some of the items, but he remained silent, and Martha always went by his judgement. Never once did she not listen to him.

If Eddie told Martha to get rid of something, then she got rid of it. If he told her that the item in question was 'good', then she listened and sold it to one of her customers.

They had a happy working relationship.

Martha walked up the steps to Eddie's office and wondered why the 'Old Bastard' didn't get an office with a lift. She didn't realise that Eddie owned the building, it was probably worth millions, and Eddie had a theory that steps kept all the tyre kickers and time wasters away.

If people were going to waste his time, then they would have to climb up some stairs to do it.

Martha knocked and Eddie looked into the CCTV Screen and pushed the button to release the lock so that Martha could enter the office come showroom.

'Hello, Eddie love,' Martha said in a sincere way, 'how are you? You look fine. Is everything all right?'

'I'm getting older and grumpier,' Eddie replied.

'Well, I've got just the thing to cheer you up, love,' Martha said as she slipped a couple of photos across Eddie's desk.

Eddie remained calm as he looked at the pictures; his eyes widened just a bit as he took in what lay before him.

'Well, what have we got here?' Eddie asked.

His brain was running at full speed, for he knew that before him was something that would place his name in the history books for eternity.

Martha had noticed the expression that for a mere split second had betrayed Eddie. She knew that she had her man hook, line, and sinker. All she had to do was reel him in.

Martha slowly smiled and said. 'A mere trinket that a couple of friends of mine stumbled across. They brought it to me as they knew that I would be able to get them a fair price. It's a bit delicate as they are divers and the wreck that they got it off is in a 'no-take' zone. If they are suspected of disturbing the site, then they will be in trouble.'

'I understand perfectly,' Eddie replied, 'discretion is the better part of valour.'

Martha didn't get it and just smiled and nodded.

'How much are they asking for this piece of treasure?' Eddie asked with a smile that would petrify a demon.

'They are not sure how much they want. They have no idea of its value.' Martha answered.

Eddie couldn't keep his eyes off the photos. 'When can I see this object?'

Martha looked at her old friend and could see that he was excited.

'They are very careful about, not letting it out of their sight. They would hate for something to happen to it.' She answered.

'Yes, yes, of course, they are,' Eddie soothed, 'I bet it's not every day that they come across something as unique as this. Tell me, Martha, have you shown this to anyone else?'

Martha looked at Eddie and smiled. 'Of course not, Eddie, you were the first one that I thought of to show it to. We have done work together and we trust each other, and I know no one has a better knowledge of this sort of thing than you do.'

Eddie smiled and nodded. He thought that he didn't trust anyone when it came to money, especially Martha, she was a survivor and they are the most dangerous. He would have to be very careful how he went about this.

Eddie's mind was racing. He had heard of a golden chalice rich in diamonds and jewels that had vanished over in England in the sixteen hundred's. It was a present from the Spanish royal family to the English royal family and had been taken by pirates or had been lost at sea. It was like a mystical treasure, worth a king's ransom. Stories had circulated for generations of the fabulous chalice, but no one knew what had happened to it or where it had gone, could this be it? Could this be the one thing that would make him stand out apart from the other dealers and would this chalice make his name a household name to be remembered for eternity?

Eddie looked at Martha the same way as a snake looks at a mouse just before it strikes.

'Tell me, Martha, can I see this piece?' he asked.

Martha knew that Eddie was more than interested. She also knew that if Teddy and Eddie were to meet that she would be there in the middle. She had never seen Eddie so animated. He was desperate for the chalice, and she was desperate for her share or more if she could.

'Eddie, I don't really know, I told my friends that I would get back to them in the next couple of days. I don't want to build their hopes up too far as they might want a lot of money for it.' Martha said softly.

Eddie nodded and said. 'I think that we should move on this with some urgency. We don't want other dealers to get involved as that will only drive the price up and confuse your friends.' Eddie smiled kindly, nodding his head. 'Perhaps they could come into my office tomorrow. They are probably busy at this time.'

Martha, had, for the very first time, began to feel uncomfortable in the presence of her friend, something wasn't quite right. 'I'll give them a ring and see what they are up to,' she suggested.

Eddie said, 'Perhaps you can ring them now, maybe I could see it this afternoon?'

'I tell you what, why don't I ring them and set up an appoint ment for tomorrow, say about eleven o'clock?' Martha smiled and Eddie nodded his head.

Martha left Eddie's office and quickly called Teddy.

Teddy answered, 'Yes, love.'

Martha said, 'I've just left a friend's office. He's a big gold and jewel dealer. He wants to see us all at eleven o'clock in his office in the city. Are you available?'

Teddy said, 'Can't we meet him at your place? It's too hard getting the entire group into the city and I don't want to carry the chalice around.'

Martha couldn't have been happier.

This way Teddy wouldn't talk to Eddie without her being there and when they were on her home turf, she felt that she was in control.

Martha rang Eddie and told him the new arrangements.

He reluctantly agreed.

Eddie couldn't sleep.

He was too excited to shut his eyes.

He kept thinking that this was it; this was why he was placed on this earth, to be the one that finally solved the biggest question of all time, what happened to the golden chalice? How the history books would embrace him as the one, the one that bought this chalice to life? He would tour all the museums of the world. Yes, it would be him that was on display. He would lecture groups of dealers and groups of the wealthiest people in the world, all would be vying to be in his presence. Yes, the world would be his oyster; he must, at any cost, get the chalice.

He knew that Martha was very smart and would be a major hurdle in his quest.

As soon as she realised that this was the find of a lifetime, she would want to share the limelight, but Eddie knew that there was room only for him.

As the dawn broke, Eddie planned for the coming day, maybe he would go to the meeting a little prepared. He knew that the chalice would be there and there was no way in the world that he was leaving Martha's house without it.

He opened his safe and withdrew several bundles of bank notes and placed them in his briefcase. There were one hundred thousand dollars in one hundred dollar notes, more than enough to startle anyone, besides the money was his licensed Glock, a semi-automatic handgun, with a thirteen-bullet magazine inserted in its grip.

He pulled the sliding carriage back to reveal a bullet in the breach. He carefully uncocked the hammer and placed it back into his briefcase. It was ready to go and so was he.

He cooked a light breakfast and noisily sipped two sweet, strong black coffees.

There was still a couple of hours to go, so he decided to go into his office and lose himself in some paperwork

Teddy rang the boys and said, 'I've arranged a meeting with Martha and a buyer. They want us to meet them at Martha's place at eleven o'clock tomorrow morning. I've seen Derek, the processor, and got our money and worked out our 'whack up'. What if we all meet and I'll give you your money and we all go over to Martha's place and see what they want us to do with the chalice?' They all agreed, so Teddy decided that he would have a quiet night and prepare for the next day's excitement.

Eddie couldn't concentrate on paperwork, so he sat in silence and decided that he needed some sort of back-up.

He knew a lot of gangsters.

Sometimes bought stolen items from them and had them melted down and sold the gold in bars. It was almost impossible to track down items once they had been melted down.

He thought for a while and made a phone call.

The man he spoke to was a professional criminal. His nickname was 'The Juggler', not a very bright person, but very willing to do anything that there was a dollar in. He explained that he was going to a meeting and that there was something there that he wanted very badly. He also said that there was a possibility that what he was going to see, the people that were holding the item, wouldn't be that keen on him taking it. So perhaps he and another friend could help persuade the reluctant ones to release the object into his care.

The Juggler understood perfectly. 'So you want us to just grab the item and belt any bastard that gets in our way?'

'Yes, you have got the picture. If they take out the item from the meeting, then you step in and grab it for me.' Eddie replied and gave the Juggler the time and place for them to be.

The juggler rang a friend and said. 'We have got a job to do, a simple pick-up. It shouldn't take us too long, and we will be rewarded handsomely. I've done this sort of thing before and always ended up well in front.' His accomplice agreed and they decided to meet in fifteen minutes.

The boys all headed over to Teddy's place and got their money.

Teddy explained how it all worked out and who got what and where it all went and they all decided to head over to Martha's place with the chalice.

They arrived, and Teddy parked behind the late model Merc. They got out and Teddy rang the doorbell.

Once again, the littlest guard dog in the world went ballistic and once again it got a kick up the arse for its troubles.

Martha opened the door and welcomed the four men inside.

She fussed around the kitchen and asked if they wanted coffee. She operated the latest model coffee machine with incredible dexterity and soon the air was filled with the aroma of freshly brewed coffee.

The boys were enjoying their beverages where the doorbell went again.

The dog went into overdrive, barking, and scratching the door.

Martha gave it a kick up its arse and opened the door and said. 'Hello, Eddie love, how are you going?'

Eddie replied. 'Well, thank you, Martha. I'm enjoying perfect health. What a lovely home!'

Martha took the complement on board and introduced the four men, sitting in the lounge room; she introduced them all by first name only, as was the custom in the underworld.

Eddie shook their hands and tried to work out who was the leader.

He soon found that Teddy was the one who did all the talking and was clearly older than the others.

Teddy started by saying.

'Good day, mate, we are a bit out of our depth. We have stumbled across something at sea and we don't really know what its worth. Martha and I have done a bit of work together and she suggested that we get you to have a look at what we have found and give us some sort of valuation.'

'Certainly, dear fellows. Let me have a look at the item in question and I will give you an appraisal, and perhaps I can even offer you a price, good business is a fast business.'

Eddie smiled a smile that made him look like everyone's favourite grandfather.

Teddy took hold of the bag containing the chalice and put it on Martha's breakfast bench, and then with a flourish, he pulled the bag back revealing the chalice.

Eddie's heart almost stopped beating. He felt an urge to burst out into tears, or laugh out loud, or even 'high five' everyone in the room.

He looked at the priceless treasure that by today's standard would be worth almost any amount of money.

Eddie managed to ask, 'Can I pick it up, please?'

Teddy answered. 'Yea, mate, grab hold of it. Have a good look. See if you can find any identifying marks, or something to say who made it or where it came from.'

Eddie picked up the chalice.

The world swam in front of him; he could imagine how the world would see this exquisite piece. He would be recognised as a real genius, the man who brought this to the public's eye.

Eddie pulled out his jeweller's loupe and studied the piece up close. Yes, it was, as he thought from the markings he could see it was over 400 years old.

'Did these fools realise how old it was? Of course, they didn't. They thought that they were dealing with something that was relatively modern.'

Eddie said out loud, 'Yes, a lovely piece of work, finely made, by a craftsman, it's years old.'

Teddy said, 'Yes, the wreck that we got it off was sunk in about the eighteen fifties.'

Eddie could see from the craftsmanship that this was made about 200 years earlier; he said nothing, just nodded and smiled.

'Yes, that would be correct.' He nodded.

'What are you planning to do with it?'

Teddy looked at his three mates and said, 'We would like to sell it and split up the 'moola' among us all, equal shares.'

The three men all nodded.

Eddie slowly said. 'I feel that this is a beautiful piece of art, and I would be willing to give you somewhere in the area of one hundred thousand dollars for it, in cash, of course.'

Teddy smiled and said. 'That's a very generous offer, and one that we will consider. But I feel because of the rarity of the object, we should perhaps take it to an auction place and see what they have to say about it.'

Eddie paused for a moment. 'I have the money here with me. At an auction place, they will charge you a twenty percent commission. So if they sell it for one hundred thousand, then you will only receive eighty thousand dollars and I am offering you one hundred thousand dollars here and now.'

Tom, who hadn't spoken before said, 'What if we get more than one hundred thousand dollars?' Eddie smiled and said, 'Well your commission goes up, the more you get, the more they take.' Dean said. 'Yes, if we get two hundred thousand dollars for the chalice, then we get charged forty thousand dollars in commission. Leaving us with one hundred and sixty thousand dollars, that's sixty thousand dollars more than you have offered us.'

Eddie smiled and said. 'To go to an auction you have to be able to prove that you own it and as I see things, that is impossible. You will lose it to the government and end up being fined for disturbing a shipwreck. You may even go to jail. The government are very hard on people who do this sort of thing.'

Teddy said to Eddie. 'Mate, we know the risks, and we are prepared to take them. Is one hundred thousand dollars your final offer? We want to get as much out of this as possible.'

Eddie felt the chalice was slowly slipping away from him. He began to panic. 'How much do you want for it then?' He asked.

Eddie felt like pulling his gun out and shooting the lot of them and taking the chalice and running, luckily common sense shone through.

Teddy looked at Eddie and said, 'We can't put a price on it until we see some other dealers and see what they will give us for it.'

Eddie said harshly. 'So this has just been a waste of my fucking time, has it? Just get me running around wasting my time, as if I had nothing better to do, fuck me dead.'

Teddy looked at him. 'Sorry, you feel this way. We just want to get some prices and take the best one.'

'Well, I will beat any price that you get by ten percent. Make sure you give me the final offer, but I would be careful walking around with something that valuable in a bag.' Eddie suggested.

Eddie picked up his briefcase and walked out the door. As he was going to his car, he saw the Juggler and his accomplice sitting in their vehicle. He nodded to the two men. The Juggler gave him a small nod of his head.

The boys said goodbye to Martha, and Teddy said, 'Eddie seemed a bit upset, hope that you and he are all right.'

Martha replied. 'Yes, he was a bit upset. I'd be a bit careful if I were you. I reckon that he really wanted that chalice, yes I'd be very fucking careful if I were you lot.'

Teddy said to Martha, 'You've got the photos, so show them around and see what you can find out and when you come up with something, give us a ring.'

'Yes, no worries,' Martha said, 'I'll let you know just what's going on. I'll give you a ring and let you know.'

With that, Teddy and the boys headed back towards Teddy's place.

They had only gone a few blocks and had stopped at a red light when a Holden Commodore ran up their arse.

'Fuck me,' Teddy said.

Tom looked out the rear window and said. 'This looks like trouble. There are a couple of bad bastards looking to have a go at us, something is not right.'

The Juggler jumped out of the car and walked towards Teddy's car, his offsider also got out and walked towards Teddy and the boys.

The Juggler had a sawn-off shotgun partly concealed under his jacket and his mate had an iron bar. Teddy waited until the Juggler got close, and as he was raising the sawn off, Teddy violently pushed open the car door. The Juggler reeled back and that was all the time Teddy needed. He launched himself at the Juggler and took hold of the sawn off shotgun's barrel and forced it up so it was pointing up in the air.

Teddy drove his fist into the Jugglers' stomach with such force that the Juggler was winded. He hadn't expected Teddy to move as quickly as he had done. Teddy unloaded an uppercut that smashed the Jugglers' head back. He still had a hold onto the sawn off. Teddy saw that the hammers weren't back, so the gun wasn't cocked. Teddy hit the Juggler as hard as he could, and the Jugglers' grip loosened on the sawn off. Teddy ripped it out of the semi-conscious man's grip and smashed him across the face with it. Blood flowed down from a gash in his forehead and ran down his shirt.

The Jugglers' offsider didn't fair very well either.

As he approached the car, Dean quickly grabbed him by his arm that was holding onto the iron bar and pulled him through into the cars interior. He helplessly flayed around and Tom leapt out of front seat and 'King hit' him a savage blow to the face, knocking him senseless. Curly ran around and started kicking the Juggler in the crotch.

Soon the fight was out of them.

Teddy threw the sawn-off shotgun into the back seat and said to the boys, 'That's the fight taken out of them. Let's get the fuck out of here.'

They drove off at high speed leaving the two gangsters lying on the ground bleeding and a heap of cars banked up behind them.

As they sped away, Teddy called Martha and told her what had happened. She sounded horrified and said, 'I told you to be careful, that Eddie is a dangerous man.'

'Point, well taken,' Teddy replied.

They drove on, Tom said, 'We will have to be a bit careful, from now on.'

They all agreed. 'Yep, we had better be on our toes,' Teddy said.

Curly spoke for the first time, 'Maybe there's a curse on the fucking thing. We haven't stopped bashing people since we got it.'

'Well, at least we are winning,' Dean commented.

The others all laughed.

Eddie the Jew was furious, angry at himself and furious at that idiot, the Juggler. It would appear that the idiot had tried to snatch the chalice armed with a shotgun and ended up getting the living Christ belted out of him and his sidekick. This calls for something a bit better planned. He started to think deeply about what to do next. Murder wasn't out of the picture. The chalice was worth a fortune. He had to do something and fast, as the news would soon spread through the underworld that something was afoot.

The 'Underworld' is the same as any organisation.

People know people and when there's something in the air, then soon plenty of people know about it, or think that they know something.

Mario and Nick, the two 'Loan sharks,' that Teddy and the boys had put into hospital after they had raped Sandy knew the Juggler. And as they had made it out of hospital, almost on the same day, news soon reached them that the Juggler and his mate had been beaten up by Teddy's crew.

They thought that this might be a good time to join forces and dish out a bit of punishment. Little did they realise that Teddy and his crew were holding on to something that was worth a fortune.

Mario got in touch with the Juggler and arranged a meeting. When they got together and realised that there was also the opportunity to actually make a good earn out of the whole deal, just by grabbing the chalice, they were all for it.

Mario and Nick were still badly shaken from their run in with Teddy and his crew and the Juggler and his mate didn't look the picture of health and vitality. They reckoned that between them all, they should end up on top.

Teddy was starting to think about what Curly said, about the chalice being jinxed and having a curse on it.

He sort of laughed it off, but the idea was still in the back of his mind, maybe there was something in all this talk about curses and the rest of it.

Teddy decided that he should hide the chalice somewhere, somewhere safe. He wrapped it up and put it up in the attic of his house. Then on second thought, he decided to put the sawn-off shotgun up beside it. Just in case he was forced to go and get the chalice, and if that happened when he came out of the attic, he would be prepared.

Martha was worried.

Did Teddy think that she had something to do with the attempted snatch of the chalice; she had better make sure that she was in the clear. She had heard, on the underworld grapevine that it was Teddy's crew that had done the loan sharks. She didn't know the full story, but it didn't surprise her when she found out.

She had a feeling that Teddy was harder than people thought; she backed her own judgement as it had proven to be correct in the past.

Mario, Nick, the Juggler and his sidekick Rick all sat in Mario's late model Merc and watched Teddy's house.

They had seen Teddy's partner head off down the street to catch public transport to go to work and they assumed that Teddy was alone in the house.

Mario said, 'I reckon that we should barge in and start belting him until he tells us where the chalice is.'

Nick agreed with him, but the Juggler wasn't so sure.

He said, 'Let's wait until we see him and maybe he will walk out with it in his hand. Then we can all jump him and grab it and take off.'

Rick nodded and said. 'At least that way we will know that we have it.'

Teddy walked out empty-handed and walked across to his car; he got in and drove away.

'Let's roll the fucking joint,' The Juggler suggested.

'Can you get inside?' Mario asked.

'Piece of piss,' the Juggler suggested.

He and Rick got out of the Merc and walked across to the front of Teddy's house.

Gaining entry was easy; all they had to do was put all their weight on the decorative front door and it soon almost silently gave way.

Rick laughed and said, 'Locks only keep the honest people out.'

The juggler nodded and said, 'Let's be quick. Toss everything onto the floor as we won't be able to hide where we have searched. Look in all the obvious places. It's big so it won't be in the fridge or anywhere like that.'

With that the two criminals went from room to room opening all the cupboards and looking in every place that the chalice could be, but alas it was to no avail. They came up empty-handed. They were soon out in the street, and when they jumped into the Merc, the juggler said, 'We couldn't find anything of value. Let alone a chalice worth hundreds of thousands.'

'You looked everywhere?' Mario asked.

'Yes, mate, every fucking where, he must have stashed it somewhere.'

'Fuck,' was all Nick had to say.

'So what do we do now?' Mario asked almost to himself. His question was met with silence.

The Juggler stated loudly, 'Well, he hasn't got it, and we can't find it in his house. He's gone out probably to meet up with the rest of his crew and decide what they are going to do next. What would we do in his situation?'

The remaining three stayed silent.

Nick said, 'Well, I would go and find someone that wanted it and sell it to them as quick as I could, get the money, and split it up and then relax.'

Mario nodded and said. 'Then we step in and take the money. That sounds like a good plan. Let's sleep on it and see what we come up with.'

Martha knew that the game was afoot.

When Teddy and the boys were attacked, she knew that there was a significant chance that Eddie was behind the attack and that he wouldn't stop just because he missed once. She knew he would do anything to get the chalice. If she could end up with it, then she was laughing, she could sell it to Eddie and really make some money, as it was obvious that Eddie was desperate for the treasure. She somehow had to get the chalice.

She was familiar with the head of a crime family.

The father and sons had done a bit with her and she found them to be easy to deal with. She had sold them some jewellery, and they had always paid her on time. Whenever they had something to sell, they always gave her first pick of it. So she rang the father and said that she needed to speak with him on some urgent business.

They agreed to meet in a restaurant in Carlton.

When Martha entered the restaurant, she saw the head of the crime family seated at a table looking at the menu.

Martha smiled her best smile and said, 'Hello, Sam, how's it hanging?'

Sam looked up and laughed. 'All the better for seeing you, Martha, how are you going?'

'I'm just fine and dandy thanks, love,' Martha said and settled into a chair. She didn't want to look at the menu as she wasn't here to eat; business always came first with Martha.

Getting straight to the matter, she said. 'Sam, there are a couple of abalone poachers in town and they have, by fluke, come into possession of a precious piece of jewellery. They had found it on the bottom of the ocean somewhere. They can't claim to have found it as they were in a no-take zone. If the government know about it, then they will prosecute the divers and fine them as an example to other divers, so they have to keep their heads down. I introduced them to a buyer, and he got greedy and fucked up the buying off them, so then he got a couple of heavies to try and take it off them but that didn't work. So now the divers will realise that they have something of great value and will understand that they are wanted men.'

Sam looked at her and decided that this was something big and there were dollars in it for him and his family.

'What do you want me to do?' Sam asked.

'Well, just grab the fucking thing and give it to me, and I'll get rid of it for the highest price and we can all share whatever we get for it,' Martha explained.

Sam looked at his old friend and asked, 'What's it worth?'

Martha smiled, seeing that Sam was interested, she replied, 'I reckon that it's probably worth, half a million dollars, maybe a little more.'

She was careful to underestimate the value.

Sam nodded his head and asked, 'Where do we find these likely lads?'

'I've got Teddy's address right here,' Martha replied.

'I'll see what I can find out about them and get back to you,' Sam concluded.

'Well, be quick, as there are other parties involved, and you might only get one chance.' Martha added.

'One chance is all we will need,' Sam assured her.

Martha went out onto the street and quickly got into her car and drove home.

Teddy, unaware that, as he drove to meet his mates, his house was being tossed over by the two criminals, was in a happy-go-lucky mood. It looked like the chalice was valuable and they would all get a bit of money out of it. It was a shame that, that Eddie got the shits and turned 'Dark' on them, but shit happens, they all would just wait until Martha came up with another buyer.

Teddy pulled into the car park of a hotel and saw that the rest of the boy's cars were already there. He pulled up and walked inside. As usual the three were together sitting at a table, half-empty pots on front of them.

'Let me get a round,' suggested Teddy.

They all smiled, and he made his way to the bar and asked the barmaid for four pots. On his return, he said. 'Well, how are you all feeling? You all look as fit as Mallee bulls.'

Tom answered, 'Yes, mate we are all going good, how are you?'

Teddy smiled and said, 'Good as gold, fella's, good as gold.'

Curly asked. 'What are we going to do with the golden chalice? Have you got any plans?'

'Yes, mate, I reckon that we should wait until Martha gets back to us and we'll have another go at selling it,' Teddy suggested.

'It's worth more than one hundred thousand dollars,' Dean said.

They all nodded. 'Well, we will just see what happens,' Teddy said.

Tom was worried. 'Do you reckon that those blokes that tried to attack us were sent by that fucking Jew?' 'It's highly possible,'

Teddy replied, 'highly likely.'

They had been there a few hours when Teddy's phone rang.

It was Rita, Teddy's partner, and she was upset and crying. 'Someone has broken into our house. The front door is open, and there is stuff all over the place. Do you want me to ring the police?'

'Fuck no,' said Teddy, 'go next door and grab Ronny, our next-door neighbour, and make sure that there's no one inside. We are on our way. Don't tell anybody.'

With that, Teddy said to the boys. 'Some bastard has overturned my fucking house. Maybe they were looking for the chalice, or maybe it was fucking drug addicts. We will all go over and see what's going on.' With that, they all jumped up and got into their cars and headed off towards Teddy's place.

When they got to Teddy's place, they saw Rita and the next-door neighbour standing out in front of the house.

Ron, the next-door neighbour, said, 'Gidday, Teddy, it's a bit of a mess inside. I waited until you came before we went in just in case.'

Ronny was an old 'Painter and Docker' and had been on the wharfs all his life.

He was a tough little rooster whose body was failing him as he had led a tough life. He was aware that Teddy and his gang were abalone poachers, and Teddy always gave him a couple of crayfish at Christmas time.

'Thanks, Ronny mate, I'll go in and have a quick look around to see what's going on.'

Teddy went inside and had a quick look around. Tom, Dean, and Curly followed him into the house. All the drawers had been opened and the contents thrown onto the floor. All the wardrobes had been opened and all the clothes inside were thrown into the middle of the room. In the kitchen, all the cupboards were emptied onto the floor. The boys stood in the mess and looked at each other.

Tom asked, 'Did they get it?'

Teddy opened the ceiling manhole and climbed up inside. The chalice was concealed under the fibreglass insulation that had been installed in the roof. He stuck his head out and smiled and said, 'No worries, fella's, everything is sweet.'

Teddy climbed down, and they all walked out into the backyard.

Curly asked. 'What do you reckon? Do you think that they were after the chalice or were it just another robbery done by some drug fucked desperate?'

Teddy said, 'I don't know for sure, but I don't reckon that anything was stolen. My good watch and other valuables weren't touched.'

'Maybe they just had good taste,' Dean commented.

All the boys laughed except Tom. 'If it wasn't a drug robbery, then we have a problem. It means that whoever it was, were after the chalice, and if they know where Teddy lives, then they will know where we live, so we will all have to be on guard.'

This thought sobered them up; they knew that what they must do is protect their families and loved ones. 'I'll give Martha a ring and tell her what's going on. I'll tell her that we will have to get rid of the chalice as soon as possible.'

Teddy rang Martha and said that his joint had been burgled and it looked like the thieves had been looking for the chalice. Martha sounded worried and asked if there was anything else taken. Teddy told her that as far as he was concerned that nothing else had been stolen. Martha came up with a plan.

She told Teddy to go to a pub in Port Melbourne and take the chalice with him. She said that she could arrange for a buyer to meet him there and he should go on his own and show the buyer the chalice.

Teddy wasn't too happy about going on his own without some back-up but reluctantly agreed, so he said he would be there.

He told the others what Martha had suggested.

Tom immediately said. 'This sounds like a set-up. I bet there would be someone there and they would grab the chalice and maybe fix Teddy up.'

The others agreed, so they started to make a plan.

The time of the meeting was in a couple of hours, plenty of time for Teddy and the boys to get there and have a look around the place.

Martha rang Sam, and he and his sons were ready to go.

This would be simple, just bash the fucking moron and take the chalice, give it to Martha and let her sell it and split up the loot, too easy.

Martha rang Eddie the Jew and told him that she should have the chalice in a couple of hours. 'Sit tight and wait,' she assured Eddie.

Eddie wanted to know just who was going to be at the meeting and where it was going to be and at what time. Martha told him everything.

Eddie then rang the Juggler and told him to be at the pub and to grab the chalice off whoever came out of the pub with it. 'This time, don't fuck it up or you will have me to deal with.'

The juggler rang Rick and said. 'We are away. I'll pick you up in an hour.'

Teddy arrived at the pub and made his way into the lounge. There was a sign on the door saying. 'Closed for a private function, sorry for any inconvenience.'

Teddy pushed open the door and saw Sam and one of his sons sitting there; right away he knew that he had been sold out.

Teddy recognised Sam. He knew that he was a very dangerous man, someone not to be messed with. Teddy started to back out, but Sam's eldest son suddenly was behind him.

'Keep walking, dickhead, we've been waiting for you. You wouldn't want to disappoint Dad, would you?' Teddy walked ahead carrying the chalice in a Target plastic bag.

Sam looked directly at Teddy and said, 'What have you got there?'

Teddy smiled and said, 'It's something that we picked up the other day. We believe that it's quite valuable.'

'Not to you, it's not. Is it worth dying for?' Sam asked.

'Nothing is worth dying for as far as I'm concerned,' Teddy replied.

'I'm glad you think like that. That makes our job so much easier. Give me the bag and let me have a look at it.'

Teddy hesitated and Sam's eldest son said, 'Give him the bag, you fucking dickhead.'

'Hang on,' Teddy said, 'how much are you going to give us for it?'

Sam looked at Teddy and said. 'You must be some sort of idiot. We aren't going to give you anything for it. You are just going to hand it over to us and then go home and think how lucky that I didn't set one of my boys on you. Because if I had done that, you would not be going home. You would end up in the boot of my car wrapped up in plastic on your way to a sea burial, understand?'

Teddy said, 'I'm not happy with that plan. We have been offered one hundred thousand dollars for it.'

Sam looked at Teddy. 'How much is your life worth, twenty thousand, fifty thousand? I can have you 'clipped' for five thousand, or I could kill you now and it not cost me anything just the price of a bullet.'

Teddy pretended to think about the offer and said, 'I'll tell you what, why don't you and your inbred sons all fuck off and go back to scaring drunks and little old ladies? I've got back-up, and right now they are getting ready to blow your fucking heads off.'

Sam's two sons looked around in a panic, but Sam just stared at Teddy.

'Sounds like bullshit to me, who would you have as a back-up?' Sam asked.

'I've just got a couple of mates with me,' Teddy replied.

Tom and Dean stepped into view from where they had been waiting for almost an hour; Tom was in the ladies' toilet and Dean from the men's toilet.

They were both holding sawn off, pump action shotguns.

Dean said. 'Step back, Teddy. I can get the three of them from here, in one shot.'

'Fuck off,' Tom said. 'I can get them easier from my side. It's like shooting fish in a barrel, that fucking easy.'

Teddy stepped away from the three gangsters and said. 'Well, it looks like our meeting has come to an end. you blokes threatened to kill me. I take that threat very seriously. You be fucking careful who you threaten from now on. If I see you anywhere near me, then I'll take that as a threat, you won't get off as lightly as you did tonight. I'll fuck more than your pride next time.'

Teddy and his two mates walked out of the pub lounge and got into their car.

For a brief second, they saw Curly. He was in an 'F100'. He pointed briefly towards a car that was parked in the car park, a late model Merc; four men were sitting in it.

Teddy gave a nod, and Curly revved up the motor, selected reverse and drove backwards into the Merc at full speed.

The Merc rocked violently, and airbags exploded, knocking the men inside around; they were caught off guard.

Curly took off in a haze of tyre smoke followed the boys they headed towards Teddy's place.

When they got there, they all sat down and Teddy said. 'That was fucking scary. Those blokes were ready to kill me or us over that fucking chalice. We are in a bit of bother.'

Curly came into the room. 'Who was in the car that you backed into?' Teddy asked.

'Well, as far as I can work out, it was those two dickheads that attacked us at the traffic lights and also those two fucking loan sharks. They all must have teamed up. I don't like where this is heading. We have got to get rid of the chalice or sooner or later we are going to get killed for it.' Curly explained.

They all looked at Teddy.

Teddy said. 'If we keep it, then we will be running all our lives, and if we sell it, then the evil ones are just as likely to come after us for the money. Boys, we are in a bind. I reckon that the only way out is to give it to someone.'

'How will that change anything? All it will do is to transfer the problem to someone else,' Tom reasoned.

The boys all thought about it; what Teddy said was true.

'There is someone,' Rita stated in a low voice.

They all looked at her.

'He is a professor at the Melbourne University, and he is an expert on ancient treasure and all stuff that's old. He lectures and all the students seem to like him. He comes into the library where I work and is always borrowing books about pirates and lost treasures. He appears to be a nice man. I think that you could trust him.'

Teddy looked at the rest of the boys. 'What do you think?' He asked.

Dean said, 'Well, we could melt it down and sell the scrap.'

Tom replied, 'That still won't get the gangsters off our backs. They will want to get something out of it.'

Teddy looked at Curly, 'Mate, it's your decision; you pulled it out of the sand.'

Curly said, 'Fuck it, let's do it, but let's do it now, right this fucking minute. Rita, can you find out where this bloke lives?'

Rita got onto her iPad and got into her files at work and came up with his address.

Professor Stanley Brian Watson was a happy man; he had just finished reading a book, a most informative book, about The Black Devil.

It was a theory about what happened to the most vicious pirate that there ever was and who disappeared never to be seen again.

Although his home office was filled to overflowing with books, he still used the local library as he assumed that it just wasn't possible to buy all the books that he wanted to read. He was in his early sixties, been married to the same woman for more than forty years. Unfortunately, they had no children, but he considered all those students that he lectured to as a sort of part family.

He was a roly-poly sort of man with a roly-poly personality. He had a magnificent comb-over, that when the wind hit it from the wrong angle would stick straight up and look a bit like a shark's fin. "Cheaper than a toupee" he would laughingly say whenever his wife commented on it.

He adjusted his 'John Lennon' type glasses to a more comfortable position on his nose. The truth is he was wearing that style of glasses long before John Lennon ever did.

There was a knock on his front door.

'I'll get it, darling,' he said.

The truth was his wife wouldn't answer the door as she was seated snug and warm in her favourite chair with the homeless moggy that had wandered into their lives. Talk about landing on its feet. She treated that cat like a Melbourne Cup favourite and dancing with the almost unknowns' was in full flight, on the TV, so there was no chance of her leaving her seat.

He secretly hoped that it was a student craving knowledge on some subject or another.

When he opened the door, he was confronted by a big man.

On closer inspection, he noted that the man wasn't a student. He also noted that he had a solid gold chain around his neck.

'Can I be of some assistance?' Professor Watson enquired.

Teddy asked, 'Are you, Professor Watson?'

The professor nodded.

Teddy went on. 'I have something of great value. I would like to show you and see what you think. There is a story about it and I need your help. May I come in?'

'Of course, of course, please come in.'

He led Teddy into his office and quickly cleared a pile of books away from a chair so that Teddy could sit down.

'How can I be of assistance?' he asked.

Teddy opened his 'Target' shopping bag and removed the chalice.

It gleamed under the light, and he put it in front of the startled professor. Professor Watson gasped; he felt his heart quicken. Before him was something of such value, historically, that it was priceless. This was something that the world had to see. This was so moving to him that he felt like bursting into tears. Imagine a man of sixty plus years bawling over something that he had just laid eyes on. His mouth went dry. He made a couple of attempts to speak, but his voice let him down.

Without taking his eyes off the chalice, he reached for a drink, and without offering one to Teddy, he swallowed a glass of scotch whiskey.

Finally, he got his voice back, 'Where on earth did you get this magnificent piece?'

Teddy said. 'Professor, I have got to be truthful with you, but you must not tell anyone that you got this from me. We are illegal abalone divers, and we found this on a wreck sit, so you can see that we have got it by illegal means. We can't sell it as there are people out there that want to take this off us. Maybe they will kill to get it, or if we sell it, then they will come after us for the money we would get for it. So we are prepared to give it to you on the condition that you go public with the find and then you put it somewhere where the public can see it. When I say go public, I mean that it has to appear on every TV channel and in every newspaper in Australia. We want for the people who are hell bent on taking this chalice away from us to realise that we don't have it and didn't receive any money for it. That way we can go about our business and be left alone. If you don't agree, then we will melt it down and it will be lost to the entire world.'

Teddy looked at the professor; he felt that he could trust him to take care of the chalice.

The professor was beside himself with joy.

There was, he was sure, nothing like this in the world. He had to think hard where would he place this and where it could be viewed by all the people. He had to examine it minutely, look at every detail, and find out what wreck it came off. There was so much to do. But first he had to thank this man whose name he didn't know.

Teddy looked at the happiest man in the world; the professor couldn't take his eyes off the chalice. Reaching out Teddy shook the professor's hand.

The professor looked deeply into Teddy's eyes and said. 'From the bottom of my heart, I thank you. I thank you for the hundreds of thousands of people that will line up to view this masterpiece, but most of all, I thank you for me. This is the finest time in my life. You have made an old man happy.'

Teddy shook his hand and walked out of the professor's house; he got into his car and drove away. He called each of the boys and told them to look at the 'Early morning breakfast shows' as he was sure that the professor would be on with their chalice.

Eddie the Jew watched the early morning news and saw the professor sitting between the early morning news team. They were all perfect teeth and hair. The professor looked like he hadn't slept at all. He was grinning like a split watermelon and trying to explain that a man that he had never seen before knocked on his door in the middle of the night and just gave him the chalice. He couldn't give a description as the man hadn't stepped out of the darkness. He couldn't be of any help to anyone about the man's identity. It all happened too quickly, and no, he didn't know why he was selected, it was all a mystery to him.

Martha sat up in bed and started to swear. Her husband asked what's wrong, and she told him to mind his own fucking business, so he did.

Sam and his two sons looked at their TV and shook their heads in disbelief. 'What an idiot!' The eldest son said out loud.

'Why do you think that?' his father asked.

'Well, they could have melted it down and sold the gold.' The elder son said.

Sam looked at his eldest son and thought, *fucking tool*!

'Well, it's a bit like this, if they say they have melted it down, we would have still been after them for the money they received for the gold. But if they gave it away, there is nothing there for us to get, so we leave them alone, they are no longer any interest to us.'

Mario and Nick looked at the Merc. It had been transported to Mario's back yard. The truck had hit them fair in the middle, and the Merc had a bend in it, a bit like a boomerang. 'Fuck me,' said Nick, 'I reckon that it's a write-off.'

Mario shook his head and said. 'We are going to square off with those bastard, if it's the last thing I do.'

The juggler and Rick looked a little lost. They had been beaten up and crashed into and had come out with nothing at all. They were too scared to catch up with Eddie the Jew. They thought that they might give him a couple of days to cool off, maybe a couple of weeks.

Teddy sat down and watched the professor describing the chalice to millions of people. His excitement was infectious, and there had, even at this early time, been people from overseas wanting to have a closer examination of the chalice. He felt genuinely happy for the professor.

Teddy was aware that a small fortune had slipped between his fingers but, that's life, as the old song goes.

Curly and the Ponzi scheme

On 3 March 1882, Maria Ponzi gave an exhausted push and her baby boy was born.

The happy parents named him Carlo Pietro Giovanni Guillermo Tebaldo Ponzi.

He would be known as Charles Ponzi. Little did they know at that time their new-born son was to be one of the biggest con people of all time. He was to start a money-taking scheme that even years after his death would carry his name – the 'Ponzi' scheme?

Charlie was such a bull-shit artist that no one would ever actually find out just what his background was. It was proved that he came to North America in 1903 and started working his way up from nothing.

He would state that when he came to America, he had $2.50 in cash and a million dollars in dreams. He washed dishes and became a waiter but was soon sacked when he was caught short-changing customers and committing theft.

He moved to Montreal and became an assistant teller in the 'Banco Zarossi'.

The bank had mainly new Italian immigrants as customers. The bank offered six per cent interest which was twice what the other banks were offering.

Charles became a manager and the bank failed.

The owner fled to Mexico, taking as much of the bank's money that he could.

Charles was penniless and stole a cheque and wrote it out for $432.00, forging someone else's name. He was charged with forgery and jailed for three years.

When he was released, he made his way back to the United States and was once again imprisoned for his involvement in a people smuggling operation. He spent two years in jail for that. But he never gave up thinking about ways to become rich.

In 1918, he married Rose Maria Gnecco, a stenographer.

Charles worked at many jobs, including his father-in-law's grocery business. He came up with a plan to sell advertising in a large business listing; unfortunately, he wasn't able to sell this idea to the large business that he wanted to and his company folded.

He received an inquiry from Spain about his catalogue, and with it was an international reply coupon (IRC). He had never seen one of these before. When he asked about it, he discovered a way to make money. Simply put. If you sent a letter from Italy where the cost of mail was lower than America's was, and then you could redeem the IRC in exchange for stamps of the country that you were in.

Ponzi claimed that after everything was taken out, he would make 400 percent profit. Ponzi immediately quit his job and got going on his latest scheme. He started his own company 'Securities Exchange Company' and offered people the chance to double their money in ninety days.

He was consumed by eager investors.

When his scheme was hit by red tape, he simply started paying people their returns out of new customer's money.

So the Ponzi scheme was born.

When the scheme failed, as they all must, Ponzi's investors were almost wiped out. Many received less than thirty cents on the dollar.

His investors lost about twenty million dollars, an enormous amount in 1920. He was tried on many charges and was jailed. When he was released in 1934 and was deported back to Italy.

Rose stayed behind as she had had enough and she wanted to remain in America.

She later divorced him in 1937.

Charles Ponzi died penniless and almost friendless in a charity hospital in Rio de Janeiro on 18 January 1949, ending a truly remarkable life.

Curly was still in bed. It was about eight-thirty in the morning, and as there wasn't anything better to do, he turned on his latest 'Flat screen TV' and caught a bit of the news.

Professor Wilson, once again, dominated the early morning news and 'Chat' shows displaying the superb golden chalice that Curly had pulled off the bottom of the ocean. He was halfway through explaining that the chalice couldn't have come off the wreckage of a shipwrecked in Australia that we knew about, as it had gone missing about 200 years before Australia was founded.

The only explanation was that possibly a ship was wrecked on the same spot as a later one was wrecked on 200 years later. The big question was what on earth was a ship doing around Australia a couple of hundred years before Captain Cook saw Point Hicks?(Known, to the locals, as Cape Everard.)

Could there be a possibility that the Black Devil, the notorious pirate, spent some time down this way?

It was on record that he and his ship were chased by the British Men of Wars in the sixteen hundred's and all were never seen again.

Perhaps, as the old salts say, they actually did fall off the face of the earth.

Curly changed channels as he was getting a bit sick of the talk about the chalice. He felt both good and bad about it, good for finding it and bad about, not getting any money from it.

It was a brilliant move on Teddy's part to give it to someone that would show the world that he got it for nothing.

He heard his mum up and about in the kitchen. Ever since his dad had passed away, Curly had stayed at home to give her some company. His big brother had moved out, and his sister had got married and had a couple of kids.

Curly was happy enough. He was making a lot of money with Teddy and Dean and Tom and had spent a bit of time and money on the house so he and his mum were comfortable. He had done up the backyard shed and put a fridge in it and a pool table and cable TV.

All in all it was pretty comfortable, and when his mates came around on a Friday or Saturday night, for a few games of pool and a drink, they were out of everyone's way.

It was on a Friday night that one of his mates, Jim, mentioned that he had met a bloke who was taking people's money and paying them ten per cent a month. Jim himself had invested a thousand dollars and was getting one hundred dollars return every month.

He knew that there were people that had invested much more than that and were getting larger returns.

Some had invested ten thousand dollars and were getting thousand dollars a month back.

Curly listened with some interest and asked, 'Where does this bloke work out of?'

Jim explained that they all met at a pub for lunch, on the last Friday every month, and they all got their interest payments.

Jim explained that they all had lunch and a couple of bottles of red wine and a steak and it was a good way to end the week.

Curly thought about it and next time when he, Teddy, and the boys had a beer, Curly told them about the scheme. Dean wasn't very interested. Tom was sceptical about such high interest, and Teddy said, 'Just, be careful, remember how the old saying goes, 'what seems too good to be true, normally is.'

Curly took all their advice on board and decided to make up his mind when he met the bloke who was running the show next Friday.

Next Friday came and Jim and Curly met at a pub in Carlton and went into the lounge bar. There was a large table set up and a few men were sitting around it. They were all relaxed and were waiting for more to turn up before they started to eat their meal.

Jim introduced Curly to all the people and explained that the main man, Patto, wasn't here yet. 'Open a bottle of red and he will soon appear,' one wit said.

Everyone laughed and they all started talking to each other.

Soon Patto arrived.

He was a short bloke, in his fifties, well-dressed in a smart jacket and neat slacks. His shoes looked new and were highly polished.

With him was a big man, about thirty-five, with a scared face, big hands, and a 'don't fuck with me' look.

He was carrying a leather satchel, also highly polished, made by an Italian company and worth about one thousand dollars.

Patto laughed and said, 'All you blokes know Les, don't you? He's giving me a hand when I shoot about and square up with all the lucky investors.'

Les didn't seem to want to go around the table and shake everyone's hand.

'Let's get down to business before we all get into the tucker,' Patto suggested.

With that, he pulled out his notebook and began reading out names and amounts.

Les put the valise onto the table and opened it. It was full of bundles of cash, fifties and hundreds all held together by rubber bands. Patto started giving out thick bundles to each of the people that were sitting around the table. Some of the men left their money in front of them and others quickly started putting their bundles of notes into their pockets.

Patto carelessly tossed two bundles of fifties on the table and said to the men that the money stopped in front of. 'You get the biggest amounts because you have got the most amount of money invested.'

The two men smiled and said, 'So we should.'

Everyone laughed.

Curly noticed that there were some people that didn't get money placed in front of them.

Jim spoke quietly to Curly, 'I think that those without the money are, like you, here to sound out what's going on.'

When most of the money was handed out, Patto said, 'Let's get a drink into us and order a steak because I'm weak from hunger.'

Everyone laughed and got stuck into ordering beers, red wine, and steaks.

When the meal was almost over, Patto came down and sat beside Curly and Jim and asked Curly, 'Mate, how's things? Did you enjoy the steak? It's not a bad meal, is it?'

Curly agreed. He asked Patto. 'How does this scheme of yours work? It seems to be a winner, the sort of thing that I would be interested in.'

'Well, mate; it's a really simple thing to get your head around.' Patto explained. 'What happens is this. My brother-in-law runs a plastic bag factory for his best mate, and he said to my brother-in-law, that if he can get his hands on a supply of granulated plastic, then he can use the plastic to make all the plastic bags that he can. At no charge. That's where I come in. He can't sell the plastic bags as he's got no contacts, and my mate is the purchasing officer for the biggest supermarket chain in Australia. No names no pack drill, got me, mate?'

Patto touched the side of his nose in a knowing way.

He went on, 'Well, I got a heap of samples and took them down to show my mate and he said, "Fucking beauty, mate, these are as good as gold. How soon can you get me a truckload of the bastards." So I said, "Mate, I can put a truckload together as soon as I can buy the raw material." So that's how it started.

I saw a couple of blokes and got a start and now we are away and flying. The more money that I get in, the more raw materials that I can buy and the more plastic bags I can sell and the more money we all end up with. Curly mate, it's a fucking ripper, I reckon that it will go on forever. I can sell as many as the factory can put out and easily afford the ten per cent a month.'

Patto laughed and said, 'Look around the table. All these blokes are happy, just sitting down and raking the money in. There are more investors than that are here. These are the ones that get out of a Friday and have a drink.'

Curly was feeling good about the deal.

He said to Patto. 'Patto, I might be able to help you out with this. How about I give you a cheque for ten thousand dollars?'

Patto smiled and said, 'Mate, it's all tax-free, so I don't want to leave a paper trail, with cheques and the rest of that sort of shit. It's easier for me if I get cash and pay you in cash. I'll give you a receipt and you hand me the money. Then each month, we will square up in cash.'

Curly asked, 'What if I want to pull my money out at any time?'

'Yes, mate, I understand. Sometimes shit happens and you need your cash. All I ask is for you to give me ninety days' notice that you want your money back, and I'll deliver it to you in cash, no problems.' Patto smiled and asked, 'Do you want in or not?'

Curly said, 'Yep, I'm in. I'll give you the money on Monday morning, and do you want to meet me somewhere?'

Patto smiled and said, 'You name the place and I'll be there.'

They arranged a place and Patto went around the table to where another potential victim was sitting drinking red wine.

He started the same conversation with the unfortunate man.

Curly and Jim headed home, and they went into Curly's shed and got out a beer and Jim said, 'Curly, mate, we are in business. I wish that I had more spare cash hanging around as I would put more into Patto's scheme, I reckon that it's a winner.'

They both agreed.

Early Monday morning, Curly went to his local bank and got out ten thousand dollars, in cash. He rang Patto's number. Patto agreed to meet him at an inner city pub. Curly agreed and was soon sitting at the bar when Patto and Les walked in.

They sat down, and Patto asked, 'Got the money?'

Curly nodded and passed the bag over; Les reached across and grabbed the bag.

Patto said, 'No worries, Curly, we will see you in a month with your interest.' With that, they shook hands and turned around and walked out.

Les and Patto had been friends for years. They really got on well together. The difference in their sizes made them look like the odd couple, Patto small and Les huge.

Although Les wasn't the smartest human on the planet, he could have been the toughest. He had done stunts in jail for drunk driving and beating blokes up and once for armed robbery, so he knew his way around.

He had a favourite trick.

Whenever he went to jail, he would ask who was the toughest bloke here? When he was pointed out, then Les would front him and say. I reckon that you are all piss and wind. See how you handle this, and he would let one go.

The toughest bloke in the jail would always answer the challenge and they would get into it, toe to toe, usually neither taking a step back until both of them were covered in each other's blood.

Les wouldn't have any problems after that.

Nobody would try to stand over him in the queue at the canteen, or gave him any lip.

He wasn't an easy person to like, but Patto had never had a problem with him.

Les had been doing it a bit tough, living hand to mouth, doing a bit of security work, but he didn't have any tickets so it was all under the counter stuff. So when he met Patto about five years earlier, he recognised a similar type of person to himself but worlds apart.

Patto was so sophisticated and knew things that Les didn't. He knew which fork to pick up in a restaurant, not that he had ever been to a restaurant before he met Patto, and how to treat people with respect. Even if you didn't like them very much.

When Patto had a bet, he didn't go to the TAB like all the other mugs. He just got on the phone and rang a 'Bookie', and Patto had an 'in' with one of the biggest 'SP'S' in Australia.

This bloke was the most prominent in the game and had been hounded out of Australia and went to Vanuatu and worked legally from there.

Yes, he was a strange one that Patto. But Patto always said, 'be nice to everyone, then when they least expect it, rob the fuck out of them.'

Yes, in a lot of ways Les looked up to Patto.

Teddy fingered his gold chain and was looking at the weather map, on the weather channel.

'Looks like a bit of fair weather coming our way,' he said, almost to himself.

'I reckon that we should have a trip, somewhere between Lakes Entrance and Mallacoota. This time we should put in at the boat ramp at Cape Conran, steam towards Mallacoota and have a jump around Point Hicks. There's a lot of bottom there and it's a Marine park and that makes it a 'no-take zone' for any seafood, so there should be plenty of abalone there. It would be better if we dived at night, but that might be a bit of a problem with Dean. He doesn't like diving in the dark in the middle of the ocean. I suppose that I can only ask him and see what he says.' Teddy muttered to himself.

Dean wasn't having any luck at all.

His last hand was a full house and he thought that he had a winner, and in most cases, he would have, but that arsehole Chinese prick had had four threes.'

Fuck me dead, Dean thought.

He had looked at him and was sure that he was bluffing, them 'Chows' only ever bluffed now and then, Dean reckoned that it was time that fucking chow was ready to bluff. 'Fuck me dead, how much had he lost?' He didn't want to think about it.'

The Chinese smiled and said, 'bed ruck, Dan.'

Dean thought to himself, 'Fuck me dead, he could hardly speak fucking English and he didn't even know my fucking name.'

'It's Dean,' Dean said to the grinning oriental, fucking Dean.'

The Chinese said. 'So solly, fucking, Dan.'

Dean didn't know if he was taking the piss out of him or not, but he suspected that he was.

'Fucking, plate face,' Dean muttered, and got up from the table and walked away. It just wasn't his day or night whatever it was outside. He needed a drink and a cash injection. He wondered what Teddy had in mind, and he hoped that he was coming up with a plan.

Tom sat with Sandy; she still wasn't completely over being abused by the loan sharks.

She liked Tom to be around and even the slightest noises had her on edge, but she was getting better. Tom seethed inside. He knew that he hadn't finished with those two dogs. There would be a time when he would shut them down, but not right now; he would wait. As the old saying goes, vengeance is a dish, best-eaten cold.

Meanwhile, he would tend to Sandy and make her as happy as he could. 'It's a lovely sunny day, why don't we go out into the garden and pull a few weeds out.'

Tom knew that Sandy loved the garden.

Teddy eventually got through to Dean.

He had tried a few times and Dean's phone had been turned off, a sure sign that Dean was involved in a high-stake card game. The other players didn't take too kindly to being interrupted by someone's phone ringing.

Teddy asked, 'How's things?'

Dean responded in a cynical way, 'Fucking fantastic, I feel like knocking myself.'

'Well, I might be able to cheer you up a bit,' Teddy laughed, 'I reckon that we should get up the coast and do a bit.'

'Sounds good to me, anything to get away from what I've just had to put up with.'

'No worries, mate, keep your phone turned on and I'll be in touch.'

Teddy then rang Tony and told him that they would be going away in the next couple of days and to fill up the four-wheel drive and the Shark Cat. Tony said he would do it first thing in the morning. As usual Tony didn't ask any questions as he knew that Teddy would fill him in as soon as he needed to know, and you didn't know who was listening on the phone.

Teddy rang the other boys and told them what was going on, and they all said that they were, willing, and eager. Tom said that he might bring Sandy around as she still wasn't one hundred percent about being on her own. Teddy said that he was happy with that and he would tell Rita and let her know that she had a visitor.

Curly was happy when Teddy rang and said they were going away, as the ten thousand dollars that he had given Patto and Les was about to be replaced. He told his mum, and she started to pack his bag.

He was sure that when the boys heard about his investment, then they would be interested.

Tony got the 'nod' from Teddy the next day and headed off towards Cape Conran, a five or six-hour tow. The boat towed beautifully, and he hardly knew that it was behind him. He kept his eyes on the rear-view mirror just to make sure that he wasn't being followed.

No problems so far. He turned on a CD of Bob Segar's, greatest hits and thought that life was good.

Teddy rang Dave and told him what was happening. Dave was ready and willing.

He rang his brother Lee and told him everything was on the go.

Lee laughed and said, 'I thought that we might be doing something soon, as the weather is good enough.'

Everything was set. Teddy and the boys were off. They were in Tom's Commodore, a run of the mill, an average family car. All their gear was in the Shark Cat, so they just had overnight bags, mainly just 'Jocks and Socks' and a change of clothes.

They drove down behind the boat and Tony.

They went through Bairnsdale, and Tony stopped and filled up the long-distance tanks at Newmerella. The boys had refuelled earlier in Bairnsdale and made their way down to Marlo and Cape Conran.

The boys pulled up in the car park at the Cape Conran boat ramp. There were a few cars and boat trailers there as the early birds had got an early start and gone out fishing for flathead and gummy shark.

Half an hour later, Tony rolled into the area and said with a grin. 'Shit, mate, this is the easiest thing in the world to tow, the F100, really pulls a treat.'

They all started unstrapping the boat and releasing the tie downs that held everything in place. Tony waited until all the boys had climbed up into the boat and then he backed it into the water. Teddy started both motors and they ticked over smoothly. He slowly reversed back off the trailer and then pulled around in a tight circle to avoid a large rock that was just under the surface. Sometimes the sea would break over it on rough days. Teddy had done his homework and knew about most of the boat ramps in the area. He slowly pushed down on the two throttles and the boat slowly got up onto the plane and they headed out to sea.

When Tony drove past the camp park in Marlo, the manager, who was outside mowing the lawn, recognised the Shark Cat as a poacher's boat.

He had been involved in the abalone industry all his life and was on good terms with the fisheries department and Inspector Wallace Trotter.

'Fuck me,' he said, 'I know that boat. I have seen it around and it's a poacher's boat. I'll give Piggy a ring and tell him there is trouble afoot.'

With that, he stopped the ride on mower and went inside to the telephone on the reception desk. He rang the fisheries and asked to speak to fisheries officer Trotter.

Fisheries Inspector Trotter known to all as Piggy, but never mentioned to his face, was sitting at his desk and was halfway through the Herald Sun crossword. He looked up irritably when his phone rang. He heaved his bulk forward in the chair and said, 'Fisheries Inspector Trotter, how can I help you?'

Piggy recognised the voice as a friend of his, whom, on many occasions, had tipped the fisheries off to the fact that there were poachers operating out of Cape Conran,

'Whoa, whoa, slow down, mate, what's the problem?' Piggy asked.

'I'll tell you the problem, mate. The problem is that a boat just got towed past and it's a Shark Cat, the same Shark Cat that was up this way earlier on in the year.' The camp park manager said quickly.

'Bastards,' Piggy roared into the handset, 'are you sure it's the same one?'

'Yes, mate, I'm sure it's the same one.'

Piggy asked a couple more questions and then hung up.

This time he would get them. This time they would find out what law and order were all about. He quickly summoned his crew about him and said, 'Let's get every available member on the ball. Let's get everyone that's not on leave ready and we'll set up watch and work out what they are up to. We know that they must have gone up north. They may be at Pearl point, or they may have gone further up all the way to Point Hicks. They may even be on the reef at "Wingham Inlet", but I reckon that that's a bit deep and tidal for them. I'll get a plane organised and we'll see where they are at. Then we will know what we should do to intercept and charge the bastards.' Piggy looked around and could sense the victory.

At last he's going to get the bastards. He had them where he wanted them, on the bloody ropes.

'Yes, I'm a chance of confiscating the boat and all their gear. At long last I've got the bastards.'

Piggy started to ring and book a plane so they could go out and have a look at where the poachers were fishing.

Teddy drove the boat in under the lighthouse, at Point Hicks, on the Lakes Entrance side.

The water looked clear and was moderately flat.

'This looks like a good spot,' Teddy assured the divers.

Tom replied, 'Any spot's a good spot, if there's abalone here.'

The boys suited up, and Teddy got things organised. The hoses were out and the compressors were running.

As always Dean and Curly worked off a 'T' piece and Tom worked off a single line.

Dean and Curly went ahead and started chipping abalone off the rocks and putting them into net bags. Then Tom would take the net bags off them and carry them to a stockpile. Dean and Curly would continue chipping abalone off the rocks. They took all sizes. Soon there was a pile of net bags in a sandy spot and the amount of abalone on the rocks had diminished.

Tom gave the boys the thumbs up and they all headed to the surface. Teddy brought the boat up beside them and they all climbed on board.

Teddy asked, 'How's it going?'

Tom replied. 'We have got ten full net bags. There are plenty down there. These 'no-take zones' are perfect for us.'

They all laughed.

As there was no fish on board, there was a relaxed atmosphere among the divers.

Tom asked Curly about his new beaut investment scheme. Curly went into great depths, about how much it was worth and how all the people who were in it were more than happy about the way that they were getting their money.

'What an excellent way to spend a Friday lunch getting drunk and making money.' He laughed.

Dean asked. 'If I were able to put in ten thousand dollars, then I would get back, one thousand dollars each month, and still have my original ten thousand dollars that I could get back?'

'Yep,' Curly said, 'but Patto want's a three-months-notice if you want your money back.'

Tom said. 'If I was to borrow twenty thousand dollars and invest it with this bloke, and I borrowed it from my bank, I would probably be paying, say ten percent, a year. And I would be getting one hundred and twenty percent back from your mate. Sounds too good to be true to me but I wouldn't mind a bit of the action while it lasted. I think that we should go and visit this Patto when we get back and see if we can get on board the gravy train.'

They all agreed that it was a good plan.

With that, Teddy drove the boat over to another position and they all started to get back into it.

When Dean and Curly went over the side Tom held back and asked Teddy. 'What do you reckon, about this investment scheme? Do you think that it might work?'

Teddy screwed up his face and said. 'It's the kind of deal that sounds too good to be true, but if it's a goer, then I wouldn't mind being involved. Maybe we should go along and see this Patto and work out what's going on.'

Excitement is infectious and Piggy and the two underlings that he had invited to go with him were excited. Piggy drove towards Bairnsdale's airport at a lot over the speed limit.

The pilot was doing his safety checks, walking around the four-seater plane.

'Are we after more of the bastards?' The pilot asked, using Piggy's favourite expression when describing poachers.

'We sure are. We know that they are in the area and they have headed down to Cape Conran. We'll go and have a look for the evil bastards, and we see just what they are up to.' Piggy suggested.

The pilot smiled to himself as he had flown Piggy on sightseeing tours a few times. The money was good as he was paid by the Fisheries and he never tired of flying over the ocean. The two underlings climbed into the back seat, leaving Piggy to sit up the front beside the pilot. They taxied off towards the landing strip and checked to see if there was any incoming traffic. When the pilot was sure that it was clear, he lined the little plane up and increased its speed. They were soon airborne and zipping across the paddocks surrounding the Bairnsdale airfield.

Piggy smiled. He loved getting up in the air.

They headed towards the coast and were soon above the ninety-mile beach.

They followed it along until they came to the entrance at Lakes Entrance. The tide was running out and you could see the dirty water mixing with the clean ocean water. The sea glinted greenly under them.

They were soon up to the mouth of the Snowy River. 'Looks like the bar's open at Marlo,' The pilot commented.

'Yes, but there's not a lot of water on, it would be too difficult to get a big boat out,' Piggy replied.

They followed the coast until they reached Cape Conran.

'Take us down lower,' Piggy asked. 'I want to see if I can recognise their F100.'

The pilot lowered the plane and Piggy looked at the car park.

'No, it's not there. The driver must have taken it and hidden it somewhere. All right, let's go up the coast and see if we can find them. Keep your eyes open in the back.' Piggy ordered.

The plane made its way up the coast, past Pearl Point and past the Bemm River bar.

'That bar's not open,' Piggy commented.

'Maybe they will need to blow it open,' the pilot suggested.

Piggy nodded, his eyes were scanning the ocean ahead of them. They were travelling north and they approached the Point Hicks lighthouse. They all spotted Teddy's boat at once. It was close to the rocks.

The pilot said, 'There's our boy,' and circled the plane around.

Teddy was in the half cabin and didn't see the aircraft coming. The noise of the compressors didn't allow him to hear the aircraft. He was hanging out of the window steering the boat along, keeping close the diver's bubbles. He happened to glance up and saw the plane circling him.

He thought to himself, it could be the fisheries or it could just be some sightseeing flight and the pilot is giving the customers a look at an abalone boat.

He walked out onto the rear deck and waved.

The pilot waved back at him and Teddy could see that the passenger had a camera and looked to be taking photos.

Piggy lined up Teddy and thought, *got you, you bastard, this will look good in court, caught in the bloody act.*

A voice from the rear seats commented, 'They must have just started as they don't seem to have any abalone on board.'

'Yes, good point,' Piggy replied. 'They have been out here for hours. I wonder what they are up to!'

They circled the boat for some time and none of the divers came up to the surface. From the air, it was easy to see the diver's bubbles.

There were two sets of bubbles that stuck together, and one set that moved from the two sets and moved away and then came back.

'I can't make out what they are doing.' Piggy questioned.

The pilot mentioned that it was getting late and that they had better make a move home as he wasn't equipped for night flying.

They had one more spin around the boat and Piggy made a decision. He rang the fisheries office in Bairnsdale and arranged for a fisheries four-wheel drive to come up and meet them at the Marlo airport. Then that would enable them to go back to Cape Conran and wait until Teddy and his crew came ashore. He also had the fisheries stake out the Lakes Entrance boat ramp so if they went down there, they would be walking into a trap.

Piggy felt that he had all the areas covered.

He told the pilot to put them down at Marlo and they would meet up with a vehicle.

One of the back-seat passengers would go back and the other one would be stuck in a 4WD with Piggy all night. He would reminisce about his years of stake outs and how he arrested this villain and this poacher, etc., etc.

They landed at Marlo airstrip and the unfortunate one and Piggy watched as the plane took off down the runway and took to the skies.

When the fisheries' four-wheel drive arrived, Piggy took control of it, and with the two hapless officers, they headed down to the now deserted boat ramp and started their long wait.

When the boys came up for a break, Teddy told them about the plane, and they all reckoned that it might be the fisheries and what would they do. There was about seven hundred kilos of meat on the bottom, that needed shelling, and they really needed another six or seven hundred kilos to make the trip work out for them.

Teddy asked. 'If we work until midnight and then unload at Point Hicks at say, three o'clock in the morning. Dave and Lee will be up and we can load them into the van and go back to the ramp and let Tony pick up the boat. He can start off back to Melbourne and we can either put our heads down or go straight back, what do you reckon?'

They chucked a few ideas around but couldn't come up with a better one than Teddy's original one. So they agreed to get back into the water and to make an effort to get as much as they could. They hit the water with new determination and as the hours went by so did the amount of abalone increased on the bottom.

Teddy rang Dave and said that they were going to unload the abalone onto the sandy beach at Point Hicks at about 3 a.m.

'What about the padlocked gate?' Dave asked.

'You will just have to cut the chain that holds the gate closed, at three am, there won't be any tourists,' Teddy said.

The lighthouse at Point Hicks is about one and a bit kilometre from the car park. There is a locked gate there to stop any vehicles driving down the track to the lighthouse as the road is very narrow and it would be dangerous for two-way traffic use.

Tourists are welcome to walk into the lighthouse area. There is accommodation at the lighthouse, in the old lighthouse keeper's quarters, and if you are staying there, you wild be given the combination of the lock, which is always changed.

Dean was constantly amazed at how much light there is underwater at night.

True, he wasn't too happy about night diving, but all in all, when you looked at it, the others didn't seem to mind. If a Great White did happen along, then his chances were one in three.

Something stirred up the phosphorous in the water just beyond his vision and he almost shit himself, but he kept on going.

He knew that he wouldn't be able to stand the horror of it for much longer.

There was something out there, Dean assured himself.

He made his way over to where Curly was working and gave him the thumbs up. Curly, who had been expecting this, gave him the thumbs up also and they headed to the surface. Teddy came over, and Dean climbed into the boat.

'There's some fucking thing out there just out of my vision,' Dean swore. He started to get out of his gear.

Teddy nodded and said. 'Well, we might as well start shucking out what we have got. I reckon that there is over a tonne of meat.'

'Do you want me to start bringing up the shells?' Curly asked.

Teddy said, 'Yes, mate, you and Tom start bringing up the shells and we will begin shucking them out.'

Soon the boat was full of abalone shells and half full draining bins. They worked on into the night. Teddy went back to the stockpiled abalone, and Tom brought them to the surface.

It was almost 3 a.m. when they were finished, and with navigation lights off, they pulled around the point and slowly motored in towards the shore.

Teddy's phone buzzed in his pocket, and he answered it.

Dave was on the line. 'Mate, I can see you. I'll shine a torch and you come into shore. It's as flat as a "shit carter's hat", so lift the motors up and you will be able to come into a couple of feet of water.'

'Sweet, mate,' Teddy answered.

The boat gently rode the small waves, and all the boys unloaded the abalone meat that had been placed in plastic bags and sealed with a wire tie on the ends. Dave and Lee ran the abalone up into their furniture van and put them into the tea chests. They were soon snookered behind a wall of furniture, out of sight.

Dave helped push the boat out into deeper water and Teddy lowered the motors. He started them and slowly made his way out into deeper water.

Dave and Lee jumped into the truck and Lee said, 'Melbourne, here we come.'

He slowly drove down the track and through the gate.

They stopped at the gate, and Dave closed it and put back the lock so to the casual glance it would appear that it was all OK.

Dave settled down and prepared himself for the long journey.

Teddy rang Derek the processor and told him that the load was on its way. Derek said, 'Thanks, mate,' and went back to sleep. He knew that Dave would ring him in plenty of time for him to get everything ready.

Wallace Piggy Trotter was in full flight, not even the lateness of the hour could put the brakes on his talking. He was going over all the ways to follow, undetected a poacher's boat and how he had tailed the very same boat, that they are now waiting on to pounce upon, from Bairnsdale to Merimbula, undetected. A feat that possibility would never be repeated, and one done with such cunning that that he should actually put it in print as a guide for younger officers.

Piggy was just about to throw himself into another riveting story when he detected lights approaching from the road leading off the highway into the boat ramp.

'Someone is coming,' he hissed.

From where they had hidden the fisheries four-wheel drive in the scrub, they watched as an F100 approached.

'That's the same one as I followed to Merimbula. The bastards are going to be picked up here. I knew it. I fucking knew it. Careful, lads, they might be dangerous. They are going to get the shock of their lives when they see us.'

Tony slowly drove down to the boat ramp and put his reversing lights on. The whole area was illuminated brightly, and he backed the boat trailer into the water and waited.

The Fisheries Officers also waited.

'We will wait until the vessel is loaded onto the trailer and then we will rush forward in the truck and block them off so they can't get away,' Piggy enthused.

He could taste the sweet, sweet taste of victory already. 'It doesn't get any better than this,' he told himself, 'no siree!'

Teddy brought the boat around the Cape and saw that Tony had lit up the boat ramp.

The ocean was calm and smooth. He drove the boat up onto the trailer, and Tony clipped the winch strap to the front of the boat and secured the boat to the trailer. He then got into the F100 and pulled the boat out of the water.

It came out smoothly; the boys all climbed down and started to stretch their legs. Tony began to tie down the boat when all of a sudden, from out of nowhere, the fisheries vehicle appeared. It screeched to a halt totally blocking the boys' way out of the boat ramp.

Piggy leapt out and with a sneer asked, 'You boys are a bit late, aren't you?'

'Yes,' Teddy replied, 'we had a bit of boat trouble and only just managed to make it back, a bit of crook fuel I reckon.'

Piggy shone a strong torch around the vessel and asked. 'What have you got aboard? Let's have a look, shall we?' Piggy started to clamber up the side, 'Let's have a look, all will be revealed.'

When the flashlight shone on the deck of the Shark Cat, there was a stunned silence from Piggy and his two offsiders. It was empty and clear of anything, nothing at all.

'What did you do with the abalone?' Piggy asked almost to himself.

Teddy looked at Piggy and said. 'Really, mate, you have got to stop accusing us of doing the wrong thing. Like I've told you on a million occasions, we are wreck divers looking for wrecks and just having a good time out and about. We aren't hurting anyone just minding our own business.'

Piggy slowly went back to the Fisheries four-wheel drive shaking his head. 'Where did I go wrong?' He asked himself.

One of the understudies offered, 'There wasn't any abalone in the boat when we saw it from the plane, so maybe what they say is true. Maybe they aren't poachers at all. Maybe they are simply divers that look for wrecks, go out and just enjoy themselves.'

Piggy looked at the young man and shook his head. *Fucking idiot,* he thought but decided that it probably wasn't the time or place to get into him.

Tony slowly drove the F100 out of the car park and started the drive to Melbourne; he took Curly with him for a bit of company.

Teddy, Dean, and Tom all jumped into Tom's car and left in the boat's wake. They had made plans to stop at the 'Billabong' Roadhouse for an early breakfast.

Piggy and his two companions drove back to Bairnsdale; the silence that filled the cabin could have been cut with a knife. Piggy looked straight ahead, deep in thought; they had come up behind a furniture van slowly driving up a hill.

For the first time, Piggy spoke out loud. 'Check these morons out, carting furniture from city to city. Bugger me, what a way to earn your money. That would have to be the lowest job in the world, dragging furniture from one house to another.'

Somewhere a light went off in Piggy's brain, but no, there was nothing there, he couldn't quite put his finger on what was wrong.

Lee looked in the rear-view mirror of his truck and said to Dave, who was half-asleep, 'Hey, mate, we have got the fisheries behind us.'

Dave jerked himself upright. 'Fuck me, are they on to us?'

Lee always the calmer of the two replied. 'No, mate, they are just waiting for a chance to get past us. As soon as we hit the overtaking lane, then they will be on their way.'

Dave wasn't as sure, but time did tell, and the fisheries vehicle went past them and disappeared into the early morning.

Dave said, 'I'll go back to sleep then.'

✧ ✧ ✧ ✧

By the time Tony had pulled into the 'Billabong' road-house, Curly had convinced him that the investment scheme was too good to be true. Tony would be a mug, not to get involved in it.

When they got out of the F100 and walked around the trailer, waiting for the boys to arrive, Tony had convinced himself that he would get involved, he might put a couple of grand into it.

Tom pulled his Commodore into the parking bay and all the boys got out.

Teddy walked up to the boat and asked how it towed. They were all standing around the trailer and as one decided to walk into the restaurant, dining room; they were greeted by an attractive, but tired-looking woman, the same one that always served them. She had a name tag on her right breast that said, Hilda.

Teddy said, 'Top of the morning, Hilda, looks like you win the prize and get to serve us again, you lucky little devil.'

Hilda gave a tired smile and thought to herself, I remember these blokes. The big one with the gold chain does all the talking and always leaves a big tip.

'Yes, boys, I'm not exactly run off my feet, as you can see; what would you like?'

'Steak, eggs and chips, for five, thanks love.'

Hilda started off to the kitchen, and Teddy and the boys got some chairs and a couple of tables together. Hilda thought that it was funny the way that they all didn't ask for their steaks to be done differently. Usually, if there were five steaks, then everyone wanted theirs done differently. She was aware that they were a pretty tight crew.

Teddy shouted out to Hilda, 'I'll get the coffee going for you, if you don't mind.'

Hilda smiled to herself and yelled out, 'Please help yourself.'

Teddy got the coffee going and they all sat around and waited for their meals to arrive.

Tony said, 'What do you blokes reckon about this investment scheme that Curly is talking about?'

The general consensus was that if it were all right, then they all should have a go at it. Tom was a bit reluctant, but as they all seemed to be a bit keen on it, then he may as well be in it too.

All they had to work out was how much to invest.

Patto and Les were happy men.

The money was pouring in at a steady rate, and people seemed to think that they were going to miss out.

It was funny, as the scheme was all bullshit.

There was no plastic bag factory and there was no big deal with leading supermarkets.

All they were doing was robbing the fuck out of everyone. By giving people ten per cent a month, all they were doing was making it sound attractive so more 'Mugs' would put more money in. That simple! And it was working; the money was coming in hand over fist. Patto kept all the book work and Les was in charge of everything else. Last week, they got their hands on twenty thousand dollars; twenty thousand dollars! It was unbelievable, and as Patto pointed out, there was no money trail. There was no way of anybody proving what they were doing. They didn't put anything in the bank, so there was no record of any money going into any account. Patto had a floor safe in his garage at his house and he kept a two-hundred litre drum (the old forty-four gallon) filled with oil that was almost impossible to shift on your own. He kept his and Les's money in that, safer than a bank they would both laugh.

Patto's phone rang; it was that young bloke Curly.

Patto turned his phone onto hands-free so Les could hear both sides of the conversation.

'Hullo, mate,' Patto said when he recognised Curly's voice. 'How are you going?' Patto didn't really care how he was going; he just asked to be nice.

Curly answered that he was well and that he had a couple of blokes that wanted to be involved.

Patto winked at Les and said. 'Hey, mate, it's a good thing that you called, as I've just signed up with another big distributor and they are keen to take another truckload of bags off us.'

Patto made a gesture like he was masturbating and Les sniggered.

'How much would you be able to take,' asked Curly, sounding a bit excited.

Patto lounged back into his chair and continued the masturbating gestures, he said, 'Just let me check.'

He asked Les. 'With what we have ordered and with what we need, and taking in the time of delivery of existing stock. Just a minute, let me find the right screen, yes, yes, here it is,ahmm, let me work this out. Yeah, yeah, mate I reckon that we would be able to do another complete run and that means that if the money's there, then we should be able to accept almost any amount. How much did you have in mind, Curly?'

Curly hesitated and said. 'Maybe about one hundred thousand. How does that sound?'

Patto couldn't believe his luck, fuck me dead, one hundred thousand. He looked at Les and stopped the masturbation antics and went into a fishing pose, suddenly striking like he had just hooked a big one.

'Yes, mate, that's no problem. When can you get it to me, as I want to purchase the raw material as soon as possible?'

Curly said, 'I'll get back to you on that as soon as I can. We are just on our way back from a trip and once we all get a bit of rest, then I'll tell you what's going on.'

'That sounds sweet, mate,' Patto replied, 'I'll wait for your call. I'll ring ahead and tell the raw product people and they will have the order ready when you drop in the money. I'll talk to you later, Curly, goodbye now.'

Patto turned his phone off and said to Les, 'Mate, there is one born every day, thank Christ, or we would starve.'

Patto said to Les, 'Mate, what do you like today?'

Les picked up the form guide and said, 'There's a horse that a bloke I know said was a goer. Now this bloke is real close to the owner and he reckons that if the track is wet, then it's a chance, it's got a good jockey on it and the tracks heavy.'

'What price is it?' Patto asked.

Les looked at the TV screen on the wall of the pub that they were using as their office and said, 'It started out at thirty to one but has come into eighteen to one.'

'Some bastards backing it, maybe the owner is loading up,' Patto suggested.

'What do you reckon that we have on it?' Les enquired.

'Well, a hundred grand looks like it's just jumped in, so we may as well have ten each way.' Patto enthused.

'Fuck it, yes, let's have a go,' Les said.

Patto dialled the SP'S number and said his name and pin number and said with a wink to Les. 'Yes, hullo, mate, we might have ten thousand each way on horse five, race four. Just to watch it go around.' He laughed at something the person on the other end of the phone said and disconnected. 'They are starting to get to know us now, mate. We must be almost their biggest punters.' Patto said with a smile.

At the other end of the line in Vanuatu, the bloke on the telephone looked at the boss and indicated that a reasonable bet had been placed. His boss decided not to lay it off as he considered Patto, a mug punter. If it had been one of his big punters that knew what they were doing, then it would have been a different picture, he would have laid some of the bets off the bet with another SP.

The boss idly wondered where this mug was getting his money from. He concluded that he was robbing some other poor bastard; he didn't think that he would be on the scene for a lot longer.

Hilda smiled when Teddy paid the bill and left a fifty-dollar tip. It was worth while staying open. She wished that all the people were as generous. She watched as Tony drove the F100 and the boat out onto the highway.

Teddy and the rest of the crew were all in the Commodore and followed.

She idly wondered what they were up to. She had been around long enough to know that things were rarely as they seemed and there was something about them that didn't quite add up. It was nothing to do with her.

Dave rang Derek, the Processor, and arranged to meet up, and when they got to the factory, Derek was waiting for them. They unloaded their van and Derek and Dave took the abalone meat around to Derek's factory. They unloaded them into the area where they weighed them and Dave started ripping open the plastic bags and tipping them onto the draining table. Derek asked Dave if they wanted any left out for the Henry, the Vietnamese restaurateur, and Dave said, 'Yes, the usual.' So they put aside one hundred kilos.

All was soon weighed up and Dave went back to the furniture van. Lee was awake and as soon as the bins were placed back inside and everything was covered up, they said goodbye to Derek and headed off back home.

Teddy rang Henry, and after a bit of idle chit-chat, they agreed that Teddy would drop in the one hundred kilos later on that night. Teddy decided that they would eat at the restaurant and made bookings for all of them. He rang around and all the boys and their partners said that they would be there.

They all met at the restaurant, and Curly and Teddy carried in the bins into the kitchen and got the money from Henry.

As they sat and had a drink, they discussed the investment scheme. Curly admitted that he had put in twenty thousand and was eager to put in more. Tom said that he didn't really care much, one way or the other. Sandy and Rita were a bit sceptical, and Dean didn't really care, but would put some in if only to be in it with the rest.

Curly explained that he had spoken to Patto and relayed on to the boys that if they could come up with it, then Patto was willing to accept another one hundred thousand. This knocked the boys back a bit as they were more or less thinking of a maximum of ten thousand dollars or less.

Teddy started to hear warning bells, no documentation, no contracts, nothing, what happened if it all went pear-shaped.

Curly was adamant that it was a goer. He said that Tony was going to put in two thousand, and if Teddy and Tom put in twenty thousand each, that made forty-two thousand. If Dean put in ten thousand, that made fifty-two thousand, he would make up the rest. He would put in forty-eight thousand, making the total of one hundred thousand; they would receive ten thousand dollars a month, easy money. He would pick it up and divide it among the others, what could be easier, money for old rope.

Their meals arrived, and as they were all sharing, then there was no talk of money. When the meal was over, Curly said, 'I'll take the money over to Patto and then you can all square me up after we get paid for this trip.' They all agreed, and Curly went home happy with himself. He was sure that he had helped all the boys get a tax-free investment scheme.

'Are you sure that your mate knows anything about fucking race horses? That mutt didn't give a kick. It started slowly and moved back through the pack. The jockey had to go five wide, and when he did that it just sat out there and did nothing, not a fucking thing.' Patto said with a tone of disgust and shook his head.

Les laughed. 'Mate, what did you expect at those odds? You know that the rich people just keep backing favourites until they win and let's face it. We've got the money. Why don't we do that?'

'Yes, mate, I reckon that you are right. Fuck, the long shots. We'll stick to the favourites.'

With that, they started back on the phone and getting into it.

By the end of the day, they had seen off sixty thousand dollars. They would have been worried if it wasn't for the one hundred thousand dollars that was on its way.

Teddy went around to Derek, the processor and picked up the money from the latest load of abalone.

He walked into Derek's office and said with a grin, 'How did you go?'

'No worries at all the money's here sixty-two thousand dollars. Do you want to count it?' Derek laughed.

Teddy said that he didn't have the time; he would split it up at home when the troops arrived. It worked out to fifteen thousand five hundred dollars each, not a bad effort for a couple of days' work. They spoke for a while and Teddy drove home to split it all up.

Soon the boys arrived and Teddy worked out what the payments were. He took out money for Dave and Lee and money for Tony.

When all the boys were settled and they were all happy, Curly said, 'Now's the time to give me your money and we can start rolling into the investment scheme. If you give me what, you can now, I'll put in the rest and we can sort things out later.' They all agreed.

Curly had been to the bank and withdrawn the amount that he needed and with what he had just received, he made his way around to the hotel where Patto and Les were waiting.

When he walked in, Patto said. 'Hullo, mate, how are you? Is everything all right?'

Curly smiled nervously and said. 'Yes, mate, I get a bit spooked when I carry large sums of money around with me. there's a lot of thieves around.'

Both the men nodded and Patto said. 'Yes, mate, Les is a great comfort to me when I do my rounds. You never know when a druggie is going to jump out at you from nowhere. I don't know, the world is getting worse and worse, you can't trust anyone these days.'

Les reached out and took the bag of money from Curly without saying a word.

Patto said. 'Well, we had better get going. We've got places to be and business to do. This is the start of an excellent business partnership between us and you, mate.'

Curly smiled and said, 'Yes, I'm sure that we will all make some money out of this.' '

Yes, you've got the easy bit. All you have to do is sit back and relax and let us do all the hard work. Away we go, Les, we will drop this money into the supplier and we should be making plastic bags all night tonight. Another hard day for us, but that's life, we do the work and the lucky ones get the money. Don't forget lunch on Friday at the same place.'

With that, they both headed off leaving Curly, sitting on his own at the table, still blissfully unaware that he was being ripped off.

Les and Patto headed to another pub and decided to win back some of the money that they had 'knocked off' the previous day.

There were races on all over Australia. So there wasn't ever a shortage of venue to have a punt on, and let's face it; as far as Patto and Les were concerned, they had a never-ending supply of money coming in. What they lost today some mug would top them up with tomorrow, that easy.

Les looked into the bag that was full of money and laughed. 'One hundred grand doesn't take up much room, does it?'

Patto laughed and said, 'this is just the beginning, mate, we'll get the pricks for millions.'

Les couldn't comprehend all the money, but he knew that whatever he wanted he could go out and buy, it was that easy. They looked at the next race meeting and decided that they should have a go at the favourite.

Patto picked up his phone and dialled.

On the other end, the man that answered the phone, in Vanuatu, took the thousand dollars each way and indicated to the boss that Patto was on the line.

The boss nodded and asked. 'Who in the fuck is this Patto? I'll look up his file.'

When he opened Patto's file, he realised that he had been betting with them for a short time. He was one of the people that one of his agents in Melbourne, Rob had arranged for him to bet with them. This wasn't uncommon as the Vanuatu project had pushed heavily for contacts in Australia to bet with them. He had always paid on time and was a good punter, as he didn't seem to really know what he was doing. Looking at his record, he saw that he had lost quite a bit of money to them in the last month or so, and this week he had really started to bet big and too lose big.

The boss rang Rob, his agent in Melbourn, and told him that Patto was into them for more than fifty thousand. He told the agent that he had better go and see him and that he had better see what was going on.

The agent Rob rang Patto's number and asked what he was up to and how was he going and how about they meet for dinner.

Rob suggested an upmarket 'Chinese' restaurant in the city.

Patto agreed, and when he hung up, he said to Les. 'These blokes in Vanuatu really know how to treat us big punters. Mate, we are invited to a knockout meal in Melbourne, in one of the best restaurants in Melbourne.'

Les was excited as he didn't frequent many restaurants and he knew that Patto knew his way around.

'Yes,' Patto said, 'they really know how to treat their big punters.'

Curly and Teddy were sitting in Curly's shed, out the back of Curly's mum's house, having a beer and talking.

Teddy asked Curly, 'Did you get the money across to your mate, Patto?'

Curly said. 'Yes, mate, I took it over to them earlier. They were a bit shocked that I could come up with that much money so soon.'

Teddy laughed and said. 'We could have come up with it a bit quicker if Dean hadn't lost most of what he's made at the card games, and Sandy hadn't knocked Tom's off at the pokies.'

They both laughed at the joke, but they knew that if anybody else had said that, then they would have looked at it through different eyes.

'When are the boys going to square up with you for the money that you put in for them?' Teddy asked.

'When they go and get it from their banks, then they will drop it around, I'm going to go and have lunch with Patto and Les on Friday and do you want to come around? You can meet them. I reckon that you will like the pair of them, Les is almost as tall as Dean.' Curly laughed.

'We might all come around and have a chat with them.' Teddy suggested.

Curly agreed with Teddy that it would be a good move to all get together.

The next night, Patto and Les got out of the taxi and entered the restaurant. They walked up the stairs and into a plush dining room. The room had red wallpaper and the tables were scattered around. Chinese waiters moved quickly around the many tables. The front of house person came up to them and directed them to a table where Rob sat on his own.

'Hullo, fellows,' Rob said to the pair, as they nervously sat down and a waiter asked them what they wanted for a drink.

'How are you both going? Patto, you look like a million dollars, and Les as fit as ever, you are both in a good paddock.'

Patto and Les grasped their drinks and looked around. 'This is the first time that I've been here,' Patto said.

Les decided to remain silent.

'Yes, well, I come here a fair bit.' Rob said. 'Mainly with clients who are going all right, just to make sure that we are doing everything we can do to make your life happier.'

The three looked at their menus, and Rob said, 'Don't worry about choosing. I'll tell the waiter to just send us the house specialities. They will keep bringing them until we tell them to stop, does that suit you?'

With that, Rob gave the instructions to the waiter and ordered some wine from the wine waiter. Within minutes, the first course was at their table and the three men hungrily started eating.

'What line of work are you two in, Patto?' Rob asked.

Patto stopped chewing and said. 'Well, Rob, we have come across a scheme that is so good, we are literally, "killing the pig". Yes, we are living "high on the hog",' Patto enthused. 'We have got into a scheme, almost by accident that is a real money maker. We have got the use of a factory that makes plastic bags. My brother-in-law runs it and we can make all the plastic bags we want.

All we have to do is supply the raw product. I've got a contact with the biggest supermarket in Australia, who will take all the bags we can produce and they pay us in thirty days.

Mate, I tell you this is a real beauty. We get money from investors, and we pay them ten percent a month. So if they invest ten thousand dollars, at the end of the month, they receive from us one thousand dollars, cash no questions asked. Mate, it's a fucking ripper.'

Rob looked at the two men and thought that he wouldn't mind a bit of this action. Ten percent a month, maybe the boss would be interested, he might want to invest a couple of thousand dollars.

The diners really got on well together, and when the bill was presented, Patto made a fine gesture of wanting to pay, but Rob steadfastly said that the 'Boss' insisted that Rob pay.

Before they left, Rob made a point of insisting that he be included in the scheme and said that he was prepared to put up five thousand dollars of his own money. If they would let him in.

Patto, of course, accepted, and they discussed just how and when they would all be in the scheme together.

When they had parted, Patto looked at Les and drunkenly said, 'Mate, if I'm not the best in the business then, well, I don't know what. Here's a bloke come and buy us dinner just to see if we can settle up with them and I end up getting five large out of the prick. Yes, mate, this is big, in fact, it's huge.'

Les agreed.

To watch Patto in action was a joy to behold; he had all the right moves and said all the right things, beautiful to watch. When they parted and went their separate ways, they both felt that they were onto a winner.

Rob rang through to Vanuatu and spoke to the boss.

He was beside himself, and sure that the boss would be in on it, but the boss said that most of his money were pretty well tied up. But if Rob thought it was a good idea for him to go ahead and get involved, then he could do what he wanted. Rob rang off after saying, 'I just didn't want to leave you out, mate.'

The boss thanked him and thought, *fuck me dead, it sounds like a scam to me.*

They are always around, anything that sounds too good to be true, usually are too good to be true.

Rob got out five thousand and rang Patto and arranged for them to meet up.

Friday arrived, and Teddy, Dean, and Tom picked up Curly and made their way to the City hotel where they were to meet Patto and Les for the first time.

They walked in, and Curly recognised some of the men from the last time he had been there. They were all sitting at a large table and there were plenty of empty seats, so they all sat down together. They introduced themselves to people that they didn't know and soon they were all talking and having a drink.

Patto and Les came in, and Patto started talking to everyone and introducing himself to the people that he didn't know. Soon it was time for business. Patto started pulling out wads of money and giving it to different people. There was a feeling of goodwill in the air. People were smiling and talking. Once again some put their money into their pockets and some carelessly left theirs out on the table.

When Patto came to Curly, he said. 'Mate, you have done well. You get some today and some more in three weeks' time. Yes, you are well and truly in business.'

Curly laughed and said, 'I want you to meet my partners in crime.'

Everyone laughed and the introductions were done.

Patto had the ability to make everyone feel like they had known him for 100 years, and all the boys immediately took a shine to him.

Les looked at Teddy and the rest of the crew and thought to himself. Yes, laugh, you dickheads. We are going to stick it up you pricks' Les thought that there wouldn't be a problem with any of them. They were all fit, but they didn't look like fighters.

The lunch went on and Patto worked the room. He joked with the investors and looked for more 'mugs'. There were a couple of smarties who kept asking questions and Patto handled them with practiced ease. Soon they were willing to put in some money. Some investors decided to leave in their money so that it would accumulate. Patto was more than happy to accommodate them in that department and others had bought more money in to invest. All in all, there was confidence in the air.

Patto was writing amounts in his book and making notice of details and generally had the air of a successful businessman about him.

Les said little, just kept his eyes on the room and continuously watched the people at the table. At the end of the meal, Patto stood up and announced that he and Les, in fact, would pick up the bill for that day's meal and drinks. As they had had the best week, production-wise, that they had ever had. 'We sent out truckloads to the supermarkets. Yes, a very productive week indeed.' Patto concluded.

Teddy, Tom, Dean, and Curly were going home after the lunch meal and Curly said. 'I told you blokes that you would like Patto. He's a real good bloke. Don't you reckon, Teddy?'

Teddy thought for a moment and said. 'Curly, he seems a terrific bloke and we were probably lucky that you got mixed up with him, but that Les bothers me a bit. He doesn't quite fit in. I reckon that we should do a bit of asking around about him, someone will have some mail on him.'

They all agreed to put their ears to the ground and see what they could uncover.

What's commonly referred to as 'the underworld' is in fact quite a small and close-knit group. There is always something going on and word gets around, so when Teddy and the boys started quietly asking around about Patto and Les, they soon discovered that Patto was a small-time con man and Les was a big-time stand over man. Which is a combination that sits well. If Patto gets sprung in some kind of scam, then Les comes in and straightens out whoever has got robbed out, usually by force. So, not only does the mug lose his money, but he could also end up with a smack in the mouth for his troubles.

Patto looked like a successful business man and even Les had upgraded his entire wardrobe. He, in fact, had some Italian suits and started wearing silk shirts and handmade Italian 'loafers', very stylish, if he did say so himself.

It was settling day with the offshore bookmakers, and there was no problem at all. The men didn't have to get into the floor safe as they had all the money they wanted to settle up on hand. They wired the money into the account and decided to go and have a meal and a few drinks in a pub that had the 'SKY channel' races on.

They both decided that this was the life.

Tom's partner Sandy was on duty when Patto and Les walked into the lounge bar.

She looked up and smiled at Patto and got him the two pots he asked for.

'How are you today, Love?' Patto enquired with a smile.

'I'm fine, thanks,' Sandy replied, 'looks like the rain has gone for a while.'

Patto thought that she was a fine-looking young woman. 'Yes, love,' he answered, 'let's hope it stays fine so the kids can get out and have a bit of a runaround.'

Patto always referred to children when he spoke to women.

Sandy agreed, 'Yes, let them burn off a bit of energy.'

They both laughed, even though neither of them had kids.

Patto returned to the table and said to Les, 'She's a bit of all right, great tits, and not bad looking.' Les took a long pull of his beer and looked at Sandy. 'Yep, she would be all right. I wouldn't climb over her to get to you, you ugly bastard.' They both laughed at the thought.

Sandy heard them laugh and thought to herself, 'Typical, bastards, there's no chance of either of them getting into my "knickers".'

Patto turned his attention to the TV and said, 'Let's see what we can do here. Surely, there are a couple of sure things that a couple of honest lads like us can get on and turn our fortunes around.'

Les kept his eyes on Sandy and thought that she was indeed a lovely piece of skirt.

The day sped past, and Patto and Les got drunker and drunker.

Patto communicated loudly on his phone and both he and Les urged on their picks as they watched TV. Working on the theory that their luck had to change, they kept betting bigger and bigger. Every now and then one of their picks would win and the two con men would congratulate themselves. They showed almost no emotion when they lost because it wasn't really their money that they were losing, it was the investors' money, and there was plenty more where that came from. All they had to do was put up their hands and some dickhead would fill it with money, that easy.

When the time came for them to go to another pub, Patto walked up to the bar and gave Sandy a fifty-dollar tip.

'Thanks, love, thanks for looking after us, and we'll see you later on, have a drink on us.'

Sandy smiled and said. 'You two are no trouble. Did you end up in front? You sure had a few bets.' Patto said, 'Well, we broke about even, maybe next time we will make our fortune.'

With that, the two men walked outside and grabbed a taxi.

Sandy looked at the fifty-dollar note and thought that it would be great if everyone were like those two, no trouble and big tippers. She wasn't sure of the big one Les. He could be trouble if you rubbed him up the wrong way. Anyway, it was time to clock off and get home and put her feet up and watch some TV with Tom.

She wondered what he was doing.

Tom was home waiting for Sandy when she drove her little car into the driveway. He walked out and smiled and thought how lucky he was, she sure was a beautiful looking girl. He wished that she would give up her job as a barmaid, but realised that with her gambling problem, it would be more of a problem. That boredom would more than likely force her out of home and into the clubs.

Tom asked, 'How was your day, love?'

Sandy replied, 'It wasn't too bad. I had a couple of big punters in and they gave me a fifty-dollar tip when they left.'

'Well, just as long as that's all, that they gave you,' Tom replied.

'No, love, they were very nice blokes. The small one was really well-dressed, and the big one looked like someone had "mail ordered" his clothes for him. He looked like he was a tough bloke, though.'

Tom was only half-listening. 'What were they up to?'

Sandy replied. 'They spent all afternoon on the phone placing bets. I don't know how they ended up. Patto said that they broke about even.'

At the sound of Patto's name, Tom was suddenly interested.

'Did you say, Patto?' he asked.

'Yes, that's what the little bloke was called,' Sandy replied.

'Was the other bloke, a big bad-looking dude, called Les?' Tom enquired.

'Yes, that's right, do you know them?'

'Not really, I've just only met them recently. Were they betting in significant amounts?' Tom asked carefully.

Sandy looked at Tom and said, 'Sometimes they bet in thousands, sometime one thousand each way.'

Tom took all this in and said, 'Well, that's very interesting. I wonder if they will be back tomorrow!'

Sandy said, 'I hope so, they seemed pleasant enough.'

Tom felt jealousness twist his stomach. That Les would be a problem, but Tom wasn't the type to worry about things like that. He had faced bigger and worse bastards than Les.

Tom rang Teddy and told him about Patto and Les and that they were at Sandy's pub all afternoon betting up big. He said that they had thousands on horses that they were pulling out of the air.

Teddy listened and said, 'That's a worry. These blokes seem like they have money to burn. I would hate to think that it was our hard-earned that was going up into the fucking air. Wait and I'll give Curly a ring and see what he reckons.'

Teddy rang Curly, and Curly was a bit worried, this wasn't what he had expected to hear. Patto had said that they would be sleeping all day as they were working all night at the plastic bag factory, maybe this was nothing or maybe they hadn't worked all night. Curly said that he would make a few phone calls and see what he could uncover.

Curly rang Patto's phone, and Patto answered, 'Hullo, Curly mate. How are you going?' Curly apologised and hoped that he hadn't woken Patto up.

He said, 'Sorry, mate, I didn't think, did you work all night and did you get any sleep?'

Patto looked at Les and smiled. He put the phone on speaker. 'Curly mate, Les and I worked all night. We got out of the factory at 5 a.m. and we hit the sack at about 9 a.m., and we have just got out of bed and thought we might have a bit of a late brecky downtown somewhere. Do you want to join us?'

'No, thanks mate,' Curly replied, 'I've got a bit on at the present time, but I'll catch up soon.'

Curly hung up and thought, *they reckon that they have been in bed and Sandy was serving them drinks all day. I wonder just what the fuck is going on.*

Curly rang Teddy back and told him that Patto was bullshitting him and saying that they had been in bed, when in actual fact they were drinking and gambling all afternoon, something isn't right here.

Teddy agreed.

'We will have to watch these blokes a bit.' Teddy suggested.

Patto looked at Les and said. 'That was a strange call. Curly rang and didn't want anything, very strange. He seemed to be checking up on us. He wanted to know where we were all day, maybe he is getting suspicious of us.'

'Well, fuck him,' said Les, 'we've got nothing to worry about, dumb fucking pricks.'

Patto looked at Les and said, 'Yes, fuck them, we've got their money and there's fuck all that they can do about it. Let's have another drink.'

Now Patto, being a bit of a lady's man had been thinking about Sandy and how she had been a bit friendly and talkative. So he decided that he might call back in and see her the next day.

The next morning just before lunch, they presented themselves back at Sandy's Pub.

They walked into the lounge bar, and Patto on seeing Sandy said, 'Hullo, Sandy, love, do you remember us?'

'Well, hullo boys, how did you pull up?' Sandy asked with a laugh.

Patto answered with a smile, 'It was a bit rough for a while, but then I said to Les, let's go back and annoy Sandy as she didn't look too busy yesterday.'

'Would you like a couple of pots?' Sandy asked.

'Yes, thanks, love, that will hit the spot just right,' Patto said.

'Now let's have a look at the races, and see what's about. Why don't you pick a horse and we'll have a dollar or two on it for an interest for you, help the time pass.' Patto suggested.

'That would be a bit of fun, but I'll pay you back if my horse wins,' Sandy said laughingly.

'I wouldn't worry about paying us back,' Patto said, 'we are on a good run at the present moment, we've got a bit coming in.'

So they started to have a bet on the races on the SKY channel.

Patto rang through their bets through to Vanuatu and started putting Sandy's bets on at the TAB counter. They were all getting on well together. A couple of hours into the afternoon, Patto was getting a bit more talkative, and seeing he and Sandy were getting on so well, he started to think that he was a chance with Sandy.

Patto boldly asked Sandy did she have a partner or a boyfriend at the moment. Sandy smiled and shook her head. 'At the present time, I'm between boyfriends. The last one I had didn't work and was a bit of a bastard, so I'm having a bit of a spell at the present time.'

Patto put on a concerned face and said. 'It must be very difficult in your current position. There would be heaps of blokes who show lots of interest. Young blokes who are only after the one thing, and you are a very attractive young woman, but they would all be broke and not very sincere. They would tell you anything, unlike us older gentlemen.' Patto laughed.

Sandy laughed along with him. She realised that Patto was lying in wait, her plan was working. Patto and Les were drinking more and more and both of them were getting drunker and drunker. When Sandy handed back Patto's change, he lightly rubbed the back of her hand and smiled.

Patto complemented. 'You have lovely hands. In fact, you have lovely everything's,' he said glancing at her breasts.

Sandy noticed his look and smiled and went to serve another customer.

Patto was sure that he was on a winner. He and Les continued to bet on the phone and kept putting on Sandy's bets. They were going bad and down quite a few thousand. 'Things had better change,' Patto said to Les, 'or we might have to get a few more investors into the plastic bag scheme.' They both laughed drunkenly.

Sandy rang Tom and said. 'They are back. Patto and Les are in the lounge, and they are betting up big. I just heard Patto have a thousand dollars each way on a roughie that wouldn't run a place in a three-horse race and it didn't run a place in a twelve-horse race. I've been talking to them, and Patto reckons that he's a chance with me, so they will stay until the end of my shift and then see how they go.'

Tom felt his blood pressure go up at the thought that someone was flirting with Sandy.

He rang Teddy and said, 'Those bastards are back at Sandy's Pub betting up big, and trying to make a move on Sandy.'

Teddy knew that Tom would be more worried about them making a move on Sandy than spending Tom's and their money.

'Well, don't fly into a panic, Tom,' Teddy said. 'You know that you don't have a problem with Sandy. She's as solid as a rock, as far as you're concerned, and our biggest problem is, what do we do? How will we get our money back? If those pair of pricks is on the con, then we are in trouble. They will have knocked off most of it by now. If, by chance, they aren't ripping us off, then we will look like idiots.'

Tom replied, 'It's better to look like a fucking idiot than end up with your dick in your hand and fuck all money.' Tom as usual got to the core of the problem quickly.

Teddy said, 'We had better have a meeting and work out what we want to do.'

Teddy rang around and called all the boys to meet in Curly's shed. When they all got there, Teddy addressed them and said, 'Boys, we have a problem, or I think that we have a problem. Sandy just rang and told Tom that Patto and Les are at the pub she works in, and were there yesterday, and they are throwing money at horses like there's no tomorrow. As you all know, we have done a bit of homework and we found out that Patto is a con man from, way back and Les is a stand over man. Sandy said that they are throwing money at anything that eats hay, so here's the problem, what do we do? Do we go over there and demand to know what's going on or do we sit tight and see what happens, in the long run.'

Curly said. 'I feel like it's my problem as I introduced them to you all, and I will make up any money that anyone of us loses. You all know that I've got the money to do that, and what I haven't got, I'll get when we go back to work. Rest assured that none of you will be out of pocket.'

Teddy said, 'Thanks, mate, but I reckon that if we act quickly we should be able to get all the money we invested.'

Dean spoke for the first time, 'Fuck this, we should go straight over and see just what's going on. If it's a con, then we want our fucking money back. If it's not a con, then we want some assurance that our money is safe. Let's just see what they are up to and if we see everything, including the factory, then I would be more than happy to stay involved. There's only one way to do that, and that's to go over and see the pair of pricks straight away.'

All the boys agreed.

Tom said he would ring up Sandy and see if they were still there.

Sandy answered the bar phone and confirmed that Patto and Les were still there.

Patto was in full swing and even Les had let his guard down a bit. He was happily drunk.

The thought had crossed both their minds about 'gangbanging' Sandy.

Patto was sure that she would be in it. Shit, even if they had to sling her a couple of hundred, it would be cheap.

Sandy was looking better and better as the day wore on.

Curly walked into the lounge bar with Teddy, Dean, and Tom behind him.

Patto's expression changed as he recognised the group.

He said to Les, 'Mate, we've got company.'

Les looked at the group and decided that they weren't too big a problem.

'Hullo, boys,' Patto called out, 'this is a coincidence, fancy meeting you here, and do you come here often?'

Curly said. 'Not as much as we used to, just every now and then. Aren't you pair supposed to be getting ready to be making plastic bags?'

'Yes mate,' Patto replied, 'we were just getting ready to go.'

Les spoke up and said, 'What the fuck has it got to do with you fucking clowns what we are doing or where the fuck we should be?'

Silence reigned and Teddy broke it by saying. 'We have a few questions that we want to be answered, number one, where's this factory? Number two, we want to meet this bloke who lets you run the factory and doesn't charge anything for it, and number three we want to meet whoever are buying all these plastic bags.'

Les spoke. 'Fuck me, you want to find out all our information so you lot can set up on your own and do us out of our money. Well, it wouldn't be too smart of us to tell you everything now would it as sooner or later you would be our opposition, and that's not good business, is it?'

Teddy looked at Les and said. 'We want some guarantees about our money, that's all, and if we don't get them, then we are going to want our money back, simple as that!'

Patto smiled and said. 'Mate, you all know that it will take one month for Les and me to get your money back. I made that clear from the outset. Now if you want your money back, I can start getting it together almost immediately, but it will take a month, that's the best, I can do.'

'That's not good enough,' said Teddy. We want our money out today.'

Les said, 'That's impossible, you fucking halfwits. We have got it tied up and we need time to get it out.'

'Fucking halfwits, are we?' Dean asked, 'how do you like this from a halfwit?' And let one go, the punch caught Les off guard and he sprawled across a table and knocked over a chair. He was up and ready for the next bit of action, whatever it was.

Tom 'king hit' Patto and he crashed to the ground. Clutching his valise, Patto said, 'I've got a gun in here.'

'Well, you had better pull it out,' said Teddy and belted him between the eyes; Patto was out of it for the time being.

Dean moved in on Les. There was no sign that Les was in any trouble.

Dean led with a straight right that Les fended off a bit and it only glanced off his face. Les then let go an uppercut that landed squarely on Dean's jaw. Lights flashed brightly in Dean's head and for a split second, he thought that he was in trouble.

When Les's left caught him on the side of the face, he knew that he was in trouble.

Luckily Teddy weighed into the fight and he slammed his fist into Les's jaw. The blow shook Les right through, but he had enough experience to be able to battle on and cover up a bit.

Teddy was still swinging roundhouse blows that bombarded Les. Les fended some off, but some got through. Teddy was beginning to wear Les down, and Les didn't see Curly working his way behind him. When Curly hit Les across the back of the head with a chair, Les hit the carpet.

Tom grabbed the valise and started to go through it. He removed some bundles of money but found no gun. He tipped everything out of the valise onto a table; there were some money and some papers.

Curly went across to the bar and got a jug of water and poured it over Patto's head.

He started spluttering and groggily looked around. 'What's going on?' he asked, 'what do you want?'

'We want our money back, you little arsehole,' Teddy demanded, 'and we want it back now.'

Patto looked around to see if Les could come to his assistance but alas that avenue was closed.

He said in a small voice, 'It will take us some time to put it all together. Like I've always said, we need time as the money is invested, like I told you blokes.'

'We want our money and we want it fucking well now,' Tom insisted.

Patto looked around and didn't see a friendly face. 'I just can't pull it out of my arse, you know, it's been invested with the plastic bag people and will take some time to get out. Like I say I need thirty days to get it together. I've got payments coming in that will allow me to square you lot up, but I need thirty days' notice.'

'That's not good enough, and you fucking well know it,' Teddy said.

They was in a bit of a bind, but if what Patto was saying was true, then he, Patto, would need time to get the money back to them.

They were in a Mexican standoff.

Tom came to the rescue. 'What about we take the money that's in the Valise and you give us the rest at the next meeting, in a couple of weeks' time, how does that sound?'

Patto was desperate to get out of this situation alive. He agreed, he would have agreed to anything by now, after seeing the boys put Les out of action. He thought that there was a chance that Dean and Tom might kill him and Les. He could see a side to them that he hadn't seen before. He was lucky that he didn't have a huge amount of money on him as these blokes would have taken the lot and then who knows what would have happened?

Les began to groan on the floor and started to get up; Dean put his foot on Les's chest and said, 'Just stay where the fuck you are. You're lucky we didn't really fuck you up.'

Les looked at Dean and said. 'That's one to you.'

Curly counted out the money and there were five thousand dollars in the valise. He stuffed it down the front of his shirt. He looked at Teddy.

Teddy gave a nod to Patto and as they walked out towards the door Teddy said. 'We'll see you in two weeks and if you don't have the rest, you're in real trouble.'

As one, they all walked outside.

Tom hadn't acknowledged Sandy as he didn't want for Patto to realise that they were together. He wanted to keep her out of it.

Sandy walked out into the bar area and asked Patto if they were all right.

Patto said, 'Yes, love, just a bit of a lover's tiff with some investors. They seem to think that we are of a dubious nature.'

Les was filthy with himself for letting things turn out like they did. 'Bastards, got behind me, and hit me with a fucking chair. Don't worry about that, I'll sort the pricks out next time we meet. It will be a joy to rob the fuck out them. Wait until we meet them again. Next time, it will be on my terms. Then we'll see just how they stand up to us.'

Patto wasn't so sure, but he said nothing. They made their way outside and caught a taxi back to their homes to clean up a bit.

Sandy had heard Les say that it would be a joy to rob the fuck out of them. Loose lips sink ships, she thought.

She rang Tom and told him what Les had said to Patto.

Tom decided he had heard enough to really believe that Curly had been conned. He reported his thoughts to Teddy.

They both agreed that there was something amiss; it was just too good to be true.

'How much money did we get out of Patto's valise?' Teddy asked Tom.

'There was five grand in it,' Tom replied.

'Well, Curly, how much did you end up putting in?' Teddy asked.

Curly thought for a moment and said, 'What with everything that we all put in, they all had to get out one hundred and thirty thousand dollars to break even.' A silence fell over the four blokes. That was a lot of money, there was a lot to make-up, and they were one hundred and twenty-five thousand dollars short.

'They had better come to the party when we meet in a couple of weeks' time,' Dean suggested.

The four went silent; all they could do was wait and hope for the best.

Patto looked at Les and said. 'Mate, if we pay out those blokes what we owe them, and what we owe the other investors when we meet them all in a couple of weeks' time, we need to come up with almost two hundred thousand, and as you know we only have about, at the best, one hundred thousand. We are going to come up one hundred thousand dollars short, and if we don't pay everyone, then panic will set in, and then we are in real trouble.'

Les thought for a moment and decided that the best defence was attack. 'Fuck them, we will tell them that they have got to wait, or they can go and get fucked.'

Patto looked at his friend and partner and thought that thinking wasn't Les's strong point. 'Mate, we want everyone to be calm and believe that everything is going along good, so we don't wish to cause any ripples. We have a couple of weeks to sort something out, and I bet that everything will be all right.'

Patto thought that the only way out was for them to get going on the punt, because after all they didn't need to come up with any money until settling day, and anyway what the fuck were the crew in Vanuatu going to do if they lost, fuck all more than likely.

The next day saw Patto and Les at a venue that had SKY channel in the lounge bar and they studied the form. It was simple, back the favourites until they started to win, and as it was all on the 'Nod', they would just keep betting up until they won.

Patto was on the phone to Vanuatu and had his first bet on a favourite in some unheard of place, a thousand each way. Sure enough, it lost, and, in fact, it didn't run a place due to an incompetent jockey and a wet track.

'For fuck sake,' Patto pointed out to anyone within earshot. 'I could have ridden the fucking horse better than that prick.'

The day wore on.

Patto's luck wasn't any better that it was on the first race. They were getting desperate, and they needed a big win just for them to break even, so they started to back some long shots, just as the favourites began to win.

By the end of the day, they were behind.

They were well behind.

In Vanuatu, the boss looked at his screens and saw that Patto was 'chasing,' that meant that he was losing and trying to recoup his losses with their money.

That was a dangerous game as Patto needed to be able to bet more and more just to break even. He instructed his phone men to let him know just how much Patto was betting, so that he could keep his eye on him. The boss thought to himself that Patto wasn't a good punter and he guessed that he was betting with someone else's money that was a bad combination. He thought that Patto was probably drunk as well. He would have to keep his eye on this bloke. By the end of the day, Patto was into them for almost fifty thousand dollars. The bad news, for Patto, was that he didn't look like backing a winner, he had, had the worst run of luck known to man.

'Mate, our luck has got to improve, surely.' Patto said to Les.

Patto and Les made their way back to Sandy's Pub.

They explained to an interested Sandy that they had had a bad day, an awful day but would be back into it tomorrow bigger and brighter than ever. Sandy listened to them and joined them for a drink as her shift had finished.

Patto was sure that he was on a winner, but after the drink, Sandy said that she had to go home as her mother wasn't well.

When she left, Patto said, 'I still reckon that I'm a chance with that Sandy.'

Les laughed and said, 'We had better start thinking about how to get out of the problem that we have got ourselves into.'

'Don't worry, mate, we will get out tomorrow, you wait and see,' Patto replied with a lot more confidence than he felt.

The next day both Les and Patto were crook from the drink. So Patto opened up the day's betting with a three-thousand dollar each way bet at a country meeting, the horse run a place, and they lost one thousand on the race, 'Things are on the improve,' Patto enthused.

Les just grunted. *Not as easy as it looks backing favourites,* he thought.

Patto continued to bet up big on the phone overseas.

The boss kept an eye on how he was going and began to feel a little uneasy. 'Listen up,' he told his people on the phones, 'I'm putting Patto and his mate on a maximum limit of one thousand dollars each way, no if's or butt's. That's the limit.'

When Patto rang next, he was told of his limits and he flew into a rage. 'That fucking bastard has put the brakes on us. He's a real prick, the bastard!'

Patto was furious. He rang the agent in Melbourne, Rob, and blew up on the phone. Rob said that he would get in contact with the boss and get back to him. When he got in touch with the boss, the boss said that all Patto was doing was chasing what he owed with the boss's money. If he wanted to do that, then he would have to bet in cash.

Of course, Patto didn't have the money.

When Rob got back to Patto, he wasn't able to get any sense out of Patto at all.

Patto was off his head with rage. Without really thinking, he rang Vanuatu and asked to speak to the boss. The boss took the call and told him what was going on; he wouldn't deviate from his line.

Patto slammed down the phone and said, 'I'm not finished with that prick yet. He's a bastard, and he can stick what we owe him up his arse as far as I'm concerned.'

Les nodded. 'Fair enough,' he said, 'what's the weak prick going to do about it anyway.'

✧ ✧ ✧ ✧

When no money arrives on square up day, the boss thought that he had better do something about what was happening. Because if you let one arsehole get away with, not paying, then it soon gets around, that he's an easy target and every dickhead will hold back on you.

The boss rang Rob, his representative in Melbourn, and said, 'Mate, we've got a problem with Patto and his mate Les. Get in touch with Sam and his two sons and get them to have a talk with these pricks.'

Sam was sitting in his favourite restaurant when he got Rob's call. He arranged to meet up with Rob for a meeting that would be beneficial to them all in a couple of hours' time. Sam rang his two boys and they agreed to meet with Rob.

At the meeting, Rob told Sam and his sons that there was a problem with Patto and Les not paying. The boss wanted for them to make an example of what happens when blokes don't pay up.

Sam, who was the head of a large criminal organization understood the situation; he had, at times, helped collect money off punters that had overstepped their limits.

Sam said that he would get straight on to it.

'Where will we find these two dickheads?' he enquired to Rob.

Rob said he would give them a ring and find out where they were.

He rang Patto and organised a meeting. He didn't tell Patto that Sam was going to be there.

When Patto and Les arrived, they were confronted by Sam and his two sons.

Patto felt a twinge of fear as he knew who Sam was and he knew that his boys were more than willing to belt the living shit out of them. Patto thought that he would be lucky to get out of this alive.

Sam started the ball rolling by saying, 'You are behind with your money, and we want it now, right fucking now.'

Patto was about to say something when Les said. 'You and your idiot sons can go and get fucked. I'm not scared of an old man and a couple of hairy arsed boys. Get the fuck out of here before I belt the shit out of the fucking lot of you.'

Sam was a bit taken back by Les's outburst; this wasn't going according to plan.

Sam said in a low voice, 'Do you know who we are?'

Les looked at Sam and said. 'You're an old drunk, and these halfwits of yours think that they are gangsters. Fuck off before I belt you.'

Patto started to think that things were beginning to look up.

Sam's youngest son took a step forward and hit Patto on the side of the head. It was a violent blow, and Patto wasn't expecting it. He fell to the ground. Les punched Sam to the side of the jaw.

Sam immediately tasted blood in his mouth. He spat out a mouthful of blood onto the carpeted floor.

Les was only starting to get going, he gave Sam's eldest son an uppercut that sent him staggering back into some tables and moved in on the youngest one.

The youngest saw him coming and realising that Les was probably a bit too much for them, he pulled out his .38 revolver and shot Les once in the chest.

The force of the blast rocked Les and he stopped going forward. He stared blankly at the young man and said. 'You weak cunt.'

Before he could say anymore, the young man pulled the trigger on the pistol twice in quick succession, both of the bullets tore through Les's chest and the big bloke hit the floor.

Les was dying.

He knew that.

There was no pain.

The carpet felt warm under his cheek.

His mind raced back to his childhood, and he was once again a happy young boy living in the country. He could smell the freshly mown front yard and see his father laughing and pushing the hand mower and half-listening to the radio which was on the sports channel. Geelong was playing, and at the start of each Melbourne race, the station would play the race and Les's father would have an interest in the horses. He loved his father more than anyone in the world. Soon it would be time for afternoon tea and his mum would bring out a tray and they would all sit down and listen to the footy and have a cup of tea. He had never felt so happy.

That all finished when his father died of a massive heart attack and his mother remarried a 'hard' man who hated Les and made his life unbearable.

His mind went back to happier days.

He smiled and died.

Sam gathered himself together first and said, 'Let's get the fuck out of here.'

Both the boys agreed and they ran out of the back bar, leaving Patto to look at his lifeless friend.

He felt a wave of sadness pass over him. He wondered why Les had a slight smile on his face.

He also took off; he was in real trouble now, without Les to back him up.

In the car, Sam said to his youngest son. 'Get home and have a shower. Throw your clothes that you have got on into the washing machine, and if anyone asks, tell them we were all together at my place all night.'

Patto was terrified. He was the only one that could put Sam and his family at the scene of the shooting that meant that he was a marked man.

He thought wildly.

Fuck the investors, fuck Sam and his crazy sons; he was going to get out as soon as he was able. He had to get back to his unit and get whatever money was there and get the hell out of Dodge City. He made it back to his place and with superhuman strength pushed the oil drum away from over the floor safe, grabbed what money was in it, and headed inside and threw some clothes into a bag. He then jumped into his car and headed out of town.

He was running for his life, and he knew it, he had to go somewhere, where no one knew him, and never set foot in this city again. He knew without reckoning that if he had to square up Vanuatu and all the investors that he was a long way short.

He thought briefly about Sandy but decided that it was a waste of time trying to talk her into coming with him; maybe he would give her a ring sometime and see if she was interested.

Teddy and the boys were talking in Curly's shed and a news flash came over. The attractive news reader said. 'And a story just breaking, there has been a shooting in a hotel in Port Melbourne. Police have stated that it might be gang related as the victim was known to them and had a record of violence.'

The boys looked at each other and said, 'Well, that's another one down.'

Teddy asked, 'I wonder if we knew him, probably not as there are a million villains out there and let's face it he was just another waste of space.'

One of Sandy's regulars mentioned that she had lost a good customer.

Sandy stopped pulling a beer and asked, 'What do you mean?'

The customer smiled, happy to be the centre of attraction. 'Those two blokes that were in the lounge bar, who were betting up big a couple of days ago, well, the big one ran into trouble, earlier on tonight. He ended up taking a couple in the chest. Guess he was in the wrong place at the wrong time.' The regular said smugly.

Sandy frowned and asked, 'Do you mean Les, Patto's mate?'

The regular beamed and said. 'Yep, that sounds about right. My mate just heard it on his scanner. He listens to all the crap that comes over the airwaves. He can listen to any police band that he wants to. You would be surprised just what he comes up with.'

Sandy stopped listening and gave Tom a ring.

When Tom answered, she said, 'That bloke that just got knocked was Les, Patto's mate. A bloke just came into the pub and said his mate had heard it on a police scanner.'

Tom hung up and said to the boys. 'That was Sandy. She has just heard that the bloke that was killed was Les, Patto's mate.'

Silence gripped the shed.

Curly asked the question that was on everyone's mind, 'I wonder what is going to happen to our money?'

Teddy said. 'Give Patto a ring and ask him what happened. Make sure that he is all right.'

Curly rang Patto's number and heard the phone ringing.

Patto was on the outskirts of Melbourne and his phone started to ring. He wound down his window and threw the still ringing phone out the window into the long grass on the side of the road.

'Good-bye, old life. Welcome to the next life!' Patto laughed and drove into the night.

Curly looked at the faces of his friends. They looked back. Curly knew that he was seriously out of pocket, as he was the one that introduced them all to the scheme, he was the one that would have to make things right. 'Don't worry, fella's, I'll ensure that you are all squared up. It will just take a bit of time.' They all looked at their mate.

Teddy spoke and it was for them all. 'Mate, don't worry. We know that you didn't rob us and let's just see what happens in the next couple of days, who knows it might turn out all right, after all. Let's have a game of pool. In fact, I'll play you for one hundred thousand that should take your mind off any problems.'

They all laughed, got themselves another beer.

Teddy said, 'Mugs away.'

Curly said, 'My break, I suppose.'

The boss in Vanuatu looked at his people that were working the phones.

'I don't know if you have heard anything or not, but it looks like Patto's mate Les got whacked last night. If Patto rings in a bet, then put him onto me, as I want to have a bit of a talk with him. He is into us for over two hundred thousand dollars. I've spoken to our agent over there, Rob, and he reckons that Patto has done a runner. Rob's been looking all over for him and he's gone to ground. If any of you hear anything, then let me know.'

The police sort of investigated Les's murder, but they knew that the only way of getting some information was going to be if they charged someone with an offence and the people that they charged knew anything about what had happened. Then they might try to plea bargain their way to a lesser sentence. They were met with dead ends everywhere they turned.

Curly started to work out how much he was down the drain.

He owed Tony two grand that he had put in. Dean had put in five grand. Tom had put in ten thousand, Teddy had put in twenty thousand, and Curly had started the ball rolling by putting in the original ten thousand. Curly had made up the difference of fifty-three thousand dollars so that they could give Patto the one hundred thousand dollars. So he only owed the boys thirty-seven thousand dollars that meant that he would be out sixty-three thousand dollars, not much if you said it slowly.

Curly rang his mate Jim, the one that had introduced him into the scam. Jim was beside himself with worry as he had also talked plenty more people to invest in the scheme. Jim said that he was at his wits end. 'What the fuck am I gunna do?' He asked Curly.

Curly didn't have an answer as he had problems of his own.

When the investors met for their lunch at the usual hotel, they all looked like beaten men.

Everyone had a tale to tell, and most of them agreed that the scheme was just too good to be true. They all cried poor and tried to find someone to blame, but it became apparent that they were in fact totally to blame as greed had gotten hold of them.

Some of the tough guys threatened to do Patto harm if they ran across him some time. They were all a bit braver now that Les wasn't on the scene, but the meal wasn't a great success.

They left in pairs or on their own all thinking what to do next. A sad and sorry bunch; not at all like the other meetings.

Patto pulled into a service station on some back road in NSW.

It was a long way from Melbourne, but it seemed to be a nice-looking area.

Over the last few days, he had worked out how much money he had and there was enough to keep him going for a while. He would have to be careful and keep his eyes open and make sure he didn't have any publicity; yes, he would be all right.

Teddy decided that they needed to get back to work and get some abalone and get some money. Maybe they would do a bit of a run out onto the islands in Bass Straight, and there were plenty of abalone to be had over there. Yes, that was an idea to get away from familiar territory and get out in the middle of nowhere, get the boys back into the water.

Bass Strait Bandits.

The Kent group of islands are in the Bass Strait, that's the strait that separates Victoria from Tasmania; they are about halfway between the northern tip of Flinders Island and Wilson's Promontory.

They are much closer to Victoria than Tasmania, but are classed as Tasmanian.

The main islands of the group are Deal Island, Dover Island, and Erith Island. There are also two smaller islands: North East Island and North West Island; the spectacular Murray Pass separates Deal from Dover and Erith.

The group were discovered by Mathew Flinders in 1798 when he was on a rescue voyage to Preservation Island to pick up survivors of the shipwreck of the Sydney Cove. It is a very rocky coastline and an excellent place to take abalone. Due to its isolation, it's regarded as an ideal location for abalone poachers to go and work undetected.

Teddy sat across from his old mate 'Bass Strait' Barry.

They called Barry 'Bass Strait Barry' because he had spent most of his life fishing the treacherous waters of Bass Strait.

Barry was an old-time fisherman and his face was a testament to the years of being out in foul weather.

He was a regular at the Port Melbourne pub. They sat in the beer garden as Barry was a non-stop smoker.

The only time he wasn't smoking he was drinking. He was in his seventies and didn't really care about his personal health. He was fond of saying, 'If a man can't have a drink and a smoke, then he may as well be fucking well dead.'

Teddy smiled at his old friend and said. 'You know the rules, mate, some people can die from lung cancer when they are thirty and some people smoke right up until they die, and they might be eighty and get hit by a truck.'

Barry laughed and said, 'Yer, mate, you don't know when your time is up.'

Barry had been on the water for all his life.

He had skippered vessels and all types of boats in the pursuit of fish, scallops, crayfish, shark, and any other thing that there was money involved in.

Like a lot of other smarties, he had seen a fortune in the 'Orange Ruffy', a species that lived in the cold depths. He and the rest of the fishermen had almost wiped out the whole population.

Being a cold water fish, their recovery was very slow. Although the fisheries had put quotas on them, Barry and his mates had seen a way around that little problem and had made fortunes out of the ugliest fish known to man.

He was retired from all the hard work and had kept his last boat and used it more for relaxation than anything else. He and his mates would go out into Bass Strait and muck about, do a bit of Cray fishing, and just get away from all the hassles of modern-day life.

Teddy and Barry had been mates for a long time. They had done some dangerous deals together and trusted each other.

Teddy rolled his gold chain through his fingers and said. 'Mate, we might be able to do some business together. Me and the boys are thinking of doing a bit in Bass Strait, maybe head over to the Kent group of islands and spend a couple of days near Deal Island. There's a shallow reef just off the lighthouse, and last time I was there, it was loaded, back to back abalone.'

Barry looked up and said, 'Green lip or black lip?'

Teddy smiled and said, 'Green lip, mate, all green lip, there was thousands of them so close that when you chipped one, then about twenty tightened up.'

Both the men laughed.

Teddy swallowed half of his pot and Barry asked, 'What do you want me to do?'

'Well,' Teddy replied. 'I reckon that if you take your seventy footer over and I take the Shark Cat over and we work off it and then we sleep on your boat and one of us run the fish back at night.'

Barry looked at Teddy and screwed his face up and said, 'I'm not that happy about running across Bass Strait in the middle of the fucking night.'

Teddy laughed and said. 'Well, I can do that and you can drive the Shark Cat when the boys are diving. How does that sound?'

Barry wasn't too happy with any of the suggestions but knew that he had to do something or he wouldn't get paid. 'All right, I'll think about it. When do you want to head off?'

Teddy thought for a while and said, 'It will be in the next couple of days.'

Barry was happy with the way the day was shaping up. He was a semi-retired fisherman and he had an old wooden clinker hulled seventy-footer. It was an ex-shark boat which he kept for sentimental reasons.

It could sleep about eight people, comfortably, and had showers and toilets, plenty of room in the galley, a big wheelhouse. It was a comfortable live aboard vessel.

He knew that Teddy was a good payer and that he could get easily a thousand dollars a day for what was only a bit of fun. Teddy would fill it up before they left and then would refill the boat when they returned. If Teddy or someone were going to run the abalone across every night, then there wouldn't be any fish on board that he could get caught with.

After a careful inspection of the weather map, Teddy reckoned that there was a few days' work in front of them in a couple of days.

Teddy rang Tony, the driver of the F100, and told him that they were going to do something in the next couple of days. Tony was an Italian bloke that was on an invalid pension, and Teddy paid him on a daily basis to tow the Shark Cat around from place to place and do a bit of running around for the group. He was reliable and could keep his mouth shut.

Tony agreed to fill up the Shark Cat and the F100 and be on the alert.

Teddy then rang the boys and told them to prepare to get their arses wet in the next couple of days. They were all happy with the news that they were going back to work.

Tom asked Sandy, his partner, if she wanted to stay at Teddy and Rita's place as she was still a bit shaken by getting abused by the two loan sharks. Sandy decided that she would be all right to stay home on her own. Tom agreed that if she felt well enough, then it was up to her.

Tom knew that there was a problem that had to be settled with those low loan sharks and he would be the one to settle it, all in good time.

Dean was sitting in a pub when Teddy rang. He answered the phone after its first ring, and when he saw it was Teddy, Dean knew that it was about work and he thought to himself, Good news, we are going back to work.

He had had a bad run at the card games over the last few weeks. Every time he had had a good hand, one that he could bet on, and then some other bastard had had a better one, fucking Orientals; they were getting harder and harder to beat.

Dean wondered just where they got their money from.

Curly was at home in his shed when Teddy rang. He welcomed the news that they were going back to work as after the investment scheme that he had talked everyone into investing in had fallen over and they all lost all the money that they had put into it. He was behind the eight ball. The boys had all been good about it. They realised that he wasn't trying to rob them he had just been taken to the cleaners by a couple of con men.

Bastards, Curly thought, *I wonder where that Patto is now. I'd like to catch up with him someday, and I bet there are a lot of people that would like to catch up with the little prick.* He shook his head and thought about diving in the middle of Bass Strait.

Teddy had mentioned Green Lip abalone; they were the pick of all the abalone and only found in South Australia and Bass Strait, very few were found elsewhere. 'Yes, it should be a great adventure, let's hope that we get a quid out of it.'

There are basically three types of abalone. Black lip, they are the most common; tiger, they have a bit of a black and grey stripped lip; and the most popular coloured green lip, they are hard to come by and there are reefs that contain them at odd spots on the southern areas in Victoria and South Australia.

Eddie the Jew was still getting over missing out on getting his hands onto the fabulous golden chalice that Teddy and his gang of fucking idiots had ended up giving to that professor. He was now an expert on the subject of sunken treasure and shipwrecks.

Every day he is on the TV telling how important the discovery of the chalice was.

Eddie was furious with himself and everyone else that had to do with it and on him missing out on it.

Eddie was a wealthy man.

He owned the building that he worked out of in the heart of Melbourne, and he had plenty of other investment properties around the place.

He was known as a precious metals' dealer, but the dark secret that no one knew about was that Eddie also imported drugs from overseas.

He was one of the 'Big Boys' when it came to drug importing. He and a group of criminals had worked out a plan of importing drugs that was fool proof, or as fool proof as you can make it when you are working with dumb crims.

He and his gang had devised a way of getting the drugs to Victoria via a Korean Tanker. One of the kitchen hands would throw the drugs overboard in Bass Strait and they would be retrieved by a fishing boat or by a high-speed leisure cruiser. The drugs would be in a sealed container with a homing device in it. As soon as it hit the water, the device would send out a radio signal that the retrieve craft would pick up and they would speed to the drum and pull it on board. From there, they would, usually under the cover of darkness, steam into port and unload it at some deserted jetty or boat ramp, where their accomplices would be waiting.

It was almost fool proof.

Tony had Teddy's Shark Cat full of fuel and was waiting for a call from Teddy.

When it came, Tony was ready to go. He drove the Shark Cat down to St Kilda marine and met Teddy and all the boys. They were all relaxed and laughing. Even Curly was happy. He had taken a big hit when the investment scheme that he had talked everyone into fell over and he felt as though he was responsible for makine up the money that they had put in. He had given Tony back his two thousand dollars and there were no hard feelings between any of them.

Tony backed the boat into the water with all the boys in it, and Teddy started the motors and slowly drove the boat away from the boat ramp. Teddy gave Tony the thumbs up and the boat accelerated away towards the heads.

Barry and an old mate of his, Des, had left a couple of hours earlier and were almost to the heads of Port Phillip Bay when he saw the Shark Cat coming towards him. Barry reckoned that he was doing about twelve knots and the Shark Cat was doing about forty to fifty knots.

The boys all gave Barry and Des the thumbs up as they sped past him. They were soon almost out of sight. Barry knew that they would find each other when he arrived at Deal Island. They settled back and watched as the Shark Cat disappeared into the distance.

Teddy was on the GPS and steered towards the Kent group of islands. He came in under the lighthouse.

The lighthouse on Deal Island is the highest lighthouse in Australia. Although it is only twenty-two metres high, it was built on an elevated site. So when it was finished, it was three hundred and five metres above sea level. It was de-manned in 1992 and is seventy-five kilometres from the Australian mainland.

The boys started to get into their diving suits.

As usual, Dean and Curly worked off a 'T' piece and Tom worked off a single line.

Dean and Curly would 'chip' off the abalone and start to fill their bags. When they were full; Tom would grab them and take them to a spot where they would be stockpiled for the day. They would do this to the first day's catch so that they didn't have any abalone on board, just in case the fisheries decided to drop in on them.

When the boys dove down in the crystal clear water, they could see that there were plenty of abalone all over the reef below them. As they swam down, they knew that they were in for a couple of big days.

The green lip abalone is a slightly different shape to the black lip abalone. The green lip seems to have a deeper shell and there wasn't as much growth on the shells as they are constantly blasted by the sand and the currents, as the Bass Strait is very tidal.

They were going pretty well and had been working, chipping abalone for about three hours. Tom gave the boys the thumbs up so that they could go up and have a bit of a spell. They all climbed into the Shark Cat, and Teddy asked them how they were going.

Curly said, 'Mate, it's a healthy reef. There are plenty of abalone and heaps of crayfish. I reckon that crayfish will be on the menu for tonight's supper.'

They all thought that that was a great idea.

Teddy said. 'When Barry gets close, I'll tell him to tell Des to fire up the barbie and we'll grab half a dozen and roast them up, that's a good idea.'

They all thought that was a good plan.

They had a bit more sun and went back into the water.

Teddy saw Barry's boat pull around the headland and soon he dropped anchor. It was starting to get dark, so as soon as the boys had had enough, they climbed into the boat and motored over to Barry's boat and climbed up.

Teddy stayed behind on the Shark Cat and filled up the compressors and stowed all the gear away for the next day. When he got onto the deck, the boys were out of their wetsuits and gathered around the barby.

Barry and Des had a heap of steaks on and the boys were hungrily looking at the meat cooking. They each had a beer in their hands and were talking about how much abalone they had stockpiled up.

Dean said to Teddy, 'Mate, this is the life, plenty of room to move around and a chef on hand to boot.'

'Yes, mate,' said Teddy, 'it's a bit more comfortable than the Shark Cat, and a bit slower.'

They all laughed.

Barry organised the meals and the boys started eating them.

Barry and Des drowned the crayfish in fresh water and split them down the middle and put some garlic and butter on the cut sides. He then put them onto the barby, cut sides up, he got a big steamer lid to cover them and let them cook in their own juices.

When the boys had eaten their steaks, he lifted the lid and the aroma of garlic and crayfish filled the air.

Teddy said, 'I wonder what the poor people are doing!'

Dean answered him and said, 'I know what one of them is doing.'

They all laughed and started to eat the delicious white meat.

When they had all finished, Teddy asked how many bags they had stockpiled under water.

Tom replied that there were twelve bags in the first stockpile and another fifteen bags in the last stockpile. 'Twenty-seven in all, that works out to about twenty-five thousand dollars,'

Teddy thought not a bad day's work.

There were a few more expenses involved when they used a big boat, but if they got more abalone, then it was all worth it. The next day would be a big day. They would work all day and then shell out what they could and then Teddy would run it across to Victoria, while the boys had a bit of a spell.

They hit the beds early as they all knew that the next day would be a big day.

Des was happy to have a couple of day's work.

He was on the pension and was a couple of years younger than Barry, and they had been mates forever.

They had drunk together and fought, side by side, in most of the sea-side hotels in and around Tasmania for a long time.

Des was always on call whenever Barry wanted a deck hand or just some company for a couple of days away. When Barry said that they were going to do a bit of work for Teddy, he knew that there would be a bit of money in it for him. As Teddy was renowned for being a good payer and a good bloke to boot.

It was great to be included, to feel as though he was wanted.

Des fitted in with all the boys and it was a happy crew.

Early next morning, Teddy and the boys were woken by Des and Barry getting breakfast ready. Pots and pans were getting banged about in the galley and soon everyone was up and sitting around the table in the saloon. Des was placing trays of bacon and eggs onto the table, and Barry and Teddy were talking about what they would do that day.

Teddy suggested that they work for a long as they could, and then everyone get in and shuck out all the abalone that they could. When it got dark, they would load up the Shark Cat and one of them would run the load across to Victoria to where Tony would be waiting at a boat ramp near Werribee.

There were quite a few boat ramps that the locals used, and there wasn't anyone around most of the time. Seeing that it would be in the middle of the night, and then it was entirely possible that it would be calm and no swell, so unloading the shelled abalone would be easy.

The boys got into their dry wetsuits and jumped into the Shark Cat.

Teddy drove the boat away over to the reef that they had been fishing on the previous day, and Dean and Curly fell backwards over the side and slowly swam down.

As it was on the previous day, the water was crystal clear and they could see the abalone sitting on rocks everywhere. They didn't muck around, and when Tom swam down to join them, their bags were almost full. Tom started to 'chip' off some abalone, and as soon as he saw that Dean's bag was full, he swapped his nearly empty bag for Dean's full one.

Tom then swam to a sandy spot beside the reef and decided that this was as good as any place to start a stockpile. He placed the net bag on the sandy bottom and swam back to swap net bags with Curly whose bag was full.

They continued this for a few hours.

When Tom gave the boys the 'thumbs up', they nodded and started to swim slowly to the surface. By rights, they should have done some decompression stops, but as they would only be out of the water for a few minutes, they both decided that they would be all right.

Teddy pulled the boat up beside them and they all got on board. They were happy with the way that they were working and at the amount of net bags that they had stockpiled on the bottom. They all relaxed in the warm sun, and soon they were ready to get back into it.

All was going well.

Ho Yee Fat was a happy man.

He had a job on a Korean container ship as cook/kitchen hand which meant that he got plenty to eat and that he also had somewhere to sleep of a night. He was paid to do what he enjoyed; yes he was a happy man.

When his cousin said to him that on his next journey, he would be paid to throw a couple of plastic containers over the side of the boat, early one morning, at a precise time in a specific location, he accepted without question. For his cousin was a well-respected man in the city and was involved in many businesses. His cousin was also very wealthy.

When his cousin mentioned that the amount that he was to receive was almost as much as he got in a month, he was more than willing to be a part of the operation.

Late one night, before they arrived in Port Phillip Bay in Melbourne, his phone rang and a voice said, 'It was time.'

Ho Yee Fat got out of bed and went to the galley of the container ship and grabbed the two plastic barrels that were labelled, in Korean, 'bread mix'. He walked out of the galley down a passage and out into the night.

When he came to the railing and looked over the side, he couldn't see much, only the dark water that was rushing past the side of the container ship. Without wasting any time, Ho Yee Fat threw the two containers over the side and they vanished in the wake of the vessel. Soon he couldn't see them in the darkness. He turned around and made his way back to his tiny little sleeping cabin.

He dialled a number and only said, 'It's done, all is well.' He laid down on his still warm bed and fell into a sound sleep, content that he had done what was required of him.

The day was over.

The divers were cold and had had enough, so they decided to start shelling out as much of the abalone as they could get shelled out. They headed back to their first day's position and Tom began to swim up the net bags two or three at a time.

Soon the Shark Cat was full of bagged abalone and sitting low in the water.

Teddy took their load over to Barry's boat and started to get the abalone shelled.

Barry and Des helped, and within a couple of hours, the abalone meat was placed into plastic bags and sealed at the top with a wire tie. These were then put into fish bins and stored up the front of the Shark Cat.

Soon the Shark Cat was full of plastic bags of abalone meat.

Teddy and Des filled the fuel tanks up with fuel that was stored on the aft deck of Barry's boat and got ready for the long trip across Bass Strait. It was about seven thirty and the sun was setting in the west.

'I'll wait until it gets dark before I take off,' Teddy said.

Des said, 'If you want some company, then I'll come along with you.'

Teddy agreed and they all started to get some food into them.

As soon as the meal was finished, Teddy said to Des, 'Are you right mate?'

Des nodded and got up from the table and said, 'I'll see you all in the morning.'

Everyone nodded and wished them all the best.

Teddy and Des climbed down into the Shark Cat and threw off the mooring lines.

Started both motors, Teddy moved off into the darkness.

As soon as their night vision improved, they picked up speed and headed off into the night.

The sea was smooth and they made excellent progress.

The big cat sped through the water.

Teddy rang Tony and told him that they were under way; Tony agreed with their ETA and got the van ready to pick up their abalone.

Teddy and Des had been going for over an hour when a big container ship came into sight; it looked massive and was heading towards Port Phillip Bay.

Teddy gave it plenty of room but still the Shark Cat almost went out of the water when it encountered the big ship's wake.

'Jesus Christ, they shift some water!' Des said to Teddy.

Teddy agreed and quoted some words from an old poem that was said to have been published by a 'Mother Shipton' in AD 1488,

Carriages without horses will go, and accidents will fill the world with woe,

Around the world, thoughts will fly, in the twinkling of an eye.

The world upside down shall be, and gold be found at the root of a tree.

Through hills, man shall ride, and no horse shall be at his side.

Under the water, men shall walk, shall ride, shall sleep, shall talk.

In the air, men shall be seen, in white, in black, in green.

Iron in the water shall float, as easily as a wooden boat.

Gold shall be found and shown, in a land that's now not known.

Fire and water shall wonders do, England shall at last admit a foe.

The world to an end shall come, in eighteen hundred and eighty-one.

The poem that Teddy quoted from was one believed to have been written by a Mother Shipton, otherwise known as Ursula Southeil, or Soothtell. Who is said to have lived in a cave in Yorkshire between 1488 and 1561. She is reputed to have published this prophesy and it was republished after her death in 1641.

Des looked at Teddy and thought that he was a pretty smart bloke.

They cruised on towards their destination.

Eddie, the Jews men watched as the container ship approached them.

They were in no danger of being rammed by the large ship as their mono-hulled power boat was far faster than almost any boat around.

It was an almost new, twenty-five foot Haines Hunter Formula hull with two 300 horsepower Mercury outboard motors on the stern. It went very quickly, to say the least.

It was set up to do exactly what it was doing. It was a drug-running boat, as simple as that, it was propped up so that it did an almost unbelievable speed across the water in almost any condition. Inside it had racing seats that supported your lower back and this boat could easily break records, but that wasn't what Eddie wanted, he didn't wish to bring any attention to him or his boat.

Two men in their thirties were in the boat. They had the physique of very fit people, Kevin and Troy. They knew exactly what they were doing. They knew what was in the plastic containers that they were going to pick up, and they knew who was behind the operation and they knew that they would end up rich as long as everything went as according to plan.

It was the deal of a lifetime. They were hard men and dangerous as well.

They both carried handguns and had used them when it was needed. They knew the rules.

Kevin's phone rang and a voice said, 'The delivery has been made, turn on your receiver and pick them up.'

Kevin said, 'Right, we are on it.'

The phone on the other end got disconnected.

Kevin said to Troy, 'Turn on the receiver and let's pick up the containers.'

Troy nodded and turned on a receiver, silence.

He started to move the dial around, still silence.

'Try another channel,' Kevin said.

Troy shifted the controls around and said. 'Fuck all, there must be something wrong. We should have picked up some signal as soon as I turned it on.'

Kevin shook his head. 'I'm fucked if I know,' he said. 'Just keep trying,'

Troy fiddled with the knob and still the receiver was silent.

'This isn't good. This isn't good at all,' Kevin said with some dread in his voice.

The pressure was starting to build, and both the men knew that they were in trouble. What was going to be walk in the park has suddenly turned into a deadly game. They both knew that if they didn't retrieve the drugs, then there would be a lot of suspicions and the finger would be pointed at them?

It had worked before. There were never any problems.

Kevin pinpointed their position on the GPS and started to worry.

He drove the boat out to about where the container boat had been when they got the go ahead and turned off the motors. He decided to drift with the currents.

Kevin reckoned that the drugs would drift as well, and when dawn broke, they should be able to see them floating on the surface. Just in case Kevin decided to have a look around with a powerful searchlight on the off chance that they might fluke spotting the drums. He and Troy started scanning the black waters.

Teddy and Des cruised through the heads flat out; they made their way around 'Indented Head' and sped towards their targeted boat ramp.

Teddy rang Tony, and Tony answered. 'Hullo, mate, all is well here. I'm on my own and there isn't anyone around at all. As soon as I hear you, I'll shine a light out to sea and you can follow it in.'

'Thanks, mate,' Teddy replied and disconnected.

Soon he and Des saw a light shining out towards them. Teddy slowed down and made their way towards the boat ramp.

When Teddy was in closer, he turned off the motors and a silence fell over the area. They could see that Tony had parked the van on the boat ramp and the side doors were open. As soon as the boat was close enough, Tony grabbed the Shark Cat and pulled it into the shallower water.

Teddy had lifted the motors and the boat started to bottom on the boat ramp.

Des began to lift the plastic bags out of their bins and handed them over to Teddy and Tony began to run them into the van.

The whole operation only took about fifteen minutes; soon the van was weighed down by the amount of abalone that was on board. Tony jumped in behind the steering wheel and started the motor.

Des and Teddy swung the Shark Cat around and pushed it out stern first.

Teddy jumped in, and Des waited until Teddy started the motors. They ticked over smoothly.

Des jumped in and Teddy asked, 'Is everything OK?'

'I'm as sweet as mate, as sweet as.' Des laughed.

Teddy backed out from the ramp and they watched as Tony drove into the night.

'Let's haul arse out of here and get some sleep.' Teddy said.

With that, he headed the Shark Cat towards the lights of Geelong and kept his eyes open.

Derek, the processor's phone, rang, and he looked and saw that it was Teddy. He was expecting a call, and when he answered, he heard the noise of a motor or motors running pretty damn fast.

'Hullo, Teddy mate, how's it hanging?'

'Mate, I'm all right. We've just filled up the van with green lips, and Tony is on his way. He should be at the factory in about an hour's time.'

'Thanks, mate,' Derek said, 'I'll give Tony a ring and tell him to meet me at the factory.'

'No wuckers,' said Teddy.

Teddy pointed the Shark Cat towards the 'Heads' and they shot out into the darkness of the ocean.

Des asked Teddy if he wanted a spell at the controls as there was not a lot to do, just steer the boat. It would be a couple of hours before they were back at Barry's boat.

Teddy handed over the controls and went and sat in the passenger's seat and tried to sleep, but it wasn't possible. Even though the sea was flat, there was always a bit of a bump when the boat went over a swell slightly bigger than the rest.

They had been going for over an hour when Des said to Teddy, 'There's a spot on the radar. It looks like a small craft.'

Teddy opened his eyes and looked at the radar screen. 'Yes, looks like someone's out doing a bit of night fishing. We'll go over and make sure that they are all right.'

Des changed course and made for the boat.

As they got closer, they saw that it didn't have any navigation lights on. They could see that their searchlight was on and they seemed to be scanning the immediate area around them.

Teddy took over the controls, and as they brought their craft towards the other boat, the spotlight illuminated them up. Both Teddy and Des were blinded by the light.

'Fuck me,' said Teddy, as he slowed the Shark Cat down and came up to within twenty feet from the other boat.

Kevin saw the boat coming towards them and said to Troy. 'Some bastards heading our way. If they stop, then we'll tell them that we are fishing and dropped our "Esky" over the side and we are looking for it. If it's the police, throw the guns over the side. We don't want to be found with handguns on us.'

As Teddy's Shark Cat approached them, they realised that it wasn't the police.

Troy said. 'I know that boat. It's an abalone boat. I've seen it around, and I think that they might be poachers.'

Kevin relaxed a bit and as the Shark Cat pulled up beside them, he said, 'Howdy boys, what are you up to?'

Teddy didn't answer the question but instead asked, 'Are you blokes all right? We thought that you might be broken down.'

Kevin replied. 'Thanks, mate, we are doing a bit of drift fishing and our "Esky" went into the drink. We thought that we might spot it, but we haven't as yet.'

'You're all right then?' Teddy asked.

'Yes, mate, right as rain, thanks,' Kevin said.

Teddy steered his boat away from the other and accelerated into the night.

Des said, 'Fucking rich pricks, boats probably worth a hundred grand.'

Teddy nodded and they headed towards where Barry and the boys were sleeping.

They finally made it and tied up beside Barry's boat.

Barry appeared and asked how it went.

Teddy smiled and said, 'It went like clockwork, easy money.'

They made their way down to their cabins and almost instantly went to sleep.

The next day, they all were up and having breakfast when Barry asked Teddy, 'Why don't you bring over a heap of net bags so that Des and I can start shucking them out. That way, it won't be such a big ask at the end of the day?'

Teddy thought about the request and said, 'I don't like the idea of having abalone on board. If the fisheries do raid us, then we can say that we are here looking at wrecks. They can't charge us with anything if we don't have abalone on board.'

Barry looked at his old mate and said. 'The chance of us getting rolled by the fisheries is pretty remote out here. If we see a boat heading our way, then we can chuck everything over the side.'

Teddy thought for a while and said, 'It's a bit risky, granted that it would save time, I've got to weigh up the risks in my head.'

Tom said, 'It would be a big time saver.'

Teddy thought about it and said, 'All right, I'll drop off a load after our first break and see how it goes. Baz you move your boat out into the open where you can see if a boat is coming your way. That will give you plenty of opportunitiey to get rid of any abalone over the side if trouble presents itself.'

The boys suited up and Teddy moved the Shark Cat away from Barry's boat.

Soon they were over a reef and Dean and Curly went over the side and swam slowly down to the bottom. They were in about thirty feet of clear water. There was abalone everywhere and they started to chip them off the rocks.

Soon Tom arrived and began stockpiling up the net bags of abalone. With the three of them working hard, time flew, and before they knew it, Tom was giving them the thumbs up. They slowly surfaced, and Teddy brought the boat up beside them. They climbed aboard.

Teddy asked. 'How is it going? Is the abalone lasting down there?'

Tom replied, 'Yer, mate, they seem to be holding, I reckon that we should be all right for the day.'

Teddy saw that Barry had shifted his boat out into clear water, so he decided that they should give him a boat load of abalone to shuck out. That would make it easier for them all at night.

Teddy asked Tom to go down and bring up the first stockpile of abalone. Tom did this, and they took ten net bags out to Barry.

Des and Barry started to shuck the abalone, and Teddy took the boys back to the reef.

Things weren't going as smoothly for Eddie the Jew's drug pick up men.

With the coming of dawn, Kevin and Troy searched the surrounding waters for the two plastic drums. All to no avail; unfortunately. They looked and drove the boat around in circles but couldn't find anything at all.

Kevin rang and told them at the other end that they were having troubles but were told to keep looking.

The message was, don't come back in without the drugs.

Eddie the Jew was very savage. That pair of fucking clowns didn't pick up the drums, or did they? Did they decide to keep the drugs for themselves? That was the question. It wouldn't be the first time that underlings had decided that they would go out on their own and start up in opposition. It was a great way to start, especially if you got your first shipment for nothing. If they weren't careful, they might end up getting a sea burial. It wouldn't be the first time that someone was 'deep-sixed.'

Eddie just hoped that they came to their senses and brought the drugs in.

The next day progressed, and Teddy and the boys were getting ready to knock off, so they filled up the Shark Cat with all the abalone from the stockpiles and motored out to Barry's boat. They all got stuck into shucking out the abalone, and soon the Shark Cat was full of plastic bags filled with green lip abalone.

Barry and Des got a bit of dinner going and soon all the boys were relaxed.

As the sun set, Teddy and Des got the Shark Cat refuelled and decided to get going.

It had come up in conversation that Teddy and Des had come across a boat out in the middle of nowhere, supposedly doing a bit of fishing. Something was a bit suspicious about the whole deal, but not a lot was thought about it

✧ ✧ ✧ ✧

Kevin and Troy finally gave up looking for the two barrels. They phoned in and asked if it was sure that the barrels had gone over the side as they had never had any problems before picking them up. They had always been led to the barrels by the radio transmitter in the drums. This time there was no signal, no signal at all. What had happened? Why wasn't there any signal? Surely, they couldn't be blamed for, not being able to pick them up. Is everybody sure that they went over the side, what proof did they have that they were even put into the ocean? How come there was no signal?

Eddie thought through the problem slowly, what had gone wrong.

Why weren't the drugs in his possession by now? Who do you trust in a situation like this?

The answer for this one was easy, you don't trust anyone, no one at all.

Eddie decided that the best place to start was at the very beginning. He knew that the drugs were put on board the container ship.

Eddie rang Ho Yee Fat's cousin and said there was a problem and explained it. The cousin immediately rang Ho and told him that he was in trouble, serious trouble as the two drums hadn't been picked up. Ho swore that he had put them over the side as he knew how thorough the customs were in Australia and he couldn't risk having them aboard the container ship when it berthed in Melbourne.

Hoe's cousin got back to Eddie and assured him that the drugs definitely went over the side at exactly the time that was requested.

Eddie was at a loose end, why didn't the beacons go off when they hit the water? That was the question.

Kevin and Troy went back to port. They got out of the boat and were taken to an office where they were questioned separately; both their stories were the same, almost exactly.

They both mentioned a boat being out there in the middle of the night. When asked about who was in the boat, Troy explained that he was sure that it was some abalone poachers, he knew of them, but that was all.

Eddie was told of the developments and a light went on in his head.

Fucking abalone poachers, could it be the same ones that had fucked up his plans to end up with the golden chalice?

Eddie thought long and hard.

Yes, that could be the answer, the poachers were doing whatever the fuck they were doing and came across a couple of barrels and just picked them up and away they went. Yes, that was a distinct possibility.

He would get to the bottom of this if it was the last thing that he did. First, he would find the poachers and question them, how would he go about that? How would he get in contact with them?

A plan started to take shape; he would ring Martha and see if she could be of some help.

Martha saw that it was Eddie's number on the caller identification and she answered immediately, 'Hullo, Eddie love, how are you going?'

Eddie replied, 'Oh, I'm okay Martha, just fine, I was wondering if you had seen those diver blokes around recently?'

Martha's mind started to race. 'No, I haven't seen hide or hair of them since the time with you when we looked at that golden chalice. It was a shame that we didn't end up with it, wasn't it?'

Eddie agreed with her and asked. 'If I wanted to get in touch with the leader of them, Teddy I think his name is, where would I run into him? Or do you have a number that I could contact on?'

Martha thought for a moment and decided that she would ring Teddy first and let him know that Eddie wanted to speak to him. 'I've got his number somewhere, but I'll have to find it and get back to you, love.'

Eddie said, 'Martha, I'm in quite a hurry to get in contact with Teddy, so if you can get his number to me as soon as possible, I would appreciate it tremendously.'

With that Eddie disconnected

Martha immediately rang Teddy's number and it went to a recorded message. Martha told the recording that Eddie was desperate to get in contact with him and he should ring him back quickly. Martha left Eddie's number and hung up.

Teddy turned his phone on and saw a message was there from Martha.

He hesitated as the last dealings he had had with her was when she set him up with that gangster Sam and his two lunatic sons over the golden chalice. He decided to ring Martha back first.

Martha saw it was Teddy's phone number and answered like nothing had happened. 'Hullo, Teddy love, how are you?'

'I'm all right,' Teddy replied, 'I just opened your call and wondered what it was all about.'

Martha said, 'I haven't got a clue. Eddie just wants to get in contact with you is all I know.'

'Thanks for passing on the message,' Teddy said, 'I'll give him a ring when I can.' Teddy disconnected.

He wasn't happy with Martha. She was an evil bitch, one to be wary of.

Martha rang Eddie back and said, 'Here's Teddy's number, I've just come across it.'

Eddie thanked Martha and wondered what to do next. He didn't want to alert Teddy that there was something out there, but if, by chance, Teddy had picked it up, then Eddie wanted it back.

Teddy and Des headed into Port Phillip Bay and made their way across it to the same boat ramp that they had unloaded the night before. Tony was there and he shone his torch out into the darkness.

Teddy rang to say that he had seen the light and they were coming in. Tony got ready for the unloading.

As soon as the Shark Cat pulled into the boat ramp, they started to unload it.

As before Des passed the plastic bags over the side and Teddy and Tony ran them the short distance up the van. It didn't take long and the van was full.

Tony jumped into the driver's seat and with a wave, he drove off and its taillights disappeared into the darkness.

Teddy and Des prepared for the long trip back.

Des captained the Shark Cat, and Teddy relaxed in the passenger's seat. They passed Geelong and headed out the heads.

Des commented to Teddy, 'I wonder if we will run into any other boats out here.'

Teddy shrugged and said. 'I wonder just what the fuck they were doing. Ah well, nothing to do with us.'

The pair remained silent for a while as the powerful boat surged along.

Kevin and Troy were in real trouble. They were, by no fault of their own, up to their nostrils in shit. They knew that the people that they were dealing with would kill them both if something didn't show up.

They found out that the drums had been put over the side. The 'slope head' had sworn that he had done what was requested of him. He knew what would happen to him and his family if he hadn't done what was asked of him, that was beyond doubt. The next thing was to find out if someone had picked the drums up, just by good luck, or if they found them, it would be bad luck for them.

Kevin wanted to know more about the two blokes in the Shark Cat, maybe by chance they had seen the drums and grabbed them. Troy had said that he kind of knew of the boat. He had said that it was an abalone poacher's boat. Kevin explained to Troy that they were fucked if the drums didn't turn up, so Troy got busy and started to ring around.

He got in contact with every poacher he knew and slowly after many hours of talking to the shadowy world of evil-doers, he had enough to put together Teddy's boat and crew.

Armed with this knowledge, he told Kevin that in fact it was Teddy who was out in the middle of Bass Strait on the same night that they were and that they also were in the same area as them.

Kevin felt a sense of relief, at least there was one other person to take a bit of the blame. Troy rang a number that had been given to him as a number that belonged to a close associate of Teddy.

Troy rang on the pretence of being a mate of Teddy and asked where Teddy was. Tony was a bit non-committal as he didn't know who he was talking to. But Troy seemed so open that Tony was fooled a bit, and when Troy said that he was supposed to meet Teddy for dinner tonight and he couldn't get an answer on Teddy's phone, he wondered if Teddy was well.

Tony explained that Teddy was away and wouldn't be back for a while, maybe a couple of days.

Troy laughed and said, 'Jesus Christ, he's a bastard, he's left me posted again. You don't reckon that he will be back for a while then.'

Tony said. 'No, mate. Teddy won't be back for a few days. He's working over in Tassie waters, but I'll be talking to him briefly tonight if you want me to pass on any information.'

'No, thanks, mate,' Troy said, 'I'll speak to him myself when he gets back.'

Troy disconnected and said to Kevin, 'That prick is working over at the islands in Bass Strait, and running the abalone over of a night to a processor.'

Kevin thought for a while and said. 'Maybe we should run into him again and see just what the fuck he is up to. If he has the drugs, then we will have to see where they are, did he pick them up on the way over or did he pick them up on the way back.'

Troy wasn't convinced that the poachers had found the drugs but what else did they have to go on. They were clutching at straws and they knew it.

Teddy watched the weather and was sure that they would get the next day in. As bad weather was closing in on Bass Strait, and when it got bad in Bass Strait, then it was impossible to do any work at all. They headed off to work and decided that rather than stockpile the abalone, they would get a boat load and then take them over to Barry's boat and he and Des would start to shuck them out so at the end of the day they wouldn't have as many to shuck out and Teddy could get going a bit earlier.

The boys started to get working.

Dean and Curly worked the 'T' piece and Tom swam the net bags up to the boat. Soon the boat was loaded up with net bags and Teddy said that they should go over and get rid of them onto Barry's boat. The three divers got on board and helped shift the net bags over. Barry and Des started to shuck out the abalone. The others went back to work.

Barry said to Teddy. 'The weather is beginning to break. You will be lucky to get all afternoon in.'

Teddy nodded and said, 'I'll keep my eyes open and as soon as it starts to get a bit lumpy, then I'll call it a day.'

Kevin and Troy started to put two and two together. They did some checking and found out where Tony lived and decided that if Tony was going to talk to Teddy tonight and Teddy was working over in Bass Strait, then there was a chance that Tony was going to meet Teddy tonight to pick up some abalone. So the two desperadoes waited in view of Tony's house. They saw that Tony had a van parked in his drive. They were sure that Tony used this van to pick up the abalone from Teddy and take it somewhere. They waited for some movement from Tony.

Tony finished his dinner and said to his wife, 'I'm expecting a call from Teddy any time now. He rings me in plenty of time so I can meet him and unload, so I'll be back late tonight.'

He wasn't surprised when his phone rang and Teddy said, 'We are about an hour and a half away. The weather has broken, so it will be the last time you have got to come and pick up from us.' Tony went out and got into the van. He drove off into the darkness unaware that a car was following him.

Kevin and Troy followed Tony; they kept well back as, not to alert him that he was being 'tailed.' When Tony swung off the freeway, Kevin said. 'I bet the bastard is going down to that little boat ramp that no one ever uses. It's probably too shallow to put in and pull out a Shark Cat, but they would be able to unload there, and it would be deserted at this hour.'

They turned off their headlights and followed. Soon they saw Tony pull up and start to wait for the Shark Cat to arrive. They got out of the car and silently walked towards where the darkened van was.

Tony sat quietly, unaware that he was being watched.

He rang Teddy's number and said, 'How far away are you?'

Teddy answered, 'About ten minutes, I reckon, get your light ready.'

Tony listened in silence, and when he heard the sound of motors running, he turned his torch out onto the bay.

He heard the motors start to slow down and saw the phosphorus from the bow wave show up. Then he saw the Shark Cat coming in towards the boat ramp.

Teddy was running off his GPS. Soon the boat was beside the ramp.

They all spoke quietly as sound seems to travel further over water at night.

'How are you boys going?' Tony asked.

'Good as gold,' Teddy answered. He stopped the Shark Cat and 'jacked' up the motors and the boat silently ran aground. Des grabbed a bag of shucked abalone and handed it to Tony. Teddy jumped over the side and Des handed him a bag also. They both headed up the ramp to the van. It was about five metres away. Soon they were almost loaded.

Suddenly, a voice came out of the darkness. 'Don't anyone, fucking well move, stay right where you are or I'll blow your fucking heads off.'

Kevin could see the three men, and they all froze, caught in the high-power LED torches that Kevin and Troy held.

Kevin walked over to the van and looked inside. He didn't see any plastic drums, and he walked over to Teddy and said, 'We are looking for a couple of plastic drums that were in the ocean last night. They have seemed to have eluded us and we thought that you might have picked them up.'

Teddy felt a wave of relief wash over him. It wasn't the fisheries, just a couple of 'dickhead' drug runners.

'No, mate we haven't seen hide or hair of any drums. It was pitch-black out there when we saw you two.' Teddy said quietly.

Teddy was putting together two and two.

He now realised just what these two were up to out in the middle of the night in the cold when they came across them.

'Mate, you can have a good look on the boat if you like. There isn't anything aboard that belongs to you, go on, get up, and have a good look.' Teddy stood back from the Shark Cat, and Kevin stepped up through the diver's door. He shone his torch around and looked in the front cabin while Troy kept everyone under surveillance.

When Kevin was sure that there were no plastic containers on board, he stepped down into the water and walked back to where Troy had marshalled the group.

Kevin asked. 'How are you doing this? Where are the others?'

Teddy decided to be honest with him. 'Mate, they are aboard the mother ship and are on their way across from the Kent group of islands. They are a few hours behind us.'

Kevin thought for a moment and said, 'So the plastic containers might be on board the mother ship?'

Teddy said, 'Look, mate, we aren't into anything but abalone. We don't fuck around with anything else.'

Kevin thought for a couple of seconds and said, 'Give me your mobile phones, don't fuck me around.'

Teddy and Tony handed over their mobile phones and Des said, 'I don't fucking well own one.'

Kevin looked at the old man and said, 'you had better not be bullshitting me.'

With that, he hurled the mobiles out into the bay, rendering them useless.

'Come on,' Kevin said to Troy, and they walked away into the darkness.

Teddy looked at the two other blokes and said, 'They were a couple of bad heads, if I've ever seen them, thank Christ we didn't stumble over the plastic drums. We would really have been in trouble. Let's get going and get to fuck out of here.'

The men loaded up all the abalone and got going.

Tony headed back to the factory, and Teddy headed back towards the middle of the bay to catch up with Barry.

Derek was waiting for Tony at the factory.

When Tony drove in, he said, 'I tried to ring your number to see what time you were coming in, but your phone was switched off.'

'Well,' Tony said, 'it wasn't exactly turned off. When we were unloading, a couple of fucking heavies trooped up and stuck guns in our ears. They reckoned that we might have picked up some plastic drums, fuck me dead I shit myself, it was really scary. First I thought that it might be the fisheries, and after a couple of minutes, I wished that it had been the fucking fisheries. At least the fisheries wouldn't have shot us and I reckon that these blokes might have done just that. Anyway, these blokes grabbed our mobile phones and threw them into the water.'

Derek looked a bit stunned. 'You mean these blokes just walked up and stuck a gun in your face and wanted to know if you had picked up any plastic drums.'

'That's exactly what happened,' Tony said.

They were both startled by Kevin's voice.

'I can vouch for that.' Kevin said loudly.

He and Troy made their way into the factory. Both of them had handguns, and they weren't happy. In fact, they really had the shits. This wasn't turning out as they had planned.

'We are just checking to make sure that you didn't drop off the drums on an earlier visit,' Kevin said as they started looking around.

Derek said. 'You guys are kidding yourself if you reckon that these blokes or I are dumb enough to get involved with anything else but abalone. We stick to what we know.'

Kevin and Troy had a good look around. Tony looked hopelessly at Derek.

Derek said. 'There is fuck all here. It's not my caper.'

Kevin looked at both the men and said, 'If I find out that you are scamming me, I'll come back and I'll let you watch while I kill all that's dear to you. Make no mistake. I mean what I say. It will be like the O.K. Corral.'

With that, he and Troy walked out into the darkness.

Derek looked at Tony and said, 'Fuck me dead that was scary.'

Tony swallowed and said, 'You're not wrong, I nearly shit myself, and I should be getting used to it by now.'

Teddy and Des caught up with Barry's boat as it made its way across Port Phillip Bay from the heads. Barry stopped his boat and Teddy came up alongside and him, and Des tied the Shark Cat to the larger boat and climbed up. They told Barry what had happened and agreed that they might get a visit from the same two blokes on their arrival.

Both Teddy and Des decided that they were dangerous, serious and deadly.

'Thank Christ we didn't see anything floating along and grab hold of it as we would have ended up with those two pricks hounding us,' Barry laughed.

Kevin and Troy were a bit stumped; they tended to believe the three blokes that they had met.

They both knew that people lie when there are drugs involved, but these blokes were already outside the law. No, Kevin reckoned that they didn't have the drums, but would he be able to convince the others? If he couldn't, then he and Troy were really in the shit, 'big time.'

Eddie the Jew wasn't getting any happier; in fact, he wanted someone to be held accountable for the present stuff up. This plan had been working for some time and he had never been in this situation,

'What to do? What to do? Go back over it and go through it bit by bit.' He said out loud to himself.

He was confident that the drugs had gone over the side. They always had been placed in a position and the pickup boat was always on hand for a quick pick up. There had never been a problem before. Nothing had been changed. Perhaps the signal buoy hadn't gone off and the drugs were still out there, perhaps Kevin and Troy had decided to go out into their own business, surely they aren't that stupid. No, he was sure that the drums had been missed. Somehow the signal hadn't been transmitted.

Eddie shook his head and got himself a coffee.

Dawn was breaking when Barry and the team tied up at the St Kilda Marina. The divers had slept on the way over and everyone was in good spirits. Barry wasn't surprised when he saw the two men walking up the jetty towards the boat.

'Here's trouble,' Barry surmised.

Kevin and Troy came aboard and asked, 'Who's running this shit heap?'

'That would be me,' Barry said.

Kevin demanded, 'We want to have a look around.'

Barry said, 'We haven't got whatever you are looking for. I can tell you that right now.'

Kevin pulled back his jacket and revealed the butt of a handgun. 'Well, we have to check, just to make sure, sit down at the table and we'll have a look around.'

Kevin and Troy were certain that this bunch of fucking idiots was under control; in fact, they were so sure that they were in charge that they didn't pull out their guns. They were sure that just the appearance of them would be enough to keep these pussies quiet.

Des was suddenly at the cabin door, feet away from Kevin, and Des was 'packing heat,' in the form of a sawn-off shotgun. The butt had been shortened and both barrels were about twelve inches long. It was a lethal weapon, one feared by all that it was pointed at.

'Put your hands up, before I blow your fucking heads off.' Des said heatedly.

Kevin hesitated, but Troy obeyed immediately.

Teddy grabbed the handgun out of his belt and pointed it at Kevin. 'Put your hands behind your head, you fucking clown. See how tough you are without a gun.'

Kevin obeyed slowly; he knew that they were in trouble.

Barry organised some plastic wire ties and soon their hands were tied behind their backs.

'What's the plan now?' Tom enquired.

Dean looked at the two men that were completely immobilised. 'Well, if we let them go, they will only come back and fuck us up. It's obvious that they reckon that we have got their shit. They will never stop hunting for us.'

Curly looked at the two men and asked. 'What are you saying? Do you mean that we have got to kill them?'

There was silence in the galley as the truth of the matter sunk in.

'There was only one way to settle this, like Black Beard the pirate was supposed to have said when burying his loot, "Dead men tell no tales". Can anyone come up with a better solution?' Teddy asked.

There was silence in the galley. 'I wonder if anyone knows that they came on board,' Barry asked.

Kevin, who had remained silent, throughout the operation said. 'We will be missed. The people that we work for will come looking for us. They will think that you have got the drugs and done away with us. They will never stop looking for you, never.'

Teddy thought about this for a while and remarked, 'Well, if we "knock" you two that will be two less "dirtbags" looking for us.'

Kevin knew that the next few seconds would either make or break the deal. 'Why don't you kill Troy to teach them all a lesson. Then they will know that you are fair dinkum, and let me go and I'll explain to them that you haven't got the drugs that you don't know anything about them and it was all a mix-up, you were just in the wrong place at the wrong time and you just go about your business and everything will be forgotten. If you kill us both, they will think that you have got the drugs and got rid of us to hide the evidence.' Kevin was starting to plead.

He knew that a decision was seconds away.

Everyone in the room looked at Teddy to see what he was going to say. Everyone knew that the final decision was going to be Teddy's.

Teddy knew that Kevin would say anything to save his life, anything at all. Teddy was gambling with all their lives. Could he trust these two violent criminals, who had probably killed before, to remain alive, would they leave them all in peace in the future?

Tom could see that Teddy was struggling to come up with an answer that would please everyone.

In a fluid movement, Tom swept up the stiletto knife that was always in his sock and said to Teddy. 'Just give the word and I'll slit both their fucking throats and bleed them out like pigs. We can wrap the bodies in chain and dump them at sea. It will all be over in a couple of seconds. All our problems solved.'

Troy felt his sphincter muscles loosen and his stomach heave.

He had been sold out by his partner, and it was obvious that the crazy Pommy bastard would kill him and then go and have a coffee latte and not lose any sleep over what he had done. This is not how it was supposed to be done. This isn't the ending he was hoping for. Where were the sunny beaches and the near-naked Thai companions that he had dreamed of?

Troy pleaded. 'Mate, forget what has happened and just let us go. We mean you no harm. We just wanted to make sure that you didn't have the drugs. We are certain of that now. Just let us go and it's the finish, the finish of all this shit. Mate, I'm begging you, on the life of my children. I promise you won't come to any harm.'

Teddy looked at Troy. He could see that he was begging him, but could he trust him to leave all of them alone?

He looked at Kevin. 'What about you? How do you feel about the situation?'

Kevin started to see a ray of light at the end of a tunnel. A stupid thought crossed his mind. *I hope it's not a train coming.*

Kevin said. 'I'm convinced that you don't have the drugs and that's all we wanted to make sure of. We have people that we have to satisfy that you don't have them. Now we are certain. Let us go and there's no harm done. We will go and you will never see us again, and if, we do pass on the street, we will remember with gratitude the kindness you showed to us by letting us go.'

Tom butted in and said. 'Yes, that would be fucking right, we let these fuckwits go and next thing we know they are waiting for us one dark night with a baseball bat or sawn off shotgun. I say end It now, once and for all. We can all go home and forget about it.'

Teddy looked at Tom and thought, *fuck me dead I hope that he's joking.*

Tom looked like he was on the verge of going completely off the rails.

Teddy had always suspected that Tom was ten pots of beer away from killing someone. Teddy looked at Kevin and said, 'You say you have got people above you that you have to satisfy that we haven't got the drugs. Well, I want to speak to them, and I want to talk to them now.'

Kevin felt that a great weight had been lifted off his chest. He nodded and said, 'the number is on my phone, untie my hands and I'll ring it for you.'

Tom cut the plastic tie with his stiletto, and Kevin moved his hands around as if they were stiff. Curly put the barrel of Kevin's revolver to the back of Kevin's head and said, 'Make one false move and it's tat-tars for you. I'll blow your brains out all over the wall. I won't miss from here.' Kevin dialled the phone.

Eddie the Jew was sitting in his kitchen having breakfast when his 'special' phone rang. He looked at the caller's number and said, 'Hullo, Kevin, you're up and about early this morning.'

Kevin replied, 'We haven't been to bed yet. I've got some information regarding the abalone poachers.'

'Tell me more,' Eddie asked.

With that, Teddy took the phone from Kevin and said, 'Mate, I don't know who the fuck you are and I don't want to know. We haven't got your plastic containers or your drugs or whatever the fuck you think we have. We just want to be left alone. We have got your two boys here and we are quite prepared to let them go, unharmed, but we want a guarantee that we will be left alone. They have promised that they will take the matter no further. We just want to be left alone to get on with what we do. If in any way we are troubled by what's happened, then one of us will track you down and kill you. Do I make myself clear? Do you understand? We will never forget.'

Eddie was a bit taken back and he said. 'I understand perfectly. There seems to have been a misunderstanding and I will do all in my power to rectify any problems. Let me speak to Kevin, please.'

Kevin took hold of the phone and spoke into it, 'We are sure that these blokes haven't got the drugs and are not involved in any way.'

Eddie answered. 'Well, just get out and come and see me. We will work out what to do next.' Kevin disconnected the phone, and Teddy held his hand out for it. He pressed the keys and took note of the last dialled number. He memorised it and carelessly tossed the phone out the galley door and it landed in the water. 'I'm just returning the complement. Tom, get Troy's phone and deep-six it.'

Tom went over to Troy, and with his stiletto in front of him flicked it across and sliced the bottom of Troy's ear lobe, blood started dripping onto Troy's shoulder. That was the end for Troy. He felt his stomach contract and he shit himself. The stench arose and everyone in the galley knew what had happened.

Tom cut the plastic tie that was securing Troy's hands and heaved him to his feet. Troy could feel the warmth of his underpants full of shit. He walked awkwardly and made his way off Barry's boat. Blood was dripping down onto his shoulder. Tom threw Troy's mobile into the water beside the moored boat and Kevin got onto the pier.

They both walked away and didn't look back.

Teddy looked around at all the boys; he looked at Des and said. 'Thank Christ that you appeared with the trusty sawn off. We would have been in all sorts of shit if you hadn't sprung that on them.'

Des laughed and said, 'Not as much as Troy.'

They all laughed.

Tony appeared at the cabin door. 'Hullo, boys, what have you been up to? I reckon that I saw those two bad bastards driving off just now. Did you see them?'

'Yes, we bumped into them. I think that they are going to go straight from now on.' Barry suggested.

Tom said, 'straight for the shower and tidy themselves up a bit.'

Everyone laughed again, more from nerves than the humour.

Teddy got into the Shark Cat and drove it onto the trailer.

When they had secured the boat and Tony had driven off, Teddy said to Barry, 'Sort out what I owe you and I'll fix it all up. I'll get the money off Derek and we shall all get together a square up.'

Kevin and Troy drove away from the marina. The air in the car was stinking.

'Fuck me dead, you stink,' Kevin said to Troy.

'Don't talk about me stinking, you fucking dog, you wanted those pricks to "knock" me so you could go and sort things out. You threw me to the fucking wolves, I won't ever forget that.'

Troy was clearly upset.

Kevin said. 'Mate, all I was doing was getting us a bit of time. That Pommy bastard is insane. He would have slit our throats and not bothered a bit. He is a fucking headcase if ever I've seen one.'

Troy wasn't convinced. He had seen a side of Kevin that he hadn't seen before, a side that he didn't feel safe with. He made a decision that they would go their separate ways after this; he couldn't trust Kevin as far as he could kick him. Troy wanted out, and he wanted out quickly but how do you go about getting out? It wasn't the public service that he had got involved in. He just couldn't give a month's notice and leave. He was aware that he knew too much, far too much.

Kevin's mind was also working overtime. He knew that telling Teddy to kill Troy was a mistake, but it was all he could come up with. Now he had to try and weigh up what was going to happen next. He knew that Troy didn't trust him and that was a problem. He would speak to Eddie the Jew about what to do next.

Kevin dropped Troy off at his unit and went over to see Eddie.

Eddie the Jew was still at home when Kevin rung the outside doorbell. Eddie asked who it was and then pressed the buzzer, and Kevin entered the luxury apartment that Eddie lived in. When Kevin walked in, Eddie escorted him into his study, a richly panelled room that had a large antique desk. Eddie sat behind the desk and asked Kevin what had happened. Kevin sat in a plush leather chair and started to tell Eddie word for word what had happened. He explained how they had tracked down Tony and followed him to a secluded boat ramp and how they had searched the Shark Cat and how they had looked through the van that Tony was driving to load up the abalone. Then how they had followed the van back to the factory and searched the factory, then how they had gone on board the fishing boat at the marina and how they had been overpowered and how they nearly got themselves killed by underestimating Teddy and his gang.

He also told Eddie about the crazy Pommy bastard that wanted to slit their throats and how Troy had shit himself out of pure terror. He also added that he suggested that Teddy kill Troy to let everyone know that they were serious.

Eddie listened in silence, and when Kevin had finished, he thought for a moment and said. 'Thank you for being so honest. I can see you made a few mistakes, but you're only human, and I know that you believe that they haven't got the drugs. I feel that you did everything that you could to get the drugs back to me. I must conclude that the drugs were never picked up, so they are still out there. They could be anywhere by now, impossible for anyone to find. How do you feel about, Troy? Are you satisfied that he is still one of us or do you think that he might have second thoughts about staying with the program?'

Kevin knew that Eddie could see through any lies that he told, so he had to be honest. 'I think that Troy isn't happy with me for suggesting that Teddy "knock" him to show that he meant business. I reckon that Troy will have a good think about what to do next.'

Eddie looked at Kevin and said. 'We may have a problem with Troy as he knows far too much for either of us to just let go. He will have to be silenced, once and for all, before he goes to the drug squad and does a deal.'

Kevin looked at his boss and slowly nodded. He knew that the axe had just fallen on Troy and he was partly to blame.

'When do you want me to do it?' Kevin asked.

Eddie slowly looked up and said, 'As soon as possible, the longer that we wait, the more likely Troy is to confess to the police.'

Eddie picked up his 'special' phone. It was a phone that was used only for the drug business and rang Troy's home number.

Troy answered and Eddie said, 'Hullo, Troy, how are you feeling?'

Troy replied, 'I'm a lot better now. Thanks, Eddie. I've had a shower and a clean-up. I'm just on my way out to buy a new phone.'

Eddie replied, 'That's great news. I wonder if you could drop in and see me! We can go over a few things that happened over the last couple of days. I can send Kevin over to pick you up.'

Troy said, 'Eddie, I'm not too impressed about Kevin's behaviour. He hung me out to dry, and he wanted those pricks to kill me, to show they were serious. I'm not happy about working with him again.'

'Yes, yes,' Eddie soothed, 'I'll speak to Kevin about that when we are all together. In fact, I'll get Kevin to drive me over and we can all sort it all out. We'll see you in about half an hour.'

Kevin and Eddie drove over to Troy's unit in Eddie's Mercedes Benz. Eddie sat in the rear and Kevin drove. When they got to Troy's unit, he was waiting outside in the drive. They picked him up, and Troy sat in the rear with Eddie.

'I hope that you don't mind us going for a drive into the country as I've got a property that I want to have a look at by the ocean. It will only take us a few minutes.

Troy said that he didn't mind and soon they were on the freeway and heading towards the ocean.

Eddie asked Troy about the events that occurred the previous day. He agreed that in his mind that the poachers didn't have the drugs and that they were probably still at sea, the homing beacon hadn't been activated, who knows where the drums will end up.

Kevin turned off the road and they made their way to a viewing point that looked over the ocean.

Eddie said, 'I love the view from here.'

They all got out of the car and walked across to the viewing platform. The wind had whipped up the seas, and they all looked out towards the ocean.

Eddie said, 'I wish that I didn't have to do this, but what else can I do?'

He shot Troy twice in the back.

Troy staggered towards the viewing area fence, his face distorted in pain.

Kevin grabbed him under the arms and heaved him over the waist-high fence, and Troy toppled over the edge onto the rocks below.

The surf picked up his body and slammed it into the cliff face.

They looked on and saw the waves crashing into Troy's lifeless body.

Eddie said, 'Come on, Kev, our work here is done.'

With that, they walked back to the car and drove away.

Teddy and Tom went around to Derek's processing factory and walked into Derek's office. 'How's it going, mate?' Teddy asked.

Derek looked up and smiled a genuine smile of friendship. 'Mate, it's good. It's splendid. Those green lip abalone are a winner. Everyone wants them. I had no problem selling them. In fact, I could sell all you boys can get hold of.'

Teddy asked, 'Did you put aside a hundred kilos for Henry?'

Derek nodded and said. 'I sure did. He will be happy when he spots these little charmers.'

'How did we end up? What was our total weight?' Teddy asked.

Derek got the weight in sheets. The first lot was twelve hundred kilos. The second lot was eleven hundred and fifty kilos. The final lot was, after we took out the hundred kilos for Henry, thirteen hundred and twenty kilos. Making the grand sum of three thousand, six hundred and seventy kilos, and at our agreed price of forty dollars a kilo, you end up with one hundred and forty-six thousand, eight hundred dollars. I've got the cash for the first two loads here, and I'm going to go and get the last lot this afternoon. The bank has got it all ready.'

Teddy smiled at Tom and said, 'Not bad for a few days' work, is it mate?'

Tom laughed and said, 'We nearly weren't here to pick it up.'

All the men realised just how close it came to being a real mess.

Teddy shook his head and said, 'Let's hope that we don't hear any more about drugs and drums floating in the ocean ever again, I wonder where those drums ended up.

Ho Yee Fat looked out the porthole of the container ship and wondered what went wrong with the pickup. It wasn't his fault that the people that were supposed to pick up the drums didn't do it the right way. He knew that he would be paid as he had done everything that was expected of him. He was aware that his was a dangerous business and that everything was good as long as everything went according to plan. He wondered if he would be expected to do the same on the next trip, who knows?

Teddy and Tom loaded up the one hundred kilos and went around to Henry's restaurant. Teddy knocked at the rear door and Henry's father opened it and said with a smile, 'Hullo, Tiddy, how are you?'

Teddy laughed at the mangled attempt of his name. 'Hullo, old mate, I'm a fit as a young bull and twice as dangerous. Where is my girlfriend?'

Henry's mother laughed and went a couple of shades red as Teddy always referred to Henry's mother as his girlfriend. All the people in the kitchen laughed at how embarrassed she got whenever Teddy came into the kitchen.

Teddy and Tom carried in the bins that held the abalone, and all the people in the kitchen crowded around. It was unusual to see green lip abalone, and they looked to be in prime condition. Henry's father beamed. Henry was very pleased as he knew that he would have no trouble in getting rid of these. He might even be able to charge a little bit more as green lip abalone was very hard to come by.

Henry got Teddy's money out of the safe and thanked him for delivering the abalone.

Teddy was tired and feeling happy that all had gone well. He and Tom called back into Derek's factory and picked up the money that was owed and they all headed back to Curly's shed for a few beers and to 'Whack up' the money.

Des and Barry got five thousand between them. Tony got one thousand four hundred. Food and fuel counted for two thousand, four thousand, that left one hundred and thirty-eight thousand to be split four ways which equalled thirty-four thousand, five hundred dollars each. Teddy still had the four thousand that Henry had given him. He would keep that aside for their next adventure; give them something to work with.

Everyone was happy, everyone but Eddie. It seemed that whenever he got involved with those fucking abalone poachers, he came off second best.

Months later, on a sandy beach in the south west of Tasmania, Wayne and Sara Henderson were walking along the shoreline of a magnificent isolated little bay.

The beauty was pristine. The sand was an almost white colour.

The hot sun shone down on them and almost as one they started to undress.

Wayne looked at his wife of three years and said. 'I feel like crying. It's so beautiful, so totally untouched by human hands, I feel like Adam and Eve. There is no one around for fifty miles.'

Sara laughed and said, 'Typical, this beauty is broken by man-made rubbish, look at those two plastic drums.' Wayne looked at the two plastic drums that had washed up into the centre of the beach; they had obviously been in the water for some time as they were encrusted with barnacles and weeds.

'I wonder what's in them,' Wayne queried.

'Probably rubbish from a Japanese trawler, they don't care about our beaches,' Sarah said.

Wayne walked up to them and stood them up. 'I'll unscrew the tops and see what's inside of them.'

'Be careful,' Sarah warned.

Wayne got to and started to unscrew the lid. It came off surprisingly easy.

'It looks like some sort of sugar or something,' Wayne said.

Sarah said, 'Unscrew the other one.'

Wayne unscrewed the other one and the same mixture was in it.

He tipped both drums out and Sarah said, 'I reckon that it's some sort of bread mix.'

Wayne looked at the pile of unappetising mix that was on the sand and said, 'I didn't know that Japanese ate bread. I suppose that they get sick of rice.'

Interest soon faded in the mess and Wayne looked at his near-naked wife and said, 'I've just had a thought, we are here all alone and you've got most of your gear off.'

Sarah looked at her husband and said, 'I've got the same idea,' and gave Wayne a long lingering kiss.

The waves gently washed away the pile of whatever it was that was in the black plastic containers.

Pedra Branca
AD 1642

bel Tasman, the Dutch explorer, looked through his telescope at the small island off his port bow and remarked to his first mate. 'This little island is in the middle of nowhere. It has a striking resemblance to Pedra Branca, that's in the South China Seas, so I think that I will name it just that.'

Tasman led the first-known European expedition to sight Tasmania, and in his journal, on 29 November 1642, he noted that the island was about 4 miles (6.4 kilometres) from the mainland of Tasmania. At the time a Dutch mile was about 5.8 kilometres, so 4 Dutch miles would be 23 kilometres which is very close to the distance Pedra Branca is from Tasmania at the South East Cape.

Pedra Branca is a 2.5-ha rock or small island about 26 kilometres south-sout-east of South East Cape, Tasmania. It is known for its inaccessibility, rich marine wildlife, wet and windy weather, interesting geology, and large waves. The weather can be extreme on Pedra Branca and freak waves have been known to, on occasion, sweep right over the low-lying area of the islet.

It is approximately 270 metres long and 100 metres wide, and a 60-metre high pillar of rock rising towards the heavens.

The name Pedra Branca means 'White Rock' in Portuguese and is only one of two places in Australia with a name of Portuguese origin, the other being the Houtman Abrolhos Islands in Western Australia.

AD 1973

Captain Nakayama studied the radar and could see that there was no other vessel in the immediate region. His fishing vessel the Nisshin Maru No 8, a steel fishing vessel of 254 gross tons. It was steaming towards Hobart for its regular mechanical inspection and he was looking forward to a couple of days off in a port that he had been to before quite a few times.

He and his crew welcomed the friendliness of the Tasmanian people, and it would be good for the crew to unwind and relax in the many waterside hotels and restaurants. He decided that he would leave a watch on duty and go and have some sleep.

He confirmed with the watch that if there was any problem, the man on duty was to alert him immediately. The crewman bowed slightly, and the captain went below, had a shower, and slept soundly.

Unfortunately, soon the man on watch also was asleep when out of the night loomed Pedra Branca.

The Nisshin Maru hit Pedra Branca at full speed, came to a violent stop, and then slid backwards and sank into deep water within minutes.

All the crew were asleep when she ran aground. The watchman was thrown violently into the instrument panel and was knocked unconscious and never knew what hit him. He drowned as the water poured into the vessel as did almost all the other crew members.

There was only one survivor of the twenty-two crew, engineer Yoshiichi Meguro, he was still alive when the fishing vessel 'Walrus' arrived, on the scene days later.

Present Day

Teddy rolled his gold chain through his fingers and looked at his old mate, 'Bass Strait' Barry.

Barry had arranged a meeting with Teddy and was sure that he had come up with a plan that would be beneficial to everyone.

'Teddy, seeing that we all work so well and everything worked for the lot of us, we should be doing something together again,' Barry suggested.

Teddy and Barry had just done a run across to the Herd Island group and it had really worked well.

By using Berry's seventy-foot boat, everyone was comfortable and being able to have a shower and being able to sit down at a table and eat was a real comfort.

Teddy knew that the divers wouldn't mind a bit more comfort, and if Barry had a plan, then he would consider it.

'Here's what I have been thinking,' Barry enthused. 'We take the big boat over to Tasmania and really get stuck into it. I know a place where the abalone is back to back. It's not deep and it's miles away from anyone. There are no planes and almost no passing traffic. We would be able to work off the big boat and really get some weight together.'

Teddy was more than interested. He thought about it for a couple of minutes.

He knew that Dean and Curly would be happy to head off and was sure that Tom would be in it, so he asked Barry, 'Where would we be going?'

Barry leaned back in his chair and said two words, 'Pedra Branca.'

The name sent a chill up Teddy's back; he could feel the hairs on the back of his neck stand up.

Teddy leaned back and asked, 'Pedra Branca, are you sure we can do that?'

It was Barry's turn to look smug. 'Yes, mate it's as easy as shitting in bed.'

They both laughed at the old joke.

Barry went on to say, 'I'll supply the boat and the food and the grog. I'll get Des to come along to give us a hand, and maybe you can do a bit in the water, give the boys a hand.'

Teddy was impressed. It was a chance for him to get back into the water and he knew that diving was something that he had been missing.

'What's the deal? What's in it for you?' Teddy asked.

Barry was ready.

He smiled and said, 'I want twenty percent of whatever we end up with.'

Barry wasn't stupid. He had seen how well the boys had worked on their last outing and he knew that Teddy was one of the best abalone divers going. So he was sure of them getting a huge load, and he knew that Teddy was on the ball when it came to organising everything. Twenty percent was enough for him; he could sling Des a few hundred and still come out a mile in front.

The fact that what they were doing was illegal didn't bother either of them as they knew the rules and either of them didn't mind breaking any of them.

As long as Dean could remember, he and Curly had been mates. They had been together when they started school, and when they went to secondary school, they had met Tom. It was an instant success the three of them had been solid friends for years. They had started poaching abalone in Port Phillip Bay to top up their wages when they all started apprenticeships.

They had been a good team, and when they got involved with Teddy, they went from being occasional abalone poachers to full-time abalone poachers, and they were good at it, very good at it.

The three of them looked a bit odd as Tom and Curly were short and Dean was almost two hundred centimetres tall.

Tom was a small, wiry Pommy and Curly had shoulder-length blonde hair. He almost looked effeminate. Dean was of a very gentle nature, like a lot of big blokes were, and Curly was a little laid back, but Tom had a dangerous temper. He always kept a stiletto in his sock. He wasn't going to be pushed around by anyone.

Tom loved Sandy. She was a barmaid and as far as Tom was concerned, she was the 'duck's guts.'

Dean had been in a relationship, but that had slowly disintegrated as Dean had a problem with the 'punt'.

No matter how much money he ended up with, he would somehow end up with what 'Paddy shot at,' nothing!

His partner got sick of it and she ended up moving in with an SP bookie that had been on the receiving end of Dean's misfortune.

Dean regarded SP's as the enemy.

Dean was in the business end of Little Burke Street in China Town, in Melbourne. He and a group of men were playing poker, in a gambling den; the room was full of smoke and 'Orientals'. Some of the men were crowded around a table playing Mar Jong, a Chinese game a bit similar to 'Dominoes' and they were laughing and yelling out. They were really enjoying themselves.

Dean wasn't.

Dean couldn't take a trick; he was down and looked like being even worse off. He threw his cards onto the table and an oriental smiled at him and said, 'Bad ruck, Dane.'

He didn't know if the Oriental was putting shit on him or not.

'It's Dean, Dean, not fucking Dane.'

Dean could see himself losing everything that he had made on the last trip that Teddy and they had been on. That didn't worry him that much as he was sure that Teddy would be eager to get going soon as it had been a couple of weeks since they had done any work. Tom would be broke and Curly was always keen to do a bit. He finished his scotch and indicated to the waitress that he wanted a refill.

She was a stunningly beautiful Chinese girl. Dean couldn't tell her age, but she was young and beautiful. Dean drank Scotch whisky as he didn't need to go for a piss as often as when he drank beer.

'Thanks, love,' Dean said when the waitress had delivered his drink.

'You are most welcome,' the waitress replied.

'What's your name?' Dean asked.

She smiled shyly and said, 'My name is Leckie.'

Her English wasn't too bad.

'That's a lovely name. My name is Dean.'

She smiled and moved away.

Hamm Nugent looked across the table at the giant of a man and wondered where he got his money from. Dean always seemed to have money and the way he played, he didn't appear to care.

Hamm was always aware of how much money he was up or down. He kept a tally in his head; you would never see him counting his money as the game went on.

He had asked around and no one really knew what Dean did for a living. Hamm thought that he probably was a drug dealer. He knew that he was an appalling gambler, yet he never seemed to worry too much about his losses. That meant that he was able to replace any money that he had lost quickly. He must find out more about this man Dean.

Teddy and Barry discussed the weather. There was a possibility that they would get a stretch of weather soon. Barry was ready to go at short notice. His boat was fuelled up and everything was ready.

Tony, the Italian that did the running around for Teddy, had been into the marina and transferred the compressors onto Barry's boat. Along with all the gear, hoses, demand valves, weight belts, and any other things that they would need.

There was great amusement when Teddy's gear went on board as it had been a while since Teddy had actually struck a blow, diving-wise.

Teddy expected a bit of ribbing and hoped secretly that he could keep up with his more youthful companions. Time would tell.

A high was approaching Tasmania and would be there in about three days.

Barry put Teddy on alert as they might be off any day.

Teddy and the boys were ready, poised on the starting blocks.

Barry rang Teddy the next morning and explained he had been talking to some Tasmanian Lobster fisherman that went around to the west coast from Hobart. They said that they were going away as the weather was just right for them.

Teddy rang the boys and they were away.

Des, Barry's mate and occasional deckhand, was happy he was included in another trip. He got on well with Teddy and his divers, and by the sound of things, they should have a great trip.

Des were younger than Barry by a couple of year, but just as weather-beaten, and they had worked around the waters of Bass Strait for many years, they had a history of not taking shit from anyone.

Things could have worked out differently if he hadn't produced the sawn-off shotgun a few weeks ago and stared down those two gangsters when they were in trouble. Yes, he had proved his worth and was readily accepted by everyone on board.

When Dean learnt that they were going away, he rang the gambling den, and asked to speak to Leckie.

As he was such a good customer, Leckie was soon brought to the phone.

She didn't seem surprised when she heard Dean's voice.

'Hi, Leckie, it's Dean, do you remember me?'

Leckie was happy that Dean had rung as she was aware that Dean had kept his eyes on her when he was playing cards.

'Of course, I remember you, you are a nice man and you gave me a big tip. I always remember big tippers.'

Dean was happy that she had remembered him. 'Well, I have got to go away, for work, and I'll be away for more than a week. When I come back, can I take you out for some dinner one night?'

Leckie answered, 'I don't know. My uncle is very strict as he is in charge of my welfare. He watches me very carefully.'

'Well, maybe I can come and meet your uncle and we can have a talk face to face.'

Leckie was happy with that arrangement. If her uncle liked Dean, then there was a chance that they could go out together.

'When will you come into my work?' Leckie asked.

Dean said. 'I should be away about a week. I'll let you know when I'm back in town.'

Leckie smiled to herself and said, 'I will be looking forward to seeing you.'

Dean disconnected the phone and smiled. He thought that he was a chance, things were looking up.

Teddy and the boys arrived together at the marina where Barry's boat was moored. They all stepped on board and Des cast off the lines and they motored out onto the bay.

The weather was improving, and it looked like smooth sailing weather-wise.

They all sat at the galley table and talked amongst themselves.

There was a certain excitement between them as they had heard about Pedra Branca and the big wave surfers that sometimes went there, but none of them had ever dived on it.

There is only one diver they had heard of that had the courage to dive on it. He had been retired from abalone diving and done a bit of shark fishing and oyster farming, for more years than they had been alive.

It was almost like diving on virgin bottom, the excitement started to grow in them.

They steamed into the vastness of Bass Strait, taking special care to avoid the islands in the middle of the strait that had claimed many ships and a lot of lives.

Barry told Des to put his head down as he would be needed to captain the craft when Barry got tired. The boys, sick of watching the ocean go past, settled in the galley and decided to play some cards.

Teddy sat up in the wheelhouse and talked to Barry.

They reflected on the last trip when they went across to the Kent Island group and got tangled up with some drug runners. Their conversation went on to their many friends that had 'passed away' over the years and some of the funny things that had happened to them over the years.

The hours passed and they drew nearer to their destination.

Tom had gone to put his head down as he would keep Des awake for some of the night when Des took over from Barry.

The automatic pilot was on, so all you really had to do was just keep awake. Barry announced that he might have a spell and went to wake up Des.

Des came into the wheelhouse and smiled at Teddy and said, 'Are we there yet?'

Teddy laughed and said, 'No mate, we are almost halfway.'

They steamed past Tasman Island and past Fluted Cape, past the mouth of the Derwent River where the city of Hobart is and went on the outside of Bruny Island.

They crossed Adventure Bay and then past South Bruny. They steered clear of the reefs and went south towards Maatsuyker Island. The sea was calm and there wasn't any wind, the swell was dropping.

Barry, who was up and in command of the vessel, turned to his GPS and headed towards Pedra Branca, it was about forty kilometres past Maatsuyker Island.

Teddy saw that they were closing in on their target.

He said to the boys. 'Hang on to your hats, boys. We are coming in on it. We should be in the water in a couple of hours.'

Excitement rippled through everyone on board.

They all felt terrific.

Soon they would be in the water.

The divers started to get their gear together.

They all saw the pillar of rock standing sixty metres (200 feet) in the distance. They were all quiet.

Teddy spoke with some authority, he said, 'Pedra Branca is an erosional remnant of the Tasmanian mainland and it has been estimated to have separated from the mainland at least 15,000 years ago.'

There was a shocked silence from the group.

Teddy said proudly, 'I looked it up on the Internet.'

'Fucking egghead,' Tom said loud enough for Teddy to hear.

Everyone laughed.

They steamed onwards towards the pillar of rock.

Soon they were within swimming distance of Pedra Branca. It was a warm sunny day, and the divers got into their wetsuits.

Barry said. 'I reckon that the tide is about two hours away from the turn. You should be able to work for about four hours before the tide gets too strong. So when you hit the water, go like buggery before you get sucked off the reef. I've had a look at the depths and it's about thirty to forty feet deep. Be on the alert as if suddenly you feel as though you are getting pulled hard in one direction, then you know a big swell is coming. Be fucking well careful.'

With that, Barry and Des got all the diving gear ready. Soon the four divers were ready to get into the water. Des had the aluminium dinghy ready and was waiting for the divers to start.

When they came to the surface with a net bag full of abalone, he would drive over and grab the net bag and roll it into the dinghy. When he had enough net bags in the dinghy, he would then go over to the big boat and Barry would winch them up and place them in the milk crates that were stacked in the tank. This gave the abalone some room to move and stopped them suffocating on board. They would stay alive for a week in the 'well'. This also freed up the net bags.

Everything was ready to go.

Teddy said, 'Let's get this show on the road,' and they all went over the side and swam down. The water was very clear, and they could see the reef; it was a flat surface with heaps of cracks across it. The reef was the size of a football field, and when they looked over the side, they couldn't see the bottom. They could see the sides disappearing into the vastness. There wasn't a lot of weed on the reef and there were heaps of abalone.

There were thousands of them.

Teddy was sharing a 'T' piece with Tom, and they looked at each other and gave the thumbs up. Both of then thought that this was like taking corn off a blind chook.

They started to work chipping off abalone as fast as they could. Although they worked close together, they had about forty feet of air line from the 'T' piece each so that meant that Teddy could go to the surface with his net bag and Tom could stay on the bottom working until his net was full and then he could go to the top and Teddy could stay down chipping abalone.

It only took ten minutes and Tom was on the surface with a full net bag.

Des made his way over to Tom, and Tom grabbed the side of the dinghy.

Des said, 'Mate that didn't take too long.'

Tom laughed and said. 'Des, they are back to back down there. There is a boat load down there just waiting for us to pick them up.' Des rolled the net bag into the dinghy, and Tom headed back down to where he had left off.

Dean was on the surface, and Des went over to him and said much the same, 'Jesus, that was quick.'

Dean looked at Des and said, 'Have the others been up yet?'

Des laughed and said, 'Yes, Tom has been up.' '

No sign of Teddy?' Dean asked.

'No, not yet, but he will be up soon,' Des replied.

Dean said. 'Keep a count of how we are going and tell us who has got the most bags when we knock off.' Des said that he would.

He looked up and saw that Teddy was on the surface. He went over to get his net bag.

'How are you going?' Des asked Teddy.

Teddy answered, 'I'm going like a steam train, just starting to warm up.' Teddy swam towards the bottom again.

Soon Curly was on the surface and Des went over and grabbed his bag. Curly just winked at Des and didn't say anything before he went down to the bottom again.

The day wore on, and Des made his way over to the big boat and unloaded the net bags into the well.

They worked like this for hours. None of the divers was slowing down. As the hours passed, the current got stronger and stronger.

Soon it was impossible to stay on the bottom and the divers were spending time holding on and it was getting harder and harder not to drift away from your companion diver when you went to the surface.

The divers came up two by two and climbed into the dinghy as they had had enough.

Teddy was exhausted. He hadn't realised just how out of condition that he was. The others were also tired. Teddy and Tom had the most nets.

Curly laughed and said. 'Tomorrow Teddy will be stiff and sore. He won't be able to do any good.'

Teddy laughed and said, 'Wait and see, you young whippersnapper'.

Everyone on board laughed.

She was a Great White Shark; she was afraid of nothing in any of the oceans anywhere in the world. Her official title was Carcharodon Carcharias, also known as great white, white pointer, white shark, or white death. She was a direct descendant of the prehistoric shark the Megalodon, a monster that would not have been afraid of anything on earth sixteen million years ago.

She had reached her sexual maturity at fifteen years of age, and she was about twenty years of age and about eighteen feet in length. She was in the prime of her life, and she had given birth twice.

Great white sharks are ovoviviparous, that means that her eggs develop in the uterus and continue to develop until birth. The Sharks' powerful jaws begin to develop in the first month and the unborn sharks eat each other; the stronger eat, the weaker ones.

She was moving towards the coast of Tasmania and was aware that, at times, seals rested out of the water on the flat areas of Pedra Branca. Instinct told her that there may be food in the way of tired seals, so she pressed on.

She was carnivorous and would eat anything such as fish, other sharks, dolphins, sea lions, otters, and sea birds. She had bitten all sorts of things to find out if they were edible. She preferred prey with a high content of energy-rich fat.

She had, like many other types of sharks, rows of serrated teeth behind the main ones, ready to replace any teeth that break off. Also like other sharks, she could detect any movement of fish or other creatures around her.

Every time a living creature moves, it generates an electric field and she was so sensitive that she could detect a half a billionth of a volt. She had swum past the boys as they were working and was attracted by their movement. She sensed them from miles away and never got close enough to them to be seen by their weak eyesight.

As the tide got stronger, Teddy and the boys gave up and they all climbed into the dinghy and then onto Barry's wooden boat. They were all tired and glad to be able to have a shower and a rest.

As the sun started to sink in the west, they gathered around the BBQ and watched as Des got some steaks going. The divers had all got a couple of lobsters on their way up, and they were about to be drowned and then split down the middle. Then put onto the grill and cooked in their own juices with a bit of garlic butter, everyone looked forward to the late-night snack.

Everyone relaxed after their meals and Des started to prepare the lobsters. He was down the rear of the boat when he thought that he saw something break the water.

Probably a seal, he said to himself and thought nothing more of it.

The great white broke the surface quietly and could sense the smell of the barbecue and she stayed on the surface with her nose out of the water for a short time. Then with a flick of her tail, she submerged and moved over towards the island and began her wait for a seal to get careless.

Everyone on board feasted on the crayfish and soon they began to get sleepy.

Teddy, in particular, was almost asleep on his feet.

He said to no one, in particular. 'That's it. I'm stuffed. I'm off to the bunk. I'm not used to working this hard.'

They all agreed that it was time to hit the sack, so they all wandered off and got into bed.

Early next morning, they were all awakened by the noise from the galley as Des and Barry started to knock up a bit of breakfast. The smell of freshly percolated coffee and freshly baked bread filled the air.

They were all in good spirits after a good night's sleep.

'This is living,' Dean said, and Tom replied, 'Yep, this is the life.'

They all moved out onto the rear deck and looked towards the pinnacle of rock that towered above them.

She had been lying in wait for a seal to swim above her and soon enough the bull seal slid into the water and started to swim around his harem, getting them onshore.

He was a fierce predator and had many scars on his body; scars that he had obtained from fighting younger male seals who wanted to get rid of him and take over his harem of females. None had been successful, he was the leader.

With devastating speed, the great white shark erupted from the bottom and surged towards the dominant male seal. She hit the seal at fifty kilometres an hour and she weighed over 2,000 kilograms.

The white pointer had the ability to be able to bite down with 4,000 lbs.

She smashed into the seal with such force that she came out of the water almost halfway. With the seal in her mouth, she smashed down back into the water causing a large splash and causing the other terrified seals to drag themselves up higher onto the rocks.

The seals that were in the water quickly got out onto the beach and rocks.

She shook her head and her serrated teeth tore through the seal's skin and blood soon spread in the water. She gulped down a huge mouthful of the rich fatty flesh and attacked the carcass again.

She then took what was left of the seal and swam away into the depths.

The boys were on the rear deck and watched in horror as the great white shark killed, then gulped down mouthfuls of the unfortunate seal, and then swam off into the deeper water.

Dean was the first to speak. 'Fuck me dead,' he gasped. 'Did you see that?'

There was a silence and then reality hit, it could be one of them, one of them could, at this very moment be getting devoured by the great white shark.

Teddy took control of the situation. 'Shit, that was one hungry shark. I bet it won't want to eat for another week or so.'

Tom looked at him and said, 'I fucking well hope not.'

Curly said, 'That's the first time that I've ever seen a shark take out a seal like that.'

There was a silence among them.

Barry said, 'I saw that sort of thing before. It takes a bit of getting used to.'

Des laughed and said. 'Yes, it certainly takes a bit of getting used to. I'm glad the fuckers don't have legs and can chase you up the beach.'

The thought of that made everybody laugh, more from nerves that anything else.

Tom said, 'Let's get into our wetsuits and we'll see what's down there.'

Teddy said, 'Yes, let's see what's going on. Barry, have we got the power heads?'

Barry gave him a nod and said, 'I've got two of them, will that do?'

Teddy nodded. 'Tom, you and I will go down and have a look around. If we see anything, then we will whack one of these into it. That should settle things down a bit.'

Tom looked at Teddy and said, 'Let's get going, and sort these bastards out.'

With that they all started to get into their wetsuits, soon they were ready to go.

Teddy and Tom carefully lowered themselves into the water and looked around, power heads at the ready. Teddy had a Hawaiian sling and Tom had a gas-operated spear gun.

The water was clear, and they could see the top of the reef.

They could see where they had worked yesterday as when an abalone is taken off a rock, it leaves what the divers call a scar. That is where the abalone sits, there is no weed growth, and the spot where the abalone sat is bare, clean rock and shows up as white where the rest of the rock is a darker colour. There were plenty of scars and even more abalone left on the reef.

Teddy wanted to get going, so he gave Tom the thumbs up and then swam to the surface and gave Dean and Curly the thumbs up. They didn't look too enthusiastic but seeing their mates were in the water, they felt that they had to go in also.

Barry threw in a heap of net bags and Des got the dinghy ready, soon they were all on the top of the reef and working away. They all kept their eyes open for sharks, but as the day wore on, they relaxed a bit more.

The day was calm and the sun beat down on Des as he went from one diver to another one in the dinghy picking up the full net bags and then returned to Barry's big boat. Barry winched up the net bags and put them into the tank.

All was going well and the seals seemed to have convinced themselves that there was no danger, so they started to play with the divers.

Dean was busy chipping off abalone when suddenly something grabbed his flipper and gave it a tug. He swung around and nearly shit himself when he saw a large form attached to his fin. It was a seal, a seal that was in a playful mood, maybe looking for a mate now that the boss seal was no longer around.

Dean looked across at Curly and saw that he was laughing at the situation that Dean was in. Dean gave Curly the finger and whacked at the seal with his abalone iron. The seal soon lost all interest and swam off, Dean's heart rate soon got back to normal.

The tide was beginning to pick up and the divers were soon in a situation that they were pushed by the force of the water current from the reef and out into the bottomless water. This was making them all very uneasy, so Teddy gave them all the thumbs up and they filled their last net bags for the day and headed for the surface and the big boat.

When the last of the net bags full of abalone were in the well and the boys had finished, they all started to get out of their wetsuits.

Teddy and Barry began to work out how many nets that they had for the two days. Barry had kept a count and by his reckoning, there were sixty the first day and fifty today, that made one hundred and ten net bags a together. If each net bag had sixty kilos of shell in them, that would break down to twenty kilos of meat that would mean that they had eighty-eight thousand dollars' worth of abalone on board.

His whack out of that was good. Barry was very happy with the results so far.

After they had finished dinner, they sat around and talked, the subject of shark attacks came up and they all recounted their own stories of their run-ins with sharks.

Teddy said. 'I stopped shooting sharks years ago as you are never going to see the shark that kills you. It will hit you from out of nowhere and at about fifty kilometres an hour and weigh a couple of tonnes. They are mainly just curious and only want to have a closer look at you. I remember when I was diving for abalone out of Eden in New South Wales, in the sixties we were getting forty-three cents a pound for abalone meat and thirty-five cents a pound for shark meat. The abalone were so small in NSW that there were about ten abalone to the pound. So whenever you saw a shark, you would immediately whack a power head into it and then swim it up to your boat and the deckhand would cut off its head, bleed and gut it, and put it under a wet bag to keep it from going off and you would sell it with your abalone.'

All the younger divers looked at Teddy and didn't know if he was kidding with them or not. It seemed like bullshit to them, but Teddy assured them that it was an actual story.

'Ahh, the good old days,' Teddy mused, 'I don't fucking well miss them at all, nope not one little bit.'

They all laughed.

Teddy, for the second night, said, 'I'm beat. I'm off to bed, good night all.' He left for bed. The others concluded that they were also tired and they hit the sack.

The next morning everyone was up and ready. Barry said, 'There is bad weather on its way. I reckon that we will get most of today in, but no more.'

No one questioned what Barry said, as he had been around too long and he had a good grasp of the weather conditions.

Teddy and Tom were first into the water and swam down to the bottom. They kept their eyes open for any sharks. They started chipping abalone off the bottom. They saw Dean and Curly swim down and start working. Teddy and Tom had taken their 'power heads' down with them and left them on the bottom just in case they had a problem with any sharks. All seemed quiet. They worked solidly for an hour.

Whenever Teddy took up a net bag, he asked Des what the weather was like. Des could see the weather was getting worse and worse and he relayed the information on to Teddy.

Suddenly the sea surged one way. All the boys hung on to whatever they could get their hands onto as they realised that a big swell was coming.

They braced themselves as the water surged against them. Teddy could see that they were all hanging on for all they were worth. Then the wave hit them. They were forced in the other direction. Tom was twisted off the face of the reef and was washed off into the clear sea. He couldn't see the bottom. When he got to the end of his air hose, he dragged Teddy into the abyss, they both struck for the surface.

The wave, which was huge and fizzling on top, hit Barry's seventy-foot boat with such force that Barry was caught off guard. He crashed heavily into the wheel and was winded. The boat shot backwards and the anchor was pulled from among the rocks, as the boat was washed away off the reef. The anchor was left dangling in the vast emptiness of the ocean.

As the seventy-foot boat was washed backwards, Dean and Curly were pulled by their air hoses into the abyss. Curly let go of his half full net bag and it fell out of sight into the murky depths of the ocean. Dean kept hold of his and quickly filled the parachute with air. Curly swam over to Dean's net bag and hung on to it for dear life.

When they reached the surface, he spat out his demand valve and said to Dean. 'Bugger me that was some sort of wave. Are the other boys all right?'

Dean removed his demand valve and said. 'Yes, I can see them. They are both on the surface. They seem OK.'

Barry frantically started the boat and made his way to where the divers were.

Des had ridden the wave out, in the dinghy, and when he saw it looming up to him, he steered the dinghy into it and rode over it. When he was on the top of it, he was almost forty feet above the ocean. He had glimpsed it before it had hit them all and was straight across to Teddy and Tom.

'Are you boys all right?' He asked.

Teddy said. 'Yes, mate we are right. How are the others?'

Des replied. 'They are both on the surface. They're all right.'

Teddy and Tom got into the dinghy and Des made his way over to the other pair. They also got on board. Dean said, 'Fuck me dead, that was a monster wave, I wonder what height it was?'

Teddy muttered. 'Both my ears popped. There was a lot of water in the bastard.'

Tom laughed, 'My arse popped when I was dragged into the middle of nowhere.'

Des drove them back to Barry's boat.

The weather was starting to deteriorate, and their diving was over for this trip. They climbed aboard and Barry said, 'I didn't see the bastard coming. It hit with such force that it bashed me into the wheel, took the wind out of me. I must be getting old. That was a stupid mistake, not seeing that coming.'

'Let's get out of our wetsuits and get dry,' Teddy suggested.

Barry wound up the anchor and they headed to sea, towards home.

'When you are all dry and warm, we will start shucking out the abalone,' Barry suggested.

Everyone was happy with that and they all went and changed out of their wetsuits.

Barry pumped the water out of the tank and Dean got down and started to pass up the wire milk crates that had held the abalone. Soon there was a stack of them on the deck. They started tipping out the abalone and everybody got into shucking them. They were shucked into draining bins so they could bleed soon the clear blood was running across the deck. After a couple of hours, Des stopped and started to get some dinner ready, soon they could smell the meat cooking.

Teddy said, 'I didn't realise how hungry I was until I smelt the meat cooking.' Everyone agreed.

Soon they were sitting down to a lamb chops and vegetables.

They 'shucked out' all the abalone and had them bagged up in thick, clear, plastic bags and stored them in the now dry 'tank'. There were a lot of them.

Barry set the course for home and they sailed into the night.

Although the weather was windy and cold outside, inside the wheelhouse was cosy and warm. Teddy and Barry spoke quietly and stared into the darkness.

'Where are we going to unload?' Barry asked Teddy.

Teddy asked. 'Will it be dark when we hit Melbourne? It's too risky to unload in broad daylight, anybody could spot us and drop a dime and report us to the fisheries.' Barry nodded.

Teddy replied. 'Yes, I reckon that we should unload some-where quiet in Port Philip Bay. That will make it harder for us to be spotted by anyone.'

Teddy thought for a while and came up with the plan that they would use the same little boat ramp that they used a couple of weeks ago. 'We'll go through the heads at night and motor over to the boat ramp near Werribee. I'll give Tony a ring and have him waiting for us with a bigger truck and we'll unload into that. Then we'll motor over to the marina and tie up.'

Barry agreed that would work. They steamed into the night.

With the sun rising in the east, Barry and Teddy were relieved of their duties, and Des and Tom took over. Barry told Des that they wanted to go through the heads into Port Phillip Bay just after dark and that they would be pulling into the boat ramp that they had visited last time they were out and about.

Barry and Teddy headed to their bunks and grabbed some sleep.

Some time later, after he had been asleep for a while, Teddy got up and made his way to the galley table. The divers were playing cards. Dean was way up. They only played for matches and Dean had a pile in front of him.

He looked up at Teddy and said, 'How come I can win when we play for matches but when I play for money, I don't do any good?'

Teddy shook his head and said. 'Mate, it's only money. When you get back, you will more than likely continue with your run of good luck.'

'I hope so,' Dean muttered.

Tom asked Teddy, 'How much meat do you reckon that we ended up with?'

Teddy had been thinking about it and answered. 'I reckon that we have got about three and a half tonne of meat in plastic bags, so when we work it all out, we should end up with about twenty-five thousand dollars each.'

All the divers looked pretty pleased with themselves.

They steamed all day and just on dark, they made their way through the heads of Port Phillip Bay. A couple of hours later, they approached the little boat ramp. Barry couldn't get right in as his boat drew about ten feet, so they lifted the dinghy off the deck and Des climbed into it. The rest of the boys started filling it up with bags of abalone meat.

Teddy asked Dean to go ashore and give Tony a hand to load up the truck.

Dean, Des, and Tony soon had the dinghy unloaded, and Des drove out to the big boat and repeated the operation. Soon all the meat was in the truck that Tony had arrived in and with a wave; he was off to the factory.

Des and Dean made their way back out to the big boat and they lifted the dinghy aboard and headed off towards the lights of the city.

Tony rang Derek the processor and said that he was on his way.

Derek drove to his factory and he and Tony weighed up the abalone. Tony counted the empty bags and they all tallied up.

There were three thousand seven hundred kilos of abalone meat. Tony rang Teddy and told him the amount. 'Thanks, mate, Teddy said, I reckoned that there was about that much.'

Teddy rang Henry at the restaurant and asked him if he wanted a hundred kilos. Henry was happy to get the abalone, and he started to ring around and sell what he didn't need for himself.

Derek and his team at the factory began to pack away the abalone meat and stacked it in the blast freezer; soon it would be on its way overseas.

Teddy and the rest of the crew motored across Port Phillip Bay and into the marina; they were all relaxed and happy that their work was done.

Dean was looking forward to making contact with the Chinese waitress that that had served him when he was last in the gambling den.

First they would all go and have a proper shower and clean up a bit, and Teddy would get them all their money and they would square up back at Curly's shed and have a beer and a game of pool.

Hamm Nugent was at the gambling den.

As usual he was looking for someone that was wealthy and stupid enough to play poker with him. He considered himself to be steps ahead of any of the other players that he encountered at this venue.

He had played at the Casino but found that it was to 'In your face.' It was like you were on display and he hated the way people crowded around you and he didn't like the friendly attitude of the Australians.

There was no respect among them. They treated him like some sort of idiot.

They didn't realise just how lucky that they were to be in a country as rich as this one.

They would have treated him differently if they knew just who they were dealing with. He was a man that had killed people, in his own country, those that stood in his way, for he had a dream and that was to be rich, rich beyond most people's dreams. He could get rich in this country and then go back to his native Vietnam and live like a king.

Hamm ran brothels, mostly illegal, and they were very profitable, staffing them was easy. He spoke Mandarin, as well as a couple of other languages. He had also mastered English, so when the girls came in looking for a job, he could speak to them in their own language and they felt less intimidated.

When he explained to them how much money they could earn, then it was all too easy. Some were unwilling at first, but they were easily persuaded to do whatever the customer wanted them to do and they got to keep a third of whatever Hamm decided to charge them.

Most of the girls were Asian.

Hamm found that the Australian men liked the smaller bodies of the Asian girls, and as most of them couldn't speak English, all they did was smile, pretty simple job really.

It was strange how the men treated the girls.

Some of the men treated them like princesses and were very polite and gentle, and some of the men treated them like slaves and were a bit rough on them. Some of the girls complained but most realised that it was just their lot and went on with business.

Hamm employed some black islanders for the girl's protection. They were enormous, ape-like people, morons who could hardly speak any language, and Hamm wondered just how they fed themselves. He laughed to himself as he knew that some of the Islanders would at times fall in love with the women in the brothels and struggle when they went into the bedrooms with drunken strangers.

Fools, he thought to himself.

He watched as Leckie, one of the young waitresses, served a drink to a man three times her age and smiled as he saw the old fool slip her a twenty-dollar note as a tip. He thought that she would be a great attraction to one of his business establishments. Yes, she would get the fools through the door. He would ask around and find out more about her.

Teddy and Tom walked out of Derek's factory with a 'Target' plastic bag full of money.

Teddy felt pretty pleased with himself.

The bag contained one hundred and forty-four thousand dollars, and he had worked out that Barry would get twenty-eight thousand and eight hundred dollars, and they would split up the rest, one hundred and fifteen thousand and two hundred dollars and they all would get about the same. The four thousand dollars from Henry's would go to paying Tony's wagers and whatever else was due to be paid. Yes, Teddy was pretty happy with himself.

He and Tom headed towards Curly's shed for the 'whack up'.

All the divers were at Curly's shed when Teddy arrived. He and Tom were handed beers and they drank them thirstily down.

'That feels better,' said Teddy, and he started handing out the money. All the boys were happy and there was laughter in the room, soon they all had their money and started to get about their businesses.

Tom headed off to see Sandy, and Teddy headed home to see Rita, and Dean thought that he might catch a few hands of poker at the card game that was always on above the restaurant in China Town. Maybe catch up with Leckie if she was there, yes that was the plan.

When Dean entered the smoke-filled room, he immediately noticed that Leckie was on duty.

He smiled at her when she looked at him. She smiled back, and he walked over to where she was waiting for some drinks to be made up for her to deliver to a group of mainly Asian men.

She tried to sound casual, but her heart was racing, 'I see you are back from your work.' Leckie said.

'Yes, I'm back,' Dean stated, 'I'm back and looking for a few hands of poker, what time do you knock off?' Dean inquired.

Leckie looked around the room and said, 'The next shift starts in about an hour's time. As soon as my replacement comes in, I can stop work.'

Dean smiled and said, 'What about coming and having a coffee with me before you go home?'

Leckie nodded and said. 'I would like that. I'll talk to you when I finish.'

Dean nodded and went and sat it an empty seat at a table.

Hamm Nugent felt his pulse quicken when he saw Dean sit in the empty space that was on his table.

He looked at Dean and said, 'Hullo, Dane, have you been away?'

Dean acknowledged the Asian man with a nod and said, 'I have been away working and I have just got back and I felt like a game of cards.'

He threw a folded wad of one hundred dollar bills onto the table and the dealer quickly counted them and gave Dean some chips.

Dean started to play cards.

As soon as Leckie was able to she changed into her street clothes and went over to Dean's table. He put his chips into his pocket and stood up.

Hamm said, 'You're not going, are you, Dane?'

Dean said, 'It's Dean, not Dane and I'm heading off. I've got better things to do than sit here with you blokes.'

With that, Dean stood up and made his way, with Leckie, to the door.

Hamm looked after the pair of them and thought that they must be together; he would ask Leckie about what Dean did for a living and where he got his money from.

Dean and Leckie walked along the street, and Dean asked where she would like to go, would she like a coffee or something to eat. Leckie suggested that they go somewhere like McDonalds. That suited Dean as he was OK with casual dining. They walked into the restaurant and ordered their meals. They took them and sat at a booth and started talking.

Dean explained that he was an abalone diver and had to work away from time to time and that he and a group of friends worked together. When they all went away, their partners stayed at home.

He explained that he, Curly, and Tom had been friends for a long time, ever since school and that they had met up with Teddy a few years ago and had worked together ever since, they were like brothers to each other.

Leckie listened and thought what a lovely person that Dean was. He was like a young boy at times when he talked about the group's adventures and she could sense that the team were very close.

Time sped by, and Leckie said suddenly. 'I must go as my uncle is very strict with me. He says that he is responsible for my safety in Australia. As my family is in China, and the only way that my Mother would allow me to come over to Australia was if I stayed with my uncle. He is very strict, but a good man and he wants only the best for me.'

Leckie got to her feet and Dean said, 'I've got my car. Let me drive you home.'

Leckie said with a bit of sadness. 'I do not know you well enough to ride in your car alone with you. I can catch the tram and then my uncle won't worry.'

Dean said, 'All right, can I come with you on the tram?'

Leckie laughed and said, 'I can't stop you travelling on the tram.'

So they caught the tram and both rode through Melbourne city and across to Richmond.

Leckie said. 'The next stop is where I get off. It's only a short walk to my uncle's apartment.'

'Can I walk you to your door?' Dean asked.

Leckie frowned and said. 'It would not be wise for my uncle to see you this soon as I will have to tell him carefully that I have met an Australian and want to see him again.'

Dean was elated that Leckie wanted to see him again, so he let her get off the tram alone and watched her walk along the street and turn into a block of flats. He had arranged to meet her again the next day night for another take away meal.

Dean was as happy as he had been in a long time.

When he got home, he rang Curly and told him about his first date with Leckie. Curly was happy for him as Curly knew just how hard Dean had taken it when his last girlfriend had left.

From then on, every day Dean went into the gambler's den and waited for Leckie to finish work. Then they would spend some time together and then they would both get the tram back to Lecki's uncle's unit.

One night when it was raining, Dean said to Leckie, 'I don't want you walking in the rain. Why don't you let me drive you home and not get wet?'

Leckie thought about this and decided to agree, so Dean drove Leckie home and said, 'From now on I will drive you home after work.'

Leckie agreed and said, 'You must meet my uncle.'

Dean agreed and they made their way upstairs to where the uncle and his wife lived.

Leckie opened the door with her key and she said something in Mandarin. Her uncle stood up and smiled at Dean as Leckie introduced them.

Leckie introduced the uncle as George.

George was a middle-aged roly-poly, a Chinese man, with a great smile and a happy disposition. He seemed pleased to meet one of his niece's friends. They stood awkwardly for a few seconds until George ushered Dean to a chair, and when George's wife timidly entered the room, Dean stood up and towered above her. She quaked at his enormous size. She smiled shyly and Dean smiled and nodded.

He said, 'I'm very pleased to meet you.'

She and Leckie went to make some coffee and left Dean and George to talk alone.

George asked, 'What do you do for a living?'

Dean answered, 'I'm a diver, an abalone diver.'

'I believe that that is a very dangerous occupation.' George said thoughtfully.

Dean smiled and said, 'Yes, it can be but you have to be very careful and not take risks.'

George nodded and asked, 'There is a lot of money in it, isn't there?'

Dean answered. 'Yes, but there are also a lot of expenses in it as well. It's like everything.'

The girls brought in the coffee, and they all sat around and talked.

Dean really liked George and his wife, and when Leckie walked him to his car, she was excited and happy that they had all got on so well with each other.

Soon Dean and Leckie was an item.

They met every night after Leckie had finished work and Dean really fell in love with Leckie.

Hamm Nugent watched with interest the developing love affair that was going on between Dean and Leckie. He had trouble understanding their love for each other as he had never been in love and thought that women were only here to reproduce and clean up the house.

They were as he understood, chattels to be used and abused.

He still had a strong idea that he could by fair means or foul get Leckie into his line of work, she was young and strong and her beauty would last for years.

He schemed and came up with the idea. He would approach her and ask her if she would start as a receptionist. Once she was there, she would realise how much money that she could earn by going with the customer rather than just welcoming them inside. He would introduce her to the 'uppers' and then the 'downers' and soon she would be hooked. She would be totally under his control.

He had done it before and it was easy.

Little by little he would gain control over her and soon she would be at his mercy.

He smiled to himself and watched as Leckie supplied drinks to the card players.

He made his approach one night when things were slow and Leckie was in between delivering drinks to the card players.

He boldly said. 'You are a beautiful young lady and my company is looking for young women to be receptionists in our many offices. The money is excellent and you get to meet lots of people.'

Leckie smiled and said. 'Thank you, I am tired of working here and just being a waitress. I would like to be doing something a bit more challenging than getting drinks for gamblers. I have quite a good education.'

Hamm smiled and said. 'I thought that you were well educated by the way you portray yourself. The job on offer is worth one thousand dollars a week to you.'

Leckie was surprised by the offer of a job.

She had seen Hamm and was told that he had a lot of money and was a business man. He dressed very neatly and with good taste.

She couldn't wait to tell Dean of her good luck. He would be in at the end of her shift.

She felt proud of herself.

Hamm knew that he had set the hook well. When he mentioned that the wages would be one thousand dollars a week, he knew that she was in the bag, so to speak. He told her that he ran a series of gentlemen's clubs and that having someone who was very attractive to greet the customers was essential. Leckie was flattered.

She asked Hamm, 'Where would I be working?'

Hamm said that she could pick almost any suburb, that he had vacancies all over Melbourne.

When Dean arrived to pick up Leckie, she was excited and told Dean about the job offer. Dean was a bit suspicious of the amount of money that was on offer. He advised her to be careful and not jump in too quickly. Dean had played cards against Hamm and found him to be hard to like.

A very sly person, Dean thought.

Lecky's enthusiasm was good to see. She was happy and waiting to tell her uncle the good news.

Leckie wasn't as stupid as Hamm thought; she was well aware that a 'gentle man's' club was just another name for a brothel. She knew that she was attractive and most men wanted to sleep with her.

She felt that Dean loved her and she knew Hamm was just after her because of her looks. She felt that with Dean's help, she could handle Hamm but not on her own.

Dean had been around and he knew the rules. Leckie was going to work for Hamm in a brothel and just be the front face. He knew that that would be the way it started, but soon he knew that Leckie would be enticed into doing something that she would regret.

Leckie had explained to him that it was her duty to send money back to help her family.

He knew that the offer of big money may sway Leckie into bed for a price, so Dean was quite simply against Leckie going to work for Hamm.

Tiny, a huge Samoan, and his sidekick Jesse were security for Hamm at his brothel.

Between them, they weighed as much as a small Japanese car.

They were dressed in black and looked quite menacing.

Their job was to keep trouble down to a minimum and not let the girls get knocked about.

Most of the cliental were good, but every now and then, someone would step over the mark and then the girl would set off an alarm and into the room they would barge and usually belt the trouble maker. They would then drag him out the back way and leave him in a bloody heap in the gutter.

They enjoyed their work and sometimes the girls would, on a quiet night, avail their bodies to the two giants. Yes, it was a system that suited everyone.

Hamm spoke to the two security men and said, 'Brace yourselves men, I'm about to bring in a girl that is so beautiful that you will be gob-smacked. She is a real stunner. She is going to work the front desk until I explain that she can make three times the money in a couple of nights on her back, the punters will be eager to be with her.'

Both men smiled as they thought that they also would end up in bed with her. They eagerly waited for their first meeting.

Hamm drove Leckie to her first night's work. When she got out of the car and saw the two security men looking at her hungrily, she wasn't that worried as she was used to men undressing her with their eyes.

Hamm introduced her to Tiny and Jesse; the two men smiled and said, 'Pleased to meet you.'

They went inside and Hamm showed Leckie around the place.

It consisted of bedrooms and a reception desk. A few bored girls sat in a lounge room and were waiting for some customers to show up. It was early in the evening and business was slow. Hamm explained the rates and how to take the money from the clients and how to put the cash into a time delay safe, all pretty simple really.

There was a pool table and a TV on in the room and the girls were half-watching a favorite show.

The way that it worked was that the customer would enter the door past the two giants and Leckie would escort them to the room. They would choose a girl and then they would pay Leckie an amount of money. Sometimes cash and sometimes a credit card and they would then go into the girl's bedroom for an agreed amount of time and they would leave. Some would hang around for a drink, but most would leave as their time would be over. The girl would make up the room, fix up her make-up, and go back out into the lounge room to await another customer.

At times throughout the evening Tiny would come in and talk to Leckie, he was friendly and didn't seem to ask any personal questions and they would have a coffee together. The night went quickly.

Leckie got a taxi back to her uncle's unit. He had gone to work and Leckie spoke to her auntie about her moving out as she was earning enough money now to be able to afford her own place. She would tell Dean about her wanting to move and she hoped that Dean would suggest that she move in with him.

The plan worked and Dean was more than happy to have her move in.

She met Teddy, Curly, and Tom and was aware that they had a particular bond between them. She realised that what they were doing was illegal, but in this land, people were more than willing to break the law, not like China where you could be thrown into jail for the simplest error.

Dean drove Leckie to work and saw the two security guards. He was happy that there was some protection for her.

Leckie introduced Dean to Tiny and Jesse. Then Dean drove off. Leckie settled into her routine and the customers started coming in.

Hamm came in and saw that Leckie was behind the reception desk, and he smiled at her. He went out and said to Tiny, 'I'll give her a week and she will be into the action.'

Tiny smiled and said, 'Maybe sooner, maybe she will be eager to make some real money.' Both the men laughed and Hamm got into his car and drove off.

Tiny had never really fallen in love with any woman, but he felt a strong desire to protect Leckie. She was like a little butterfly. She needed someone to keep her safe.

He had seen her boyfriend Dean and was sure that he wouldn't be a problem. If he stuck his head in, then he would get it belted, that simple.

What sort of a man would let his partner work in a joint like this? The other girls were sluts and would do anything for money. Some were on drugs, most from broken homes, they were rubbish, not at all like Leckie, and yes he would protect her.

Tiny told Jesse about how he felt and Jesse laughed and said, 'Hey, bro, you know the rules, don't fall in love with a hooker and don't back slow horses.'

Tiny took offence to Jesse calling Leckie a hooker.

'She's no hooker.' He defended.

'Not yet anyway,' Tiny responded,

'I'll protect her. I'll make sure that she will be all right.' Tiny insisted.

Jesse had never seen his friend fall in love with a prostitute. They had worked together for years and never before had Tiny ever tumbled into one of the girls before. He would have to keep his eye on Tiny as he was very protective of Leckie.

Dean, Curly, Tom, and Teddy were talking in Curly's shed and Dean was explaining about where Leckie was working.

Teddy laughed and said, not unkindly, 'Mate, if she is working in a brothel and she's not on the game, the chances are that she will be soon. It's human nature. She will be seeing the other girls earning in a night what she is making a week and next thing you know she's in there with them. You have already said that her boss, this Hamm, is as slippery as an eel. He is definitely not to be trusted, so why would you let her get caught up in this sort of stuff for.'

Dean thought for a while and rationalised that with what he was earning, Leckie would still be able to send some money home to her family.

Dean looked at his friends and asked, 'What should I do?'

Tom said grimly, 'You say that there are a couple of "cocanut heads" working as security guards?'

'Yes,' said Dean, 'they are fucking monsters.'

Teddy smiled and said, 'We should all drop by and Dean explain that he doesn't want Leckie working in that environment. Tell her to get her arse into our car and away we go. If the gorillas attempt to stop us, then we'll just have to show them who is running the show.'

Everyone agreed.

The four friends got into Teddy's car and away they went towards the brothel.

Tiny saw the car pull up and saw that there were four people inside.

He thought *a car load of 'Horney' blokes, that's what we need to get the party started.*

Then he recognised Dean.

Trouble, he thought, this doesn't look good.

Dean made his way up the three steps into the house and Tiny said, 'What do you want?'

Dean said, 'I've come to get Leckie. I don't want her working here.'

'Well, that's up to her, isn't it?' Tiny asked.

Dean said. 'Get out of my way. I'm here to talk to Leckie.'

Jessie asked, 'Is there a problem, bro?'

Tiny said, 'I don't think so. Dean is just leaving.'

'Like fuck I am, I want to see Leckie.' Dean interjected.

Tiny drew himself up to his full height and said, 'Piss off, sunny boy, before you get hurt.'

Dean swung an uppercut and it landed on Tiny's point of his jaw. Tiny staggered back a couple of feet. Teddy ran up the steps and threw a punch at Jessie's jaw and Jessie reeled back.

Tiny rushed Dean and wrapped his massive arms around him. Dean could feel all the air being crushed out of his lungs. Curly drove his fist into the side of Tiny's head, but Tiny still hung on to Dean.

Tom said over the noise of the fighting, 'Go for the bastard's body as you can't hurt the pricks if you bash them around the head.'

Teddy kept up the relentless barrage onto Jessie and Jessie felt the fight go out of him. Tom hit him on the back of the neck and it was good night nurse for Jessie.

They all turned to Tiny.

Tiny was literally battered to his end. There were simply too many of them. He felt himself lose consciousness.

Dean made his way into the reception area and said to Leckie. 'Come on, Leckie, this is no place for you to be working. Let's get the hell out of her, before we do any more damage.'

Leckie was hesitant to leave, but Dean said, 'Come on, out of here now, we will talk it over tonight when we get home.'

Leckie saw the two disabled security and she followed Dean out to Teddy's car.

'Are the security men all right?' Leckie asked.

Teddy said, 'They will have a few bumps and bruises, but they will be as right as rain.'

Dean got Leckie home and they had a talk.

He explained that she wouldn't have to work anymore as the two of them were a unit and he could afford to give her a weekly wage for her to keep the house full of food and some money to send over to her family, and she wouldn't have to work anymore.

She agreed.

Hamm was furious when he found out that Leckie wasn't working for him anymore. When Tiny rang and explained what had happened, Hamm got madder and madder.

'That little bitch,' he darkly muttered.

Tiny was a bit embarrassed that he and Jesse had been overwhelmed by the group.

'What do you want us to do?' Tiny asked Hamm.

Hamm responded by saying, 'Just keep your eyes on the place and don't let anyone else kidnap any more girls.'

Moron, he thought.

Back at Dean's place, Dean and Leckie sat and talked about where their future was going. Dean realised that he couldn't keep gambling like he was doing and still have enough money for him and Leckie, so Dean decided that he would act more responsibly than he had been.

They agreed to give it a go and see how the future panned out.

Epilogue

The Vagrant

The vagrant wandered down the street from the spot where he had spent the night sleeping. He was a bit refreshed as he had slept well. There hadn't been any disturbances. No young blokes poking him with sticks or trying to set him alight.

He wandered past the phone shop that he had bought a mobile phone for a bloke with the thickest gold chain he had ever seen and wondered what he was up to.

Deals like that don't come along every day.

He secretly hoped that he might run into him again and get him another phone. He sure could use the money.

Dean and Leckie

When Dean had bought Leckie home from the Gentlemen's club/brothel, they had talked for most of the night. Dean had explained that he would be more that happy to send over money to Leckie's parents if that was what was expected of him. He explained to Leckie that he earned a lot of money out of his working with Teddy and the boys.

He convinced Leckie to continue with her university courses, run the house for the two of them and take care of the money coming in.

Dean explained that this was the Aussie way.

Curly

Curly missed his big mate Dean, but he knew that he was happy being with Leckie and in all honesty who wouldn't be. She was lovely. Beautiful to look at and had a great way about her.

Curly decided to extend the backyard garden shed, which he and his Dad had spent many Saturday afternoons pottering around in.

Slowly he started to extend the shed and it turned into a real 'Man-cave'.

He missed his Dad and had decided to stay at home and be a bit of company for his dear old Mum. With the shed he had somewhere that he and his mates could meet and not mess up his mum's house.

Tom and Sandy

Tom loved Sandy. He loved her more that he had loved anyone or anything in his life. She was his everything. He had never let on to anyone but when she was raped by the loan sharks he had nearly given up going away with Teddy and the crew. He reckoned that it was his job to protect the one he loved. He felt that he had let Sandy down by not being there to protect her.

Not a minute went by that Tom didn't think about revenge. He was familiar with the old saying; *vengeance is a dish best served cold.*

It was only a matter of time and he would have those men on their knees.

Wallace (Piggy) Trotter

Wallace was in a state of bother. He knew that Teddy and his bunch of abalone poaching bastards were up to no good but as yet he couldn't seem to grab them with the abalone that he knew, deep inside him, that were illegally taking.

He knew that they hadn't been seen up in his area so that could only mean one thing, they were working somewhere else.

He would have to put his ear to the ground and wait until he came across a bit of news.

Then he would strike. He would suddenly appear and catch the bastards red-handed. He would show the world that no one gets away with messing with Wallace P Trotter.

The Restaurant Owner

Henry was happy with the world.

His parent's restaurant was really going ahead.

It was full almost every night and the compliments that he received from his customers were pleasing. He relayed them back to his father who was the head chef; they were both very pleased with the results.

Henry's illegal abalone business was thriving thanks to the constant supply of abalone that he was receiving from Teddy and his crew.

Everything was going along fine, but Henry couldn't understand his father's thoughts of something bad were going to happen.

His father felt that the more they stood out, the more they were likely to become victims of the gangs, of Vietnamese that preyed on the shopkeepers and restaurateurs, which were always there to offer protection.

Henry laughed and said. 'Father we have Teddy and his divers. They are our friends and if we get into trouble, they will help us out.

'Sometimes friends are only here for the good times. When dark clouds gather then, they disappear.' Henry's father said sadly.

'You will find this, not to be the case with Teddy and his crew. Teddy told me that he wants to do business with us for many years.' Henry said.

'Time will tell.' Was all that Henry's dad said?

He went to prepare some dishes for tonight's meals.

The Loan Sharks

The loan sharks had gotten over their injuries inflicted by Teddy and the boys.

They had both raped Sandy, Tom's partner, and, of course, didn't predict such a violent reprisal.

Mario said to his brother Nick, 'We were lucky those crazy bastards didn't kill us both.'

Nick laughed and said, 'Mate she wasn't a bad root. Once I got her moving she was pretty good.'

Shaking his head, Mario answered. 'There is no more of that stuff for me; I'll fuck the easy ones at the Casino.'

Their car was written off when that crazy bastard had reversed into it in a small truck when they were waiting for someone to come out of a hotel with that golden chalice.

They had the two other clowns in with them; they weren't worth a pinch of goat shit when the pressure was on.

The two men got ready for another night at the casino.

The Golden Chalice

The Golden Chalice was being shown to the world by an excited Professor Stanley Brian Wilson.

He couldn't believe his luck, that somehow he was the one that was taking this almost priceless chalice around the world.

The Melbourne University had fallen over backwards to give him all the assistance they possibly could. Doors that would have been slammed in his face were opened by eager universities who wanted to display this unique piece of history.

He was as hot as a lecturer gets.

His old students were now saying. 'Professor Wilson? Yes, yes I have attended lectures by him. He is almost a personal friend.'

The good professor's phone was running red hot. People, who couldn't have cared less about him, a few years ago, were now ringing and chatting away just like they had been friends for years.

Yes, things have changed, and it was all because of the big bloke with the gold chain.

Professor Wilson often wondered about the man. Where he was and what was he doing? Were he and his team still out there poaching abalone?

He was thinking about all this when his phone rang he picked it up and said, 'Professor Wilson, how can I help you?'

Martha

Martha was still doing what she did best and that was buying and selling gold and precious jewels.

She, at times, thought about the golden chalice. In fact, she was getting sick of that professor sticking his head into every TV show and smugly displaying that bloody chalice.

She thought that she was all right with Teddy. He was a good bloke she thought.

Eddie the Jew

Eddie the Jew had spent plenty of sleepless nights thinking about the chalice. He had been so close yet so far and he had ended up with what Paddy shot at, fuck all.

That idiot 'The Juggler' and his half-witted offsider had tried to help, but all they did was muddy the waters. And as for the plastic drums that were missing, well he was keeping a close eye on Kevin.

In this business, you couldn't trust your mother.

Bass Strait Barry

Bass Strait Barry and his offsider Des were sitting in the beer garden of Barry's favourite pub in Port Melbourne. They were relaxed in each others company.

They had worked together for so long that they almost knew what the other one was thinking.

'I reckon that we should do a bit more with Teddy and his crew.' Barry said.

Des agreed, 'He's a pretty smart bloke that Teddy. He's put together a crew of young blokes and they all get on well together.'

'Yer, I reckon that there's a quid to be made with them.' Barry admitted.

'What about that fucking Great White taking out the seal at Pedra Branca?' Des laughed.

'Jesus Christ, did you see the look on Dean's face?'

Barry agreed, 'I thought that they would want to pack up and fuck off.'

'There was no chance of that with Teddy running the show. Did you notice he said he thought the shark wouldn't eat for a week after eating the seal?'

Des chipped in, 'then without a moment's hesitation him and Tom went into the water to see if it was still hanging about. That took a lot of guts.'

Barry lamented. 'There's no question that Teddy isn't game. I've known him for years and I've never known him to take a step back.'

'Yer, he's a good bloke.' Des said nodding his head.

Both the men took long pulls from their pots of beer.

Muddy the Biker

Muddy the biker's wounds were healing. He was still in a daze about how those abalone poaching sons of bitches had given them all a walloping.

Like there were only four of the bastards, but fuck it all they went off like a bomb.

He knew that he had lost a lot of respect by ending up in the hospital, but he was unconscious when he was taken there. They suspected that he might have had some brain damage. It took him a couple of days to get over it all.

Just wait, yer, just wait. Next time, he and his gang tangle with them poachers it will be a different story. They will see the inside of a hospital, not him.

Teddy

Teddy was happy with the way things were going. The money was rolling in and everyone was happy as far as he could see.

He was more that happy with the way the three young blokes were working. There were never any problems and they all got along fine.

The fact that they could work out of a big boat or the Shark Cat was great.

His old mate Bass Strait Barry and Des were welcome additions and everyone got on fine. He could see a bright future in front of them.

Teddy was waiting for his partner Rita to come home from her work as a Liberian at the local library.

He thought how lucky he was to be in a stable relationship.

He sipped a beer and looked at the sky as the sun set.